Praise for
New York Times and USA Today Bestselling Author

Diane Capri

"Full of thrills and tension, but smart and human, too."
*Lee Child, #1 World Wide Bestselling Author of Jack Reacher Thrillers*

"[A] welcome surprise....[W]orks from the first page to 'The End'."
*Larry King*

"Swift pacing and ongoing suspense are always present...[L]ikable protagonist who uses her political connections for a good cause...Readers should eagerly anticipate the next [book]."
*Top Pick, Romantic Times*

"...offers tense legal drama with courtroom overtones, twisty plot, and loads of Florida atmosphere. Recommended."
*Library Journal*

"[A] fast-paced legal thriller...energetic prose...an appealing heroine...clever and capable supporting cast...[that will] keep readers waiting for the next [book]."
*Publishers Weekly*

"Expertise shines on every page."
*Margaret Maron, Edgar, Anthony, Agatha and Macavity Award Winning MWA Past President*

# BLACK JACK

*by DIANE CAPRI*

Published by: AugustBooks
http://www.AugustBooks.com

ISBN: 978-1-942633-08-2

Original cover design by: Cory Clubb
Digital formatting by: Author E.M.S.

Published in the United States of America.

Visit the author website:
http://www.DianeCapri.com

# ALSO BY DIANE CAPRI

## The Hunt for Jack Reacher Series:
*(in publication order with Lee Child source books in parentheses)*

Don't Know Jack (The Killing Floor)

Jack in a Box (*novella*)

Jack and Kill (*novella*)

Get Back Jack (Bad Luck & Trouble)

Jack in the Green (*novella*)

Jack and Joe (The Enemy)

Deep Cover Jack (Persuader)

Jack the Reaper (The Hard Way)

Black Jack (Running Blind/The Visitor)

## The Jess Kimball Thrillers Series

Fatal Enemy (*novella*)

Fatal Distraction

Fatal Demand

Fatal Error

Fatal Fall

Fatal Edge

Fatal Game

Fatal Bond

Fatal Past (*novella*)

Fatal Dawn (*coming soon*)

**The Hunt for Justice Series**
Due Justice
Twisted Justice
Secret Justice
Wasted Justice
Raw Justice
Mistaken Justice (*novella*)
Cold Justice (*novella*)
False Justice (*novella*)
Fair Justice (*novella*)
True Justice (*novella*)

**The Heir Hunter Series**
Blood Trails
Trace Evidence

# CAST OF PRIMARY CHARACTERS

Kim L. Otto
Carlos M. Gaspar

Charles Cooper
Lamont Finlay
Reggie Smithers
Houston Brice
Alan Deerfield
Lisa Harper
Jodie Jacob
John Lawton

and
Jack Reacher

*Perpetually, for Lee Child, with unrelenting gratitude.*

# BLACK
# JACK

# RUNNING BLIND
## (UK title THE VISITOR)

## by Lee Child

## 2000

"Maybe they weren't looking for a killer. Maybe they were looking for somebody who would *kill* a killer," Jodie said.

"Why didn't they just ask me straight?"

"They can't just *ask* you.... It would be a hundred percent illegal.... Because then they own you, Reacher. Two vigilante homicides with their *knowledge*? Right under their noses? The Bureau would *own* you the whole rest of your life."

# CHAPTER ONE

*Monday, January 17*
*8:35 a.m.*
*Garrison, New York*

HE'D NEVER BEEN LUCKY before, but today was different.
Reed could feel it in his bones. The daily nausea and abdominal
pain was barely noticeable for the first time in weeks, which was
lucky right there. Otherwise, he might have been sleeping and
missed his big break.

The original plan he'd worked up had been excellent. One
adjustment to take advantage of his luck and the plan became
absolutely brilliant. All the elements had fallen into place with
zero effort. Even the winter weather had become a willing
accomplice. How lucky could one guy be?

Weak sunlight had finally melted the last of the snow on the
driveway yesterday. Temperatures above forty were a welcome
respite from the early, bitter cold that began in late October and
never let up. A white Christmas had come and gone, which meant
New York residents were grateful for the brief winter thaw.

A nor'easter was forecast tomorrow, and more storms would follow, which was also lucky, as it turned out. He'd already planned to take advantage of both the thaw and the storms, but now, when this opportunity coincided with his preparation, he seized the chance.

He'd been watching the abandoned house for a while, which was the kind of simple task he could easily perform in spite of his worsening symptoms. Very few vehicles traveled the two-lane road in front of the house at all because of the deep snow. Only a couple of neighbors with four-wheel drive SUVs occasionally drove past to reach the small town seven miles south. The road was never plowed out, and neither was the driveway. Which made it easy to see whether anyone came or went. No one had. No visitors, no deliveries, nothing.

He took many long naps and longer breaks without missing anything at all. He knew he hadn't missed anything because afterward, he zoomed through the recorded video, simply to be sure. Not once in all these weeks had any kind of vehicle pulled into the long driveway.

He grinned. Until today.

He'd slept several uninterrupted hours for a change, which was another lucky thing because he felt rested and ready. The sunrise awakened him when the first light cleared the trees. A moment to urinate and stretch out the kinks in his muscles before he poured his last cup of hot, black coffee from the thermos, and he was alert and watching at the very moment his luck arrived.

He'd already swallowed half the coffee when the red Lexus rounded the corner and came into view. The sun glinted off the windshield as the driver slowed and turned into the driveway.

He found his long lens camera and snapped a few quick shots of the sedan. The license plate was New York blue and gold, but road grime obscured the number, which was perfect. Lexus sedans were common in New York. Without a specific plate number, the car could belong to almost anyone. The driver pulled all the way up to the big double garage door and parked.

Through the lens, he watched the driver's side door open, and a woman climbed out. Which was the moment he realized how lucky he really was.

He continued shooting as he watched. She was covered from the neck down by a black leather coat and gloves, black pants and boots. The warmer weather had encouraged her to forego her hat and scarf, but she'd donned stylish oversized sunglasses. *This just keeps getting better and better.*

Even from this distance, she was beautiful, in an ethereal way. Tall, blonde, almost painfully thin. Mid-thirties. Or close enough.

He watched her through the long lens as she walked up the sidewalk toward the house, empty-handed. At the front door, she entered a code on the real estate agent's lockbox, removed the key to unlock the door, and went inside.

*Damn! How great is that?* Reed's grin consumed his whole face. He relaxed in his seat.

He glanced at the clock so he'd know precisely where to find her arrival on the video feed later.

The house was totally empty. It was also cold and dark. The electricity had been off for weeks. Cell phone signals were weak in this area for commercial carriers, too. She wouldn't stay inside very long.

Almost like he felt the wheels turning in his head and clicking into place, the improved plan unfolded quickly. When he had it all worked out, he gulped the cold dregs from the plastic cup, screwed the top onto the thermos, and dropped it onto the seat. He wanted hot coffee and plenty of it, but he couldn't get more just yet.

He rechecked the clock. Twenty-two minutes so far. Reed wondered what she might be doing inside the house. Taking photos or video with a cell phone, probably. Nothing else was the least bit likely.

Twelve minutes later, she stepped out through the front door and turned to close it solidly. Reed raised his long lens camera to his eye again and snapped photos in long bursts. She bent to return the key and punch the code to secure the lockbox again, closed the storm door, and tested the handle. She slipped her sunglasses on before she faced the bright sunlight, which probably seemed intense after she'd become accustomed to the dark interior of the house.

She returned to her car and reversed the Lexus out of the long driveway. At the road, she turned toward Garrison and drove the speed limit until she rounded the corner out of sight.

Reed checked the clock and noted the exact time. All he had to do was edit the surveillance video to remove all evidence of her departure, which he accomplished before the coffee finished brewing. The video now showed her arrive, go inside, and never come out. He didn't even need to move the car.

No one would check the video for a while. Why would they? No reason to check it until after the body was discovered inside the house. And if they checked the video first, before the body was found? That was okay, too. Because they'd go inside looking for her.

*It's all good.* It had been a long time since he'd felt good about anything.

Reacher would find out. How long would it take him to come running? For her? Not long, probably.

Reed shook his head, still smiling. He refilled his thermos with the fresh coffee. Within minutes, he was on the road tailing her red sedan. He knew right where he'd find it. He had plenty of time. The snow wouldn't start until early tomorrow morning. Around two o'clock or so, according to the weather guys.

He looked at his eyes reflected in the rearview mirror. "You're one lucky bastard, you know that?"

# CHAPTER TWO

*Monday, January 17*
*11:00 p.m.*
*Garrison, New York*

HIS LUCK WAS HOLDING. Cloud cover blocked the moon and the stars. The closest neighbors were out of town for the season. The rest of the neighborhood was already in bed for the night. The only ambient light originated across the river in the back of the house. After midnight, even that would diminish. But sound carried across the water, which meant his mission must be completed as silently as possible.

The storm was forecast to begin after 0200 hours and continue tomorrow. At least six inches of heavy snow was expected. He'd have the body in place well before the snow made it impossible to enter without leaving tracks that could be traced and identified later. Tracks that would prompt a search inside the house too soon.

Reed checked the clock. The mission launched precisely at 0100 hours. Two more hours to kill.

He checked the existing video feeds first. Constant video without snags, stalls, or time gaps in the feed was essential. Afterward, he'd edit his activities out as flawlessly as he'd edited out her departure this morning. Sophisticated forensics could locate the edits, but the analysis would never be requested because no one would have a reason to ask.

Olympic athletes trained off the field with repeated mental rehearsals, one step at a time, emphasizing success and handling obstacles. He'd perfected his plan the same way.

The mission would last sixty minutes. Sixty-five, max. Start to finish. Delivering the paint into the tub was the slowest activity and the only segment that couldn't be rushed.

Don gloves, cap, mask, boot covers, and protective clothing.

Disable all lights on the inside and outside of the SUV. Back the vehicle slowly and quietly down the driveway to the attached garage. Get out and open the big garage door manually because the power to operate the electric opener was turned off, which had also disabled the automatic light on the opener.

Return to the vehicle. Move it into the garage far enough to prevent any casual observation of activities from the road while permitting access to the cargo. The SUV would not fit completely inside because of the garage's interior layout. Which meant he couldn't close the garage door. He relied on stealth and total darkness to cloak his activities.

Open the back hatch. He now had access to his supplies and equipment.

He visualized her naked body lying prone inside the body bag on the plastic sheet. She'd been dead long enough to be somewhat flexible again. He'd previously removed her clothes and placed them in a plastic garbage bag to limit the potential for transferred trace evidence and reduce the amount of time he spent inside the house.

He carried her into the bathroom inside the body bag and placed her in the tub. He removed her from the body bag and posed her body like a corpse in repose. The oversized tub had grips on the bottom to prevent her from slipping lower into the paint.

He returned to the garage with the body bag and stowed it carefully. He collected the plastic bag containing her clothes.

Over the past few weeks, he'd bought fifteen gallons of olive green oil-based paint from several sellers in New Jersey, Connecticut, and New York using small cash purchases. Earlier today, he'd emptied the cans into the big shop vac with a pumping feature and disposed of the empty cans at three different landfills.

He saw himself hefting the battery-powered shop vac inside the house.

In the bathroom for the second time, he dropped the plastic bag of clothes on the floor at the foot of the tub. He flipped the switch on the shop vac to low volume and used the pumping feature to let the paint flow slowly through the hose into the bathtub.

He emptied the clothes from the bag and placed them as if they'd been casually dropped when she undressed before stepping into the bath. Panties first, nightgown next. No bra.

He watched the paint flowing into the tub until the paint line reached above her shoulders to the base of her neck. He pressed the off switch on the shop vac.

He used his flashlight to check the room. Satisfied with his work, he carried the shop vac and the plastic bag out to the garage again. He relocked the interior door that connected the house to the garage.

He lifted the shop vac into the plastic sheet covering the cargo area of the SUV and stuffed the plastic bag in with the body bag. He returned to the driver's seat and pulled slowly out of the garage.

He lowered the big door to the ground and then pulled away.

He checked the clock. Another half hour yet.

At precisely 0100 hours, before the snow began to fall, he executed his plan exactly as he'd visualized it. Not one snag. How lucky could he get?

Back at his site, Reed pulled off his protective gear and stuffed everything into the plastic bag that had held her body. He edited the video footage to eliminate all evidence of his activities.

When he'd finished, three inches of snow was already on the ground. The unblemished white blanket covered the lawn and the driveway of the house. He smiled with satisfaction.

On his circuitous route home, he stopped at four appropriate dump sites to dispose of the body bag, the protective gear, the remaining paint, and the dismantled shop vac.

The only thing left to do now was to wait until the body was discovered and the media did what they always do.

Reacher would be here soon.

# CHAPTER THREE

*Eleven Days Later*
*Friday, January 28*
*2:30 p.m.*
*New Windsor, New York*

FBI SPECIAL AGENT KIM Otto landed at Stewart
International, a secondary airport about seventy miles north of
Manhattan, ten minutes behind schedule. The flight's altitude
had been high above the clouds until the pilot forced his way
through the heavy cloud cover for landing.

She'd popped her tenth antacid just before the bouncy
landing, and she was grateful to be on the ground in one piece.
She'd been seated near the front of the small jet, which meant
she could grab her bags and deplane ahead of the slower
passengers.

At the end of the jetway, she spied the signs pointing her
toward ground transportation on the lower level. She stopped
briefly in the restroom and then hurried to the exit. An unmarked
black FBI SUV waited at the curb.

The driver, a large black man who resembled a human tank, lowered the window and showed his photo ID badge. "Agent Otto?"

"Alive and well, no thanks to the flight gods." She nodded. "Unlock the back door, and I'll stow these bags. We can be on our way. Maybe make up a little time on the road."

She stashed her travel bag and her laptop case behind the front passenger seat. She climbed up onto the running board and then tucked into the cabin. She fished her cell phone out of her blazer pocket and turned it on, which would ping whoever might be tracking her location, for better or worse.

She grabbed the large alligator clip she kept in her overcoat pocket, fastened her seatbelt, loosened the shoulder harness to a comfortable length, and placed the clip at the retractor to hold the webbing in place. The tight steel grip held the harness in position as comfortably as possible, given the physics of it all.

The driver watched her organize herself as if she was an unusual lab specimen of some kind. The alligator clamp business triggered a wide grin. He extended his hand.

"Agent Reggie Smithers, at your service." His voice was a pleasant rumble like he should be hosting a late-night radio call-in show for lonely women.

She placed her small hand inside his oversized paw and gripped for the handshake as well as she could. "Seatbelts in these big SUVs invariably cut across my body at an angle guaranteed to behead me in a crash. Even if the airbags deploy," Kim said, deadly serious in reply to his obvious amusement.

"Yeah, I can see how that might happen. What are you? Four-ten, and ninety pounds soaking wet?" His smile displayed teeth resembling an entire set of white piano keys.

"What are you? Six-five and three-ten in your birthday suit?"

Kim shot back. When he roared with laughter, she shrugged. She liked him already.

"Are we still waiting for your partner? Agent Gaspar?" Smithers asked.

Kim shook her head. "He's on medical leave. I got called up three hours ago. Nobody I could bring along on short notice. So it's just me, for now."

"Got it." He pulled the SUV away from the curb, still chuckling. "We're less than fifteen miles from Garrison. But another eight inches of heavy snow fell in the past twelve hours. Plows can't keep up. Probably take us about twice as long as usual to get there, if there's no crashes ahead to tie us up."

When he'd entered the flow of slow-moving traffic along the snow-covered pavement, she relented. "Four-eleven and ninety-seven pounds of absolutely terrifying power, if you must know."

He nodded and kept his eyes straight ahead, but the corner of his mouth twitched. He cleared his throat. "You came in from Detroit, right? About a ninety-minute flight, give or take?"

"A little slower today, due to the weather. They de-iced the plane twice. It's pretty cold out there." Kim hated flying. Human error being almost a given, added to bad weather, terrorist alerts, and everything else, air travel was always a recipe for disaster. She absolutely despised air travel in winter, which never came close to the best conditions. Not even remotely.

She saw a drive-through fast food joint up ahead on the right. "Pull in over there, and I'll buy you a coffee."

"We're already running behind." Smithers frowned. "My orders were to get you to Garrison as quickly as possible. We don't have much daylight left."

Kim shrugged, an all-purpose gesture she'd stolen from Gaspar because it could mean anything or nothing. Properly deployed, it stopped conversation, too. Worked as well for her as it did for him.

But when they reached the entrance to the coffee place, the traffic had stopped, and a sea of red taillights stretched at least half a mile ahead. Smithers turned the big SUV into the driveway and pulled around to the order window.

"How do you take it?"

"Large, hot, and black," Kim replied pleasantly, wiggling her eyebrows like Groucho Marx.

Smithers roared with laughter again. "Okay. I deserved that. No more personal appearance remarks from me."

"Good plan." Kim smiled. Smithers was competent. He wouldn't be an FBI Special Agent otherwise. He was human, too. Which wasn't actually a given. Some agents could be absolute jerks. She'd met way too many of them.

He ordered two large black coffees to go. Kim handed him a ten-dollar bill. He gave her the change. In less than five minutes they were parked behind the taillights with everyone else again.

When the coffee proved too hot to drink just yet, she said, "You work out of the New York Field Office, I assume."

"Organized Crime Unit. Protection rackets, mostly. You know. Old fashioned mobsters," he replied.

She nodded. "Any idea why I've been called to Garrison?"

"Not exactly. And I'm under orders not to discuss what I do know."

"Why?"

"Because they want you to have fresh eyes when you get there."

She cocked her head. The explanation made sense as long as the situation wasn't an armed shooter or another imminent danger.

Whatever was going on wasn't immediately life-threatening, at least.

Which got her hackles up. "Why was I ordered to rush out here with no intel at all, if this isn't an immediate threat?"

"Sorry, Otto. I understand why you're annoyed, believe me. I'm not thrilled about any of this, myself. But I can't answer that question, either. You'll see for yourself soon enough."

"Okay." She took a breath and held on to her patience. "Tell me about Garrison then."

"What I know about the place won't take much time to tell. It's a little hamlet over in the next county. Established back when Moses was a pup. Active tourist place now. Country dwellers. Yankee Doodle Dandy and all that." He craned his neck to see around the traffic. "Across the Hudson River from West Point."

Kim smiled. "So you're not a fan of Garrison?"

"I'm not planning to live there, no. Fortunately, not many mobsters live there, either, so I won't be required to move." He punched a few buttons on the navigation system. "Looks like Interstate 84 is the only reasonable way to get across the river. Guess we'll just grunt this out. Unless you want me to order up a helo?"

"Way too cold, windy, and dark out there to get me in a helicopter. No thanks." She shuddered. Again, she took his comments to confirm that the situation in Garrison wasn't urgent. Which limited the possibilities. She tried not to jump to conclusions about the job, but so far, she'd seen no reason to be on full alert.

After covering very little ground for another two miles, Smithers turned on a jazz station. They traveled the remaining miles across the river on the interstate without conversation, which was fine with her. Just because two people were in a vehicle together didn't necessarily mean they had to talk to each other, Gaspar often said.

After they crawled across the Hudson behind the line of traffic, the navigation system identified a secondary state road running south along the east side of the river down to Garrison.

"How about we take the scenic route? We can get out of this traffic, at least." Kim pointed to the estimated drive time. Nineteen minutes to cover the distance, not taking the snow into account. But at least they'd be moving.

"Works for me." Smithers put the SUV in four-wheel drive and turned south following the nav system's directions.

They traveled through mostly unoccupied countryside bedecked with snow suitable for a Currier & Ives Christmas card. Kim hoped they wouldn't need to walk around out there. She hadn't packed proper clothes for hunting evidence under two feet of snow.

Smithers drove over the twisty road with the confidence of a man used to handling all types of road conditions. Kim liked him more by the minute.

The headlight beams bounced along the semi-darkness caused by the heavy cloud cover, even though it was not quite half-past three and the sun was technically still above the horizon. He kept the SUV between the ditches and made up some lost time by accelerating on the straight, flat sections, but on the curves, he was forced to slow.

"Good thing my partner isn't driving. Gaspar's from Miami. Probably never seen this much snow in his life," Kim said when they entered the township of Garrison, which seemed to be nothing more than a wide spot in the snowy forest. "So this is it?"

"We're almost there. Another couple of miles." Smithers had both hands gripped onto the steering wheel. "Thing is, these houses can have a Garrison zip code and be way off the beaten track, you know?"

The navigation system identified the next turn onto an even narrower country road. Fresh snow covered the two-lane here, but at least one vehicle had driven through. Deep ruts in the snow suggested a heavy vehicle. When Smithers lined up the SUV's wheels in the prior vehicle's ruts, Kim figured they were getting close.

Above the snow line, the top rail of decorative rough timber ranch fencing marked the edge of the properties off the shoulder. Mailboxes were visible about a hundred yards apart, suggesting driveways leading to residences might be under all that snow. Poles held cables above the treetops. She could see West Point across the river between the houses.

The ruts Smithers was riding led into the next driveway ahead. He turned right and followed them in toward the house. Kim glanced at the mailbox as they passed, but the aluminum letters that had listed the name above the address had been removed.

The SUV's headlights illuminated a long driveway. At the end was a low, sprawling house barely visible in the approaching darkness. The headlights provided enough wattage to identify dark cedar siding and a big stone chimney. There were no lights on inside or outside the building. Kim glanced at her watch. It was now only 4:30 p.m., yet the place had an abandoned, dead-of-night feel.

At the end of the driveway, in front of the double garage door, another FBI unmarked SUV was parked, lights off and the engine running. An agent was seated behind the wheel. No one else was in the vehicle.

Smithers drove up close and slipped the transmission into park. He opened the console and moved a few small boxes around until he found what he wanted.

"You'll need these." He handed her paper booties to cover her boots, a paper cap to cover her hair, and gloves. "Agent Brice is waiting for you inside."

She'd have asked more questions, but there was no point. He'd told her everything he was authorized to say, and he wouldn't say more. She appreciated his ability to follow orders.

The agent in the first vehicle on the scene turned off his engine and walked back to join them. He was bundled up against the weather. She stuffed the protective covers into her overcoat pocket and pulled her alligator clamp from the seatbelt. When the passenger door opened, a cold wind blew inside the cabin.

Smithers said, "Agent Kim Otto, this is Agent Terry Poulton. Also Organized Crime Unit."

His sandy red hair and freckled face reminded her of that actor, what was his name? Caruso, maybe? Poulton might have been a little older. They shook hands and changed places. He handed her a flashlight.

Kim slipped out of the front seat and stood on the running board before she stepped down into a snowdrift that almost reached the hem of her coat. Dry snow swirled everywhere. She stuffed her hands deep into her pockets and trudged around the front of the SUV.

"The sidewalk is just ahead on the left," Agent Poulton called out before he stepped into the warm vehicle and closed the door.

Smithers left his headlights on for her, which meant she didn't need the flashlight outside. She might need it inside the house from the looks of it.

Everything around the house was very quiet. The air smelled crisp and so cold that inhaling burned her nostrils.

The river was behind the house. West Point would be visible a mile away, probably. But the world beyond the headlight beams was black and empty on this side of the house. No visible stars or moon or ambient light of any kind. Which might mean that the neighboring homes were also unoccupied, at least for the winter months. Or maybe there were hedges or something else blocking any spillover of illumination. Hard to say.

She followed the single set of Poulton's footprints in the snow. Easier than breaking her own trail, and it could help to preserve any potential evidence that might be out there. Even so, each step meant lifting her foot in a high parade march all the way to the sidewalk and then up to the entrance.

The front door was open behind a full glass storm door. When she stepped up onto the stoop, a flashlight turned on inside. Smithers punched off the headlights. She glanced back toward the big SUV, but it had blended into the blackness.

"I'm FBI Special Agent Houston Brice. Thanks for coming on such short notice." He wore paper booties, a paper cap, and gloves. She couldn't see his face yet. "Sorry for the radio silence. We wanted you to have fresh eyes."

"Yeah, that's what Smithers said. Of course, I'd have been more prepared if you'd told me anything at all." She stomped the snow off her boots and swiped her clothes to remove as much moisture as she could.

"Sorry. Following orders, myself. You'll understand in a minute," Brice said.

"No problem." She leaned against the siding to slip her feet into the paper booties. Her hair was already captured in a low chignon on the back of her neck. She slipped the paper cap over her head and pulled the gloves on as she walked across the threshold.

Inside, she pulled the flashlight out of her pocket and flipped the on switch. Then she waited for her eyes to adjust. The first thing she noticed was the cold. Probably well below thirty degrees in here. The temperature outside had been in the teens or lower.

"No heat?"

"The forced air heating system is gas. But it takes electricity to operate the blower." He shrugged. "There's no electricity in here."

"Why not?"

"Turned off by the electric company. The house is unoccupied. Listed for sale. We're running that down now."

She nodded. "I hope they've done something about the pipes to avoid freezing, then."

Brice replied, "The house will be a mess if they didn't, and it's a pretty nice house."

"How old is this place? Thirty, forty years?" Her guess was based on the size of the lot and the location. Property on the Hudson River, even sixty miles from Manhattan, wasn't cheap. Lots as big as this one were divided up and sold by developers looking for big bucks these days.

"Probably at least thirty years, for sure. But it's been renovated more recently." He stood to one side and aimed his flashlight around a large, open floor plan. "Older homes weren't designed like this. And the kitchen looks like one of those cooking shows on television where all the high-end stuff is built in. Even has a big wine cooler. Like they have in the fancy restaurants. I'm guessing someone paid a few hundred grand to renovate. Maybe more."

She moved further into the house. After the cold and the open floor plan, the next thing she noticed was nothing. Literally nothing. As in no furniture at all.

# CHAPTER FOUR

*Friday, January 28*
*4:45 p.m.*
*Garrison, New York*

IN THE HUGE SPACE, sounds echoed across the hardwood
floors and bounced from flat walls.

Heavy blackout drapes covered the windows. Otherwise,
the room would have been colder and absolutely cavernous,
because she'd have been surrounded by the vast darkness
outside as well.

So far, her fresh eyes hadn't seen anything at all, useful or
useless.

Brice said, "We're running short on time. You'll have a lot
of questions. We all do. But for now, please just make your
observations, and we can talk more after we're done here.
Understood?"

"No problem. So far, I don't see anything to ask questions
about, other than why you dragged me out here."

"Follow me. This is a crime scene, so be careful not to

disturb anything." He turned and walked toward the back of the house, flashlight pointed at the floor.

Kim followed behind him, using her flashlight to check things out as they walked.

The hallway was wider than most. Seven feet at least. Doorways opened off the left and right sides. She pointed her flashlight beam inside each room, briefly. All were empty of furnishings, except window coverings of various types.

At the end of the hallway, a double door was ajar. Brice pushed it open and walked inside.

"This must have been the master suite, I suppose," Kim said, as she followed Brice past a massive walk-in closet larger than the bedroom in her Detroit apartment.

"That's what it looks like. For a woman with a lot of shoes." He kept walking deeper into the huge suite, also empty of furniture, with heavy drapes on the windows.

"This whole suite was probably an addition to the original house," Kim said. "City property tax records would reflect that, I assume? Adding square footage to any existing structure increases property taxes where I'm from."

She followed him through another double doorway that led to an enormous master bathroom, about twenty feet square. He stood near the center while she got a sense of the place.

Everything in the room was white. Walls, floor, ceiling, doors, cabinetry, countertops. All white. The tile was Carrera marble. The fixtures were gold.

Across the room from the double door entrance, the entire width was devoted to an oversized shower enclosed in glass. Plenty of space for an orgy inside. Maybe even fit a few spectators. On each of the three walls of the shower, a showerhead the approximate size of a dinner plate protruded. Gold, of course.

When she'd had a moment to scan the room, Brice moved aside.

"Ah," Kim said when she saw what must have been the reason they were here.

A white claw-footed porcelain bathtub with gold fixtures occupied center stage in the middle of the room. The oval tub was deeper and longer than standard. The fixtures were mounted on the side instead of either end. With a pillow affixed to the head of the tub, a man taller than Michael Jordan could stretch out inside and sink up to his neck in a bubble bath.

The current occupant of the tub was significantly shorter than Michael Jordan and definitely not enjoying a bubble bath.

Directly in the bather's line of sight at the foot of the tub was a floor-to-ceiling window. Like the other windows in the house, this one was covered by blackout drapes. But in daylight, the window likely offered an amazing view of the lawn and the river beyond it.

Unfortunately, the woman wasn't looking at the view. Her eyes were closed and probably had been at the time of death. From the looks of the body, she hadn't seen anything in quite a while.

Kim walked closer to the tub, careful not to disturb any trace evidence.

"What is that green liquid she's lying in?" She asked. "Hard to tell, but it looks thicker than water, even with additives like they use in spas."

"I promise to answer all of your questions," Brice said. "But first, tell me what you see here."

"A thin, blonde woman. Fine boned. Blue eyes, I'd guess, given the fair hair. The skin looks bad now, but when she was alive, it might have been pale and translucent. Probably taller than average, although it's hard to say since I can't see her feet. Maybe thirty-five-ish, give or take. Again, hard to say, but she doesn't look ten years younger or older. Obviously dead for a while. Sitting in a tub less than half full of thick green liquid. The light isn't good enough to determine whether there's a skin on the surface. A pile of clothes on the floor beside the foot of the tub, probably hers."

"What else?"

"The room is spotless. No green liquid splashed anywhere I can see with this flashlight. No empty containers that might have held the green liquid before it was added to the tub, assuming it's not water that flowed from the tap. No indication of how the green stuff got here or why the original containers are gone."

"Got a guess on time, manner, and cause of death?"

"Seriously? I'm not a coroner, and I haven't touched the body." When he said nothing more, Kim shrugged and played along. "The manner of death is obvious. Homicide. Could be a very brilliant suicide, but unless there's a lethal dose of self-administered drugs in her system, I'd say murder. First-degree intent to kill. No clue on the exact time, but she's been here awhile. Very little visible decomposition, probably due to how cold it is in here. A mortuary refrigerator would be warmer, and those can store bodies for months."

"Cause of death?"

Kim shook her head. "She looks peaceful. No empty pill bottles or blood mixed with the green to suggest self-mutilation. No visible trauma to the head and neck, although when the full body is examined, the coroner may find something on autopsy."

Brice nodded. "You've never seen or heard of anything like this before?"

"I don't do much actual homicide investigation. Usually not

necessary," Kim replied. "My cases tend to involve pretty obvious murders. You know, gang executions, organized crime hits, terrorist bombings, kidnap for ransom goes bad. Stuff like that. How about you? Seen this before?"

He ignored the question. "What about the green liquid? Know what it is? Or does it remind you of anything?"

"I'm not much of a green person. I like FBI blue. But this looks like army green to me." She tilted her head toward the river. "With West Point over there, army green paint makes sense."

Brice nodded and reached into his pocket to answer his vibrating cell phone. "Yeah.... Okay... Thanks." He disconnected the call and dropped the phone back into his pocket. "Come on. We have to go."

"Why? We just got started."

"We'll come back later. One of the neighbors has reported a burglary in progress here. They must've driven past and seen the vehicles in the driveway. We don't want to be here when the locals arrive."

"Why not? Maybe they can get the electricity on, and we can help process all of this. There's at least a full night's work ahead. We're all on the same side, aren't we? Truth, justice, and the American Way and all that?"

"I'll explain on the road. Come on. We'll be back. But for now, we're leaving." He turned and hurried toward the front exit before she could ask him where they were going.

She fished her phone out of her pocket and shot a quick video around the bathroom and then a few stills of the body in the tub and the pile of clothes. She took one last, long look to be sure she hadn't missed anything obvious. Or left anything behind.

She slipped her phone out of sight and hurried to catch up with Brice.

He stood on the outside stoop holding a large evidence bag into which he'd dropped his booties, cap, and gloves. He handed the bag to her to do the same while he locked the front door.

They hurried to the SUV. She hustled around to the passenger side while he started the engine. Smithers and Poulton were already gone. Brice grabbed a white-knuckled grip on the steering wheel and backed the SUV down the driveway, careful to stay within the ruts. At the road, he headed away from town.

Kim heard sirens in the distance, coming closer. Before the flashing lights approaching the house became visible, Brice pushed the heavy SUV fast enough to reach a big curve in the road and ducked out of sight of the first responders.

# CHAPTER FIVE

*Friday, January 28*
*5:30 p.m.*
*Newburgh, New York*

THE TWISTY TWO-LANE WASN'T any better on the way out than it had been on the way in, but Brice pushed the big vehicle north as hard as he dared. He wasn't the man Smithers was, in several respects, including driving ability. The back end fishtailed a couple of times and slid onto the shoulder more than once, but he kept moving in the right direction.

Kim said, "Leaving the scene of a homicide is a felony in every jurisdiction."

He didn't reply. His grip on the wheel never relaxed. White lines appeared around his nose and mouth, attesting to his level of concentration.

"It's also a violation of FBI policy and procedure. Is that how you do things around here? Pick and choose which homicides you report and which ones you ignore?"

He said nothing, demonstrating more resolve and dedication to a plan than she'd given him credit for.

"You're kidnapping me, Brice. An FBI Special Agent. It's not likely you'll get promoted while you're serving time in federal prison."

He shot her a glare, then returned his full attention to the treacherous driving conditions.

Five miles from the house, he took a chance. He lifted one hand off the wheel and made a short phone call.

"Get the ball rolling," he said and hung up. His hand was off the wheel less than a full minute.

"What's that about?" Kim asked.

"We've got a lot of legwork to do. I don't want that body moved until we get someone officially on the scene." He watched the road and handled the driving, but he was also preoccupied with something else. He wasn't inclined to discuss the case with her now. She'd begun to wonder whether the woman in the tub was an FBI case at all.

She pulled out her phone and typed the address of the house into an internet search. The cell signal was weak out here in the countryside, but with a few clicks and a bit of patience, she found the real estate listing. Her connection wasn't good enough to watch the video tour of the property, but there were still photos on the realtor's website. She chose a group of interior and exterior shots. They loaded with the speed of an exhausted sloth.

The real estate photographer had presented the property well. The pictures had been shot in the fall when the lot's elaborate gardens were in bloom and the trees cooperatively dressed in vibrant autumn colors.

The back of the property used its riverfront location to full advantage.

A large patio ran the length of the house, and outdoor furniture gathered around a well-designed fire pit close to the water. The patio featured an outdoor kitchen and dining area sufficient to accommodate eight to ten seated guests. Three seating groups were placed at spacious intervals to allow private conversations.

None of the photo angles offered a good look at the master bathroom window, but she'd acquired a solid mental image of its location.

She flipped through the interior photographs. They'd been shot on a clear day when sunshine spilled into the house from the oversized windows in every room. The designer was as talented a genius as the photographer.

The open floor plan for the common rooms seemed simultaneously massive and cozy. The kitchen was spectacular, as Brice had hinted. But the showpiece was the master suite, which rivaled any modern palace.

The property, taken as a whole, was ostentatious in the extreme. She lost her cell connection between towers and the website shut down. She'd seen enough for now, anyway.

What kind of people lived in places like that? Not Army generals, in Kim's experience. Not the honest ones, anyway. Celebrities and criminals were more likely residents.

Brice had finally piloted the SUV to the interstate. His concentration remained intense, and he still wasn't talking.

About an hour after they'd fled the homicide scene, Brice pulled the big SUV into the almost deserted parking lot of a chain restaurant off I-84 in Newburgh and killed the engine.

"How about we get a bite to eat, and we can talk. Then we'll go back to the house. See everything officially. All that good with you?" The light from the restaurant bathed his face in pink and green, accentuating the stress lines she hadn't noticed in the dark.

"Last flight back to Detroit from Stewart is already gone." Kim shrugged. "My time is your time."

They went inside, washed up, and Brice requested a quiet table in the back. The hostess didn't even crack a smile, although every table in the place was pretty quiet at the moment. The restaurant was almost deserted.

The waitress brought water and plastic menus thick enough to require a curly spine, with pictures of the food on every page. Several of the pages were stuck together. "Coffee?"

"Yes, please. Black," Kim replied.

"Same," Brice said.

"You got it. Be right back," she promised, a cheerful smile on her face. Working for tips, and it would be a slow night. She had to make the most of every chance.

Kim paged through the colorful sandwiches, salads, and various desserts, none of which would look remotely like their pictures if she actually ordered them. She settled on a vegetable omelet and toast to soak up the grease in her stomach after she ate it.

The waitress returned with a plastic insulated pot of coffee and two brown plastic mugs. She took their orders and hurried to the kitchen.

"Thanks for your patience. I know you've got questions, so fire away," Brice said with the kind of grin he'd probably practiced in the mirror, trying to look open to anything.

This was the first chance she'd had to size him up properly, and she did it in half a minute. Average and unremarkable. He was about forty-five. Brown eyes, brown hair, boring haircut. Serviceable suit, white shirt, plain tie. No wedding ring. The kind of guy women passed on the streets of every city in the country and never even noticed. Probably played by the book, followed the rules, and took orders from hot shots without protest.

Which meant he'd be easier to manipulate, once she knew the right pressure points.

"First, you catch me up. Then I'll ask questions if I have any." Kim sipped the coffee, which tasted way better than she'd feared. "Faster that way."

He looked down at the table, frowning, not too pleased with her proposal. Probably wanted to limit what she knew and worried that he'd let something slip that she wouldn't have known to bring up.

Perhaps he was a bit smarter than she'd assumed. Good to know.

"The house is for sale. The family that did the renovations moved out four months ago. He was transferred to the west coast." He led with the safest thing he could offer since she'd already seen that the house was empty and on the market.

Kim nodded, waiting. No questions yet.

Perspiration popped out on his upper lip. "The utilities have been off since then, according to records."

He paused a beat or two, probably hoping she'd signal his next move. She sipped her coffee, thinking about how that liquid got into the tub. Water wouldn't run without a pump, and pumps required electricity. Unless the body had been there when the utilities were turned off, how did whatever the liquid was get there?

"We've been trying to find the real estate agent, but the storm's been getting in the way all day today." Another pause. More perspiration, on his forehead this time.

She'd learned what she'd wanted to know. He wasn't authorized to read her into anything significant on the situation. He was a flunky, following orders. Nothing more. His boss was probably an asshole who would make his life miserable if he colored outside the lines, too.

She'd been on the receiving end of that kind of relationship. So she threw him a bone. "What kind of work does the owner do?"

He looked so relieved that she almost laughed. "We don't know yet."

"What's his name?"

He glanced down at the menu, avoiding eye contact. "Don't know that yet, either."

"So the woman in the bathtub is the guy's wife?"

His eyebrows shot up, and he gaped at her. "What? Why would you ask that?"

She shrugged. "Seemed reasonable. Sorry for the interruption. Go on."

He paused, maybe trying to think up something safe to say. "At this point, we don't know who the woman is."

"But you do have a guess, don't you?" Kim finished the first mug of coffee and poured a second. "And that's got something to do with how you knew she was in that bathtub. Also has something to do with why I'm sitting here."

"What?" His surprised look was almost comical by now. If she had any chance of getting intel from this guy before she took the situation up with his boss, he'd need to relax a little.

She softened her tone and explained the simple logic quickly. "You didn't discover the body accidentally. The house has been abandoned since well before the last half-dozen snow falls. All the windows were covered, so you didn't just happen to see inside. There were only two sets of tracks on the driveway, identical tires, depth, and so on. Both caused by the two SUVs we drove, which means no one else has been going in and out. That body might have stayed there undiscovered until spring when the temperature warmed up, and someone smelled the decomp. But you found her today, from the way this all went down. Only two ways that could have happened. Either you got a tip and chased it down. Or you already knew she was in there."

His eyes had widened as she'd laid it all out as if she was a genius or something. Which made her suspicious. Brice couldn't possibly be that thick. He'd never have made it into the FBI with a sub-normal IQ unless his grandpa was J. Edgar Hoover or something. Why was he pretending to be a clueless idiot?

He cleared his throat. "We were watching the house. We saw her go inside ten days ago. We didn't see her come out. So we got worried."

Kim cocked her head. "That's a lot of budget and personnel. Around the clock surveillance on an empty house in the middle of nowhere for weeks is a big spend. Can't be authorized by an agent at your level. What's so important about that house to justify all of that cost to the bean counters?"

He sat bolt upright. His face turned bright red and then a funky blue. His eyes bulged. His mouth opened and closed like a dying fish.

His reaction to the question was almost comical. He looked like he'd just swallowed his tongue.

Kim wasn't worried. He shouldn't die of asphyxiation for about three to five minutes, even if he had actually swallowed his tongue. She had plenty of time. Probably.

The waitress saved him after only a second or two. She brought the food along with a fresh pot of coffee. She didn't hang around for chitchat.

The interruption offered Brice a chance to compose himself. When the waitress moved away, he dug into his burger like a man who hadn't eaten in days.

Kim's appetite wasn't so keen. She ate a couple of bites of the toast, considering the possibilities. Nothing within the realm of standard FBI policy and protocols fit the few facts she knew.

One possibility remained.

Brice's operation at the house could be a black ops assignment. The FBI engaged in plenty of those these days. She should know. Her Reacher case was such a project.

If this were a black ops assignment, the budget and personnel outlay wouldn't have gone up the regular chain of command. Bean counters might not have been given the chance to kill it. Means and methods would have little to no supervision or formal consequences attached to them.

Not many FBI bosses had the power to authorize off budget black ops. She knew of only a handful who could officially approve those.

But there were black ops so deep that no one ever knew about them. Or where those ops originated or who authorized them. When black ops like that were discovered, usually years or even decades later, the truth was either buried so deep no one could find it, or already destroyed.

Which was when the connection slipped into place with a jolt to her gut and then traveled up like a Taser charge to her brain. Her personal threat meter rose from a comfortable yellow to full red alert.

Brice wasn't the one sitting at the table who was too thick to comprehend the obvious. Kim was. She chuckled wryly to herself, not at all amused.

# CHAPTER SIX

*Friday, January 28*
*5:50 p.m.*
*Newburgh, New York*

AS IF HE'D NOTICED her epiphany, Brice swallowed a big mouthful of burger and washed it down with the last of the coffee in his mug. To his credit, he simply picked up where the conversation had left off.

"Good burgers here. You should try one next time," he said as if they might have more opportunities to dine together in the future. "As for the stakeout, desperate times call for desperate measures, and all that, I guess. We've got a case we can't solve, and there's a very old, very tenuous connection to the house. We were hoping for a break, even a thin one."

"When she went into the house, that wasn't the break you were hoping to get."

Brice shook his head. "But we weren't unhappy about it, either. Which is why we didn't just walk up and ring the doorbell."

"I'm not following you." At least, not exactly.

"The house once belonged to an Army general. Leon Garber. Died a few years ago." He thumped the center of his chest with the flat of his fist. "Bad ticker. Did you know him?"

"Should I have?" Kim shook her head. She hadn't known Garber, but she'd seen his name several times in the past ninety days. In Reacher's Army files. But everything to do with the Reacher assignment was strictly under the radar, by orders from the very top of the FBI food chain. Her stomach was acting like a terrified jackrabbit.

"Garber had a daughter. She was divorced at the time he died, different last name. A lawyer. Jodie Jacob. Do you know her?" He reached into his pocket, pulled out his phone, and thumbed through a few photos until he found the one he wanted. He passed the phone over to Kim. "That's a few years old."

Kim studied the photo. Pretty woman. Some men would say beautiful, probably. Blonde, blue-eyed, pale skin, fine bones. Thin enough to make a living on the Paris fashion runways. Which is to say practically death-eating-a-cracker skinny. She looked about thirty years old in the photo. She'd be mid-thirties or so now.

"Sorry. I don't know her. Never heard the name before." All true. Jodie Jacob's name appeared nowhere in the Reacher files the Boss had provided to her. Nor had she seen the name anywhere else. She shook her head and handed his phone back. "You think she's the woman in the tub?"

He shrugged. "Possible. She's got a connection to the house. And a definite resemblance between that photo of Jacob and the body, don't you think?"

"Hard to say, even given the minimal level of decomp. All I saw was her head and face. The rest of her body was submerged

in green goop. Forensics should be able to answer that, though."
The omelet was way too greasy to eat. Her panicked stomach
wouldn't accept it now. Even the aroma was nauseating.

Kim pushed the plate aside and munched another piece of
toast to soak up the acid in her gut. "If Jodie Jacob's alive, she's
reachable. Lawyers are generally pretty easy to find."

Brice grinned, showing average teeth, probably straightened
by orthodontia as a teen. "Yeah. It's getting rid of lawyers that's
the problem, right?"

"You know I'm a lawyer, right?" She frowned, just to mess
with him.

The grin fell instantly from his face. "Oh. Uh, no. I didn't
know. Sorry. No offense intended."

He'd rolled over. No fight in him. Too easy to win. "Just
kidding, Brice."

Brice frowned, slightly confused. "You're not a lawyer?"

"I am a lawyer. But I'm not offended. No worries." She
smiled and shook her head, for good measure. This guy had no
talent for witty repartee. God, he was boring.

She missed jousting with Gaspar. He had a quick rejoinder
for everything she tossed at him. The verbal warfare kept them
both alert and focused. She wondered what he'd make of Brice
and the whole situation here.

Gaspar was recovering well, he'd said when she'd called
him at home in Miami yesterday. But only thirteen days ago he'd
suffered a gunshot wound. A glancing blow, but the injury to his
already weak and damaged right leg was healing slower than
he'd hoped. He wouldn't be back on the job for a while yet.

Which wasn't much of a problem since the Reacher case had
gone quiet right after the Palm Beach situation, anyway. For the
past week, she'd been back in Detroit, but the work she'd loved

for years before she'd been called out on the hunt for Reacher all of a sudden felt dull and lifeless.

She'd never thought of herself as an adrenaline junkie, but maybe she was.

Brice wiped three fries in a pool of ketchup with his fingers before popping them in his mouth. "Jacob was a partner in a big Manhattan law firm. A few years ago, she was transferred to Europe. We haven't had any luck locating her so far."

"Which is one reason you're thinking that's her in the tub."

"Plus the connection she had to the house at one time. I mean, her father owned the place. If anybody described the body in the tub, that description could match Jacob. Even the Jacob photo I showed you looks like the dead woman. It's a reasonable hypothesis." He seemed a bit defensive. Maybe the Jacob theory was something he'd come up with on his own.

"Why did you go into the house today?"

"What?" His eyes widened as if the question was startling. This time, the wide-eyed act didn't fool her. He was stalling.

"You said you'd been watching the house, and the woman went in ten days ago. You never saw her come out, I gather. So why did you go in there today instead of, say, yesterday or last week or tomorrow?"

"I'm, uh, not exactly sure. My boss told me to go in and check around. Maybe he was tired of waiting. Or maybe he got a tip or something." Brice shrugged. "You can ask him. He wants to see us when we're done here."

"Who's your boss?"

"Alan Deerfield. Assistant Director of the New York Field Office. Do you know him?"

"By reputation only." Kim sat back in the booth and sipped her coffee. "People say he's a hard-ass. Pugnacious. Should have been promoted years ago, but his attitude held him back. That true?"

Brice grinned and dipped his head in what she interpreted as tentative acquiescence. "There's some support for that view, I guess."

Well, that's just swell. The last thing she needed was some jerk in Manhattan on her back. She already had more of those types to deal with than she needed.

Kim finished the coffee and returned the empty mug to the table. "Why call me in on this? I don't have any particular expertise that would be helpful here. Could be a suicide or some clever murder. Nothing suggests the body is anything other than a matter for the local PD. Not yet, anyway. Even if it's an FBI case, New York has one of the most competent teams in the country. Deerfield must know that, and he's proud of it, too, I'll bet. So why call me?"

"He'll tell you all about that when we see him."

Before she had a chance to press further, his phone vibrated on the table beside his plate. He picked up the call. "Uh, huh... I see... Okay. Who is it? Thanks."

He disconnected and drained the last of his coffee. "The body's been found. The local detective assigned to the case is on the scene. The electricity's turned on."

Kim said nothing.

"Let's go see what we can find out." He stood up and tossed two twenty-dollar bills on the table. "Come on. I know you want another look at that crime scene."

"You think so? Brice, you don't know me at all. But trust me when I say that I don't appreciate being jerked around." Kim made no move to leave her seat. "Tell me why I'm here. Otherwise, I'm done."

He was torn, she could tell. He frowned. He looked down. He cocked his head.

"I'll handle Deerfield if you need me to cover for you," she said. "But I'm going nowhere with you until I know what the hell is going on."

He sat down again and cleared his throat, still frowning. He jiggled his leg under the table nervously.

She could feel the vibrations.

Brice eventually came to the only possible solution. But he was miserable about it. "It's complicated."

Kim hid her smile behind her hand and coughed to cover her laughter. What a wuss.

"You been to the DMV lately?" His puzzled expression would have been funny if he wasn't so dense. Kim shrugged, giving him a mental time limit to make up his mind. She tired of waiting. "Everything is complicated, Brice. We just suck it up and do what we need to do. What's it going to be? You tell me what's going on or I'm leaving. Your choice."

He cocked his head and frowned, perhaps considering how much trouble he'd be in if she didn't go back to the Garber house. His bouncing leg jiggled the whole table now.

After another minute, he'd run out of alternatives, yet continued to resist the only choice available.

As her mother often said, when there's only one choice, it's the right choice.

Kim fished her phone out of her pocket. She opened an app and ordered a car. It would take a while for the limo service to get here, given the driving conditions. She'd need more coffee. She raised her hand to flag the waitress over.

"I could simply pick you up and toss you into the SUV," Brice said like he'd seriously thought that one through.

"You'd want to make damn sure you succeed on the first attempt," she said reasonably. Better men than Houston Brice had tried to coerce her. They always regretted the effort.

He narrowed his eyes and lifted his chin, like a defiant teenager. "You're every bit as impossible as they say you are."

"So I've been told," she replied. The waitress arrived with another pot of coffee, poured two fresh cups, and left again. "Just leave my bags inside the door over there on your way out."

He ran a hand through his hair in frustration and finally gave up. He took a deep breath. "We requested you because you have information about a possible witness."

"A possible witness in this case? I don't see how. I didn't even know the case existed until I walked into that bathroom." She cocked her head. "Who is this witness, anyway?"

"Guy's name is Jack Reacher."

# CHAPTER SEVEN

*Friday, January 28*
*6:40 p.m.*
*Newburgh, New York*

HER ENTIRE BODY TENSED like a giant bungee cord at the bottom of a free fall. She rapidly processed the known facts.

No way Brice could have made the connection from Garber to Reacher and then to her.

A complete stranger like Brice starting with Garber and possibly connecting him to Reacher and then definitely connecting Reacher to her was a monstrous level of terrifying.

Because if Brice could do it, others could, too.

Garber had retired after decades of military service. He had connections to every Army officer that had ever served during those decades.

Reacher was one officer among thousands.

Parsing through all those names, locating known associates, even with an entire team of agents, would have taken Brice months, if not years.

Which meant that Garber's name alone, even accompanied by a thorough FBI background check, could not have sent Brice or Deerfield searching for her. At least, not so quickly.

But even if Brice had been lucky and found records suggesting Reacher could somehow be a good lead for whatever he was doing with Garber, the connection to Kim didn't exist in any records anywhere. Never had.

Her Special Personnel Task Force background investigation on Reacher was deep black ops. Not an approved undercover operation, which would have produced a paper trail, but totally off the books.

No eyes on the operation at all. Not even high-security clearance personnel knew about it.

No one even had a good reason to look at her, the SPTF search, or Reacher.

She and Gaspar had been running the job independently, supervised only by the Boss, who was several levels above any Assistant Director in any FBI field office, including New York.

The Boss would never have read anyone at that level into this particular operation.

Not in a million years.

Yet, Deerfield knew.

Because Brice knew, and he could only have been sitting on that house and now across the table from her like a petrified deer caught in the headlights of an eighteen-wheeler, if Deerfield had told him.

Only two ways that could have happened.

An informant.

Or a leak.

She shoved that thought aside. She'd come back to it. She needed more intel to work with first.

"What does Reacher have to do with this?"

Brice said, "He's a person of interest."

She wouldn't have been more shocked if he'd said Reacher was a Martian. "*Reacher*? A person of interest in that Garrison bathtub case?"

"Not exactly," he glanced down again.

Kim held herself in check. What she wanted to do was choke the intel out of him. "Then what, *exactly*, are you saying?"

"See, Jodie Jacob was Reacher's girlfriend. The one that got away, from what we can tell." Brice cleared his throat again. "Jacob left him for a job in Europe. He wasn't okay with that. Didn't want her to go. Didn't want to stay here without her. She didn't want him to come along. Get the picture?"

No.

Because Reacher was a love 'em and leave 'em guy. She'd met enough of his women to know that much about him.

All those women were still alive and breathing, by the way. So far, none of them had been the least bit concerned that Reacher would kill them and stuff their bodies in a bathtub full of green.

She shook her head. "Spell it out for me."

"You've had the same training I had." Brice shrugged. "Nine times out of ten a woman's murdered, it's her lover who killed her."

"Right," Kim said sarcastically, although those statistics could be relevant. For starters, the body in that tub had been dead for at least a week. She absolutely believed she'd seen Reacher in Palm Beach thirteen days ago. Air travel being what it was, he *could* have returned to Garrison and killed Jodie Jacob.

"When Garber died, he left the house to Reacher. When he and Jodie Jacob were together, Reacher lived there."

"Which makes him a killer who would hide the body in his

own house?" Kim didn't buy it. She could understand why Brice and Deerfield would, though. They didn't know Jack Reacher. Knew nothing about his character. She didn't know a lot about the guy, but she would never believe he did this based on what little evidence she'd seen so far.

What did Brice and Deerfield know? Maybe they'd looked at his Army files and found the bodies piled up. Reacher was one of the best-trained killers the Army had ever produced.

But she'd learned the hard way that there was more to Reacher than the Army's records revealed. A lot more. Some of it better and some of it worse than what was in those old files.

Kim knew in her bones that committing a twisted murder, like the woman in the tub, was not the kind of thing Reacher would do. For starters, he didn't kill women. At least, none she'd identified so far.

Every woman Kim met who'd been involved with Reacher was a living, breathing, Reacher fan. Astonishingly so. It was one of the many confounding things about the guy.

So why would he kill Jodie Jacob?

Because she left him? Was Brice right about that?

Possible, she supposed. Some guys, especially tough guys like Reacher, couldn't deal with rejection from women. Kim simply didn't believe Reacher was one of those guys.

And if Reacher had killed that woman, Brice and his pals were watching the house. They'd have seen him around, the same way they saw her. It's not like Reacher was invisible. Far from it. The guy was almost as big as Reggie Smithers.

Brice was barking up the wrong tree.

Which meant something else was going on here.

She needed to find the source of the leak to Deerfield and plug it.

The fastest approach was straight through Brice.

Kim began to breathe normally again. Her alert level backed a hair off the full stop at the end of the red line.

She rose from the table and slipped her coat on. "Okay. You convinced me. Let's go."

Wisely, he said nothing else to make her change her mind. He followed her outside.

# CHAPTER EIGHT

*Friday, January 28*
*7:45 p.m.*
*Garrison, New York*

THE THIRD TRIP ALONG the snow-covered route that followed the Hudson River was no faster than the first two. Almost an hour after they left the restaurant in Newburgh, the SUV came around the last dark curve into a light show that almost blinded Kim and Brice, even through the windshield.

The surreal scene at the house bustled like a Las Vegas traffic jam along the strip. Flashing red, blue, yellow, and white lights were everywhere. Dozens of pedestrians moved hither and yon like ants hard at work on dismantling a picnic.

In the driveway, on the shoulder, and lining the road on both sides were squad cars, a small fire truck, and two unmarked NYPD sedans, along with vehicles for paramedics and crime scene techs.

The only official vehicle Kim didn't see was the second FBI SUV. Smithers and Poulton had skipped the party.

Also on the shoulders were three media vans, all with satellites on top. Reporters and camera operators were staked out at various spots, setting up for their live shots.

The house was ablaze with interior and exterior lights, some placed temporarily by the various first responders. Hardly an inch of the entire property remained in the shadows, which irrevocably altered its deadly vibe. Only the real estate photos she'd found persuaded Kim this was the same house where they'd seen the body in the bathtub mere hours ago.

Nothing about a single homicide should have generated this level of response.

"Brice," Kim's anger flared. "Why are all these people here? What do they know that I don't?"

"Beats me," he replied as if he had no clue. "But we'll find out soon enough."

She didn't believe him. Not even remotely. She fumed in silence.

He parked on the shoulder at the end of the line of official vehicles, and they climbed out of the SUV. The temperature had dropped down into single digits, and the wind had picked up. The wind chill factor made it feel sub-zero in an instant.

They trudged through the packed snow, collars turned up, heads down, and hands pushed into pockets.

At the driveway's entrance, a uniformed police officer from the local cop shop checked ID and turned the media sightseers away.

Brice and Kim showed their badges, and he waved them through. They covered the packed snow path toward the front entrance quickly. Along the way, various professionals passed as they worked to collect and preserve the evidence inside and outside the house.

Another local police officer was posted at the front door. Brice showed his badge and Kim did the same. This time, the officer didn't wave them inside, and Kim was freezing.

Brice nodded toward the officer's nameplate, pinned above the left breast pocket of his shirt. "Chambers, right? I'm FBI Special Agent Brice. This is Special Agent Otto."

Chambers nodded, but he frowned, and he didn't move. "We didn't request assistance from the FBI."

Kim stomped her booted feet on the sidewalk in a futile effort to warm up, while Brice tried to reason with Chambers until he'd exhausted her patience. She stepped onto the stoop and moved through the doorway.

"Where do you think you're going?" Chambers demanded. He glared as if he might shove her back outside.

"You're not in charge here," Kim replied. "Who is?"

"NYPD Detective Mariette Grassley," Chambers said as if the name should mean something in particular to all sentient beings.

Brice sputtered. "NYPD has no jurisdiction out here."

"We don't have the resources to handle a case like this." Chambers said. "We invited NYPD to take the lead."

This was excellent news. Competent cops were always better to work with than incompetent ones.

"It's too cold to stand around out there. We can find Detective Grassley ourselves if you need to man your post," Kim said as if she had authority to deliver orders. "Or we'll wait inside while you let her know we're here."

Chambers looked from Kim to Brice and back again. He spent another full second thinking things over before he made his choice. "Wait here."

He turned and walked toward the master bathroom, leaving

his post unoccupied, which allowed Brice to come in from the cold.

Kim looked at the big, open room. She'd imagined the room bright and inviting, as the real estate photos depicted. Without furniture, it seemed both larger and smaller than it was. The drapes were shabby, and the floor was scuffed and worn. The walls were marred by holes, scrapes, and evidence of hard use. They badly needed Spackle and at least two fresh coats of paint.

The kitchen, on the other hand, was as magnificent as the photos. The appliances and fixtures, cabinetry and countertops, cost more money than Kim earned in five years. But here, too, the room was well used, and the floors and wall paint were damaged.

When Chambers returned to his post, as if he was announcing the impending arrival of the Queen of England, he declared, "Detective Grassley will be right with you."

Kim waited until he turned his back. Then she headed toward the master bedroom. She'd covered ten feet of the distance when the detective stepped out of the room to block her path.

"Where do you think you're going?" Chin out, shoulders back, fists clenched at her side, she resembled a Valkyrie ready for battle. Red curly hair held back in a scrunchie, flashing blue eyes, caramel freckles across her nose, and a chip on her shoulder the size of Devil's Tower completed the image.

"You're Detective Grassley?" Kim asked because she couldn't resist. She showed her badge. "FBI Special Agent Kim Otto. This is Special Agent Houston Brice. We'd like to see the body."

"We didn't ask for your help, Agent Otto." Grassley's tone made it clear she didn't want any help, either. But she would. Very soon. "Why are you interested in this case?"

Brice replied ingratiatingly. "We'll explain, Detective Grassley. But we'd like to see the body first."

Grassley folded her arms across her chest and refused to budge. None of the uniformed personnel were overtly watching, but they were paying attention to the war of wills. The prudent thing was to let Grassley win the skirmish and save face, which Brice-the-wuss would probably do.

"To be clear, are you denying the FBI access to view the body? Because if that's the case—" Kim pulled her phone out, refusing to back down. Bullies only respected one thing. Equal force. "We'll make a call to the Director to resolve the issue."

The standoff ended when a crime tech called Grassley to return to the master suite. She narrowed her eyes and stared at Kim, then Brice, and then back to Kim again. "I assume you have your own gloves?"

Brice pulled gloves from his pocket and pulled them on. Kim did the same.

Grassley said, "Follow me."

# CHAPTER NINE

*Friday, January 28*
*8:15 p.m.*
*Garrison, New York*

BRICE FOLLOWED CLOSE BEHIND Grassley, moving ahead quickly. Kim hung back, observing what she hadn't been able to see in the dark when she was here before. The high-end, looped Berber carpet ran the length of the hallway and into the master bedroom. It was clean and looked relatively new. She didn't notice any obvious green stains anywhere. If the green liquid in the bathtub had been carried in over this carpet, the containers must have been sealed to avoid spills.

She opened each of the doors and looked inside the rooms. They were unoccupied, and the windows were covered by the same heavy drapes as the common room. The real estate photos had shown three of the rooms furnished with beds and the fourth had been an office. The same light-colored Berber covered all the floors. The carpets still showed dents from heavy furniture, which made visualizing the layouts easier. She saw no green liquid stains anywhere.

The paint on the walls in each of the rooms and in the hallway had faded. Artwork had hung on the walls long enough to preserve the original colors in random squares surrounded by the washed-out hues.

Kim paused at the threshold of the master bedroom. Like the other rooms of the house, this one was flooded with bright light from temporary sources supplied for processing the scene. Techs were working in several areas, blocking her view, but overall the room was starkly harsher than it had seemed in the micro-beam.

She looked for green stains and saw none.

Deep dents in the carpet suggested a heavy king-sized bed had been placed against one long wall, with bedside tables on either side of a square headboard. A large chair might have occupied one corner. Perhaps a chest of drawers had rested across from the bed. A television probably sat on top of the chest, because a cable connector outlet was mounted on the wall seven feet above the floor, but there was no visible evidence suggesting a wall mount. Next to the electrical outlet behind one of the bedside tables was a landline telephone plug.

The paint was as faded here as everywhere in the house. Darker color squares dotted the walls here and there. The same thick drapes covered the windows. The big closet was as empty now as it had been before.

The double doors to the bathroom were open wide. Crime techs were documenting, collecting and preserving trace evidence here, too. The bright lighting ricocheted off every surface of the white room. Kim paused at the threshold and looked down, to allow her eyes to adjust to the sharp, painful glare.

Grassley, Brice, and a woman in a white lab coat gathered around the bathtub. The body and the green liquid were exactly as Kim had seen them originally. Crime techs collected samples. A photographer snapped photos of the room and close shots of the body.

"These folks are FBI Special Agents Houston Brice and Kim Otto." Grassley identified them first and then named the others. "Dr. Sonya Spielberg, Officer Melanie Brennan, and Officer Greg Cortez."

Everyone nodded.

Brice asked, "Have you identified the victim?"

"We know she's not the owner of this house. We're running facial recognition, but no hits yet," Grassley replied. "We need to get her out of there before we can do dental records and DNA. We didn't find her wallet or any kind of ID. It's not likely we'll find good fingerprints, either."

"Any preliminary guesses on time, cause, and the manner of death, Dr. Spielberg?" Brice asked.

"Too early to say. The body temperature is very low. Which has helped to mask the time of death. Could be a couple of days or a couple of weeks. Probably not more than a month," the woman in the lab coat replied. "We'll know more when we get her back to the morgue and do the autopsy."

"When do you think you'll have the preliminary completed?" Brice asked.

"Maybe tomorrow, late, if we're lucky. Probably not until Monday."

Kim said, "Have you identified the green liquid, Officer Brennan?"

The tech collecting samples replied, "Not definitively. But if forced to guess right now, I'd say it's oil-based paint. The right viscosity, no obvious separation or color deformity, no visible ice crystals. Oil paint dries slowly, but this has been here long enough for a skin to form on the surface."

"Latex paint is more common for house interiors, isn't it?" Kim asked. "This place looks like it could use a good paint job."

"Yes, and we found several gallons of latex in the garage, but none of it's green. No empty cans that once held green paint, either," Brennan said. "Latex is water based. It should be stored between sixty and eighty degrees and would freeze at thirty-two degrees. Temps have been well below freezing for the past five to six weeks. The stuff in our bathtub here shows no obvious signs that it's been frozen."

Kim inhaled a few times before she asked, "Shouldn't we be able to smell chemical odors coming off an oil-based paint?"

"Hard to say. Usually, the odors dissipate in maybe two to four days. This stuff has been here a while, but this is a lot of paint, and it's not dry at all. Some of the odor should have dissipated anyway," the tech replied. "But the skin on the top is probably helping keep the odor down, too."

"Could she have been poisoned by the paint?" Kim asked.

Grassley replied, "Possible. If she ingested it or breathed it into her lungs, maybe it's likely. We won't know the cause of death until we get the autopsy."

Cortez, the photographer, ignored the conversations as he moved around the room adjusting angles and grabbing snaps. When Brice blocked Grassley's sight line, Kim moved toward Cortez and tilted her head toward the bedroom. He walked along with her.

Kim pulled a business card from her pocket and offered it to him. He returned a card of his own.

"I'd like a copy of your photos. I can make a formal request and go through channels, which will take a while. So I'll get that process started as soon as we leave here. But I'd like to get moving on our end of this quickly. Any chance you could help me out?"

"Yeah, sure. No problem. We're all on the same team here, right?" Cortez replied easily. "How about I give you a call when I'm done here, and I can shoot a set up into the cloud for you?"

"Perfect. My cell number is on the card. Thanks, Cortez."

Kim rejoined the team in the bathroom. Grassley was conferring with the techs working in the massive shower. Brice stood back to watch Dr. Spielberg processing the body in the tub.

Brennan had completed her sample collection. She'd hooked up what looked like a fifty-five-gallon drum vacuum and stood near the foot of the tub with the hose.

"Sorry for the noise," she said before she placed her hand on the switch. "I'm going to vacuum this liquid out of the tub, and we'll be able to see the body."

"How long do you think that'll take?" Brice asked, checking his watch.

"The tub is oversized and probably holds about sixty gallons or more for a bubble bath. But the killer didn't want her head submerged, so he only added less than twenty gallons of the green stuff." Just before Brennan flipped the switch, she said, "Shouldn't take too long."

The vacuum roared to life, and all further attempts at conversation were futile. Brennan put the hose beneath the surface at the foot of the tub. The hose was clear so she could watch for foreign objects if she happened to pick up any. Once the tub was empty, the vac would be taken to the lab where the liquid could be analyzed.

The green liquid traveled sluggishly through the hose, and

the level in the bathtub dropped incrementally. Cortez ran a video of the entire process.

The first thing Kim noticed were the tips of Jane Doe's toes. Her feet were splayed, each foot pointing toward its side of the tub. Slowly, her feet became visible to her shins.

Her legs were positioned in a V-shape from her pelvis. Her hands were crossed low over her abdomen, left over right, elbows close to her body. Her torso was next.

The vac continued to draw the green liquid until she was fully exposed in the bottom of the tub. She was naked. Green liquid had collected in thin lines along the natural crevices of her body emphasizing each one. Her skin showed very little deterioration, considering the conditions.

On the front of her body, she had no visible tattoos and wore no jewelry. The only body piercing Kim could see was one hole in each earlobe, which had collected a tiny dot of green paint, making the holes easy to spot.

She was a natural blonde. Her body was achingly thin but well proportioned. And other than the two holes in her ears, there wasn't a single visible traumatic mark on her. She looked as peaceful as a corpse in a coffin.

Brennan turned off the vac. Cortez stopped recording.

The whole team saw the entire body for the first time simultaneously. No one spoke. No one moved.

Brice clasped his hands over his stomach, unconsciously mimicking the body's pose. His mouth was set in a firm line. His brow furrowed.

Grassley was the first to speak. "Let's get back to work everybody."

The team broke up and returned to their various jobs, but the room was much quieter now. Spielberg took charge of the body.

When she was satisfied that the team was okay on their own, Grassley motioned to Brice and left the room.

Kim pulled out her phone, snapped a few photos of the body, and dropped it into her pocket before she followed them. Her photos were automatically uploaded to a secure server, in addition to the photos and the video she'd shot earlier. The Boss should have access to them at this point. If he was paying attention.

# CHAPTER TEN

*Friday, January 28*
*10:05 p.m.*
*Garrison, New York*

THEY WALKED DOWN THE corridor to the empty room that
had been an office. Grassley closed the door and leaned against it.

"Why is the FBI interested in this case, Brice?" Her voice
was calm and her tone civil. One colleague to another. She
looked exhausted. "The NYPD and the FBI work together now,
since nine-eleven. We all understand the jurisdictional lines.
Routine homicide is not an FBI matter. You're here. So what's
going on?"

Brice took a deep breath. He looked tired, too. "The truth is
that we don't know. Not exactly. We may not be interested in the
case at all. That's why we needed to see the body. But until you
identify her, there's nothing more I can say."

"My people handle homicides all day every day. We can all
agree that this one is weird. If the FBI believes something more
is involved here, we need to be prepared. I can't put my team or

the public at risk because you haven't read me in." Grassley was right, of course. Kim would have answered her questions. But she didn't know any more than Grassley knew.

"I hear you. I understand." Brice nodded. He wrapped his right palm around the back of his neck, elbow akimbo like he was considering the problem. "At the moment, it's a homicide. It's your case. When you identify the body, and the cause, manner, and time of death, things could change. The sooner we know what we're dealing with here, the better for all of us."

"What are you worried about?" Grassley's face pinched. "Is she carrying a contagious disease? Is she filled with explosives?"

All good questions, Kim knew. Common sense said that a dead body was harmless. Common sense was wrong and had been for a couple of decades now.

"Not that we know of. Nothing like that." Brice shook his head again. "But as you said, standard protocols are in place, and we should all follow them, Mariette."

She looked steadily into his eyes for a few moments. "I've got to get back to work. Thanks for stopping by."

"Let's keep in touch," Brice said, as Grassley left the room.

She flipped him the bird on her way out and didn't look back. Kim grinned, but she didn't comment.

"They're going to be here all night. We won't find out anything more until tomorrow." He grimaced but said nothing about Grassley's parting salute. "Let's go. We can talk in the car."

They trudged through the frigid cold toward the SUV without speaking.

Kim tried to puzzle things through. Start with the obvious. Brice hadn't been straight with her or Grassley. Nothing about this whole thing passed the smell test.

Brice said Reacher was a person of interest in the case and that's why the New York Field Office had reached out to her. But the setup, the location, the bathtub, the cause of death, and even the paint? No. All of it was way too convoluted for Reacher.

Yet, something odd was going on here. She simply didn't know what it was. Or why and how it involved her. Until she knew, she couldn't leave. Forewarned is forearmed, and all that. She'd become constantly vigilant since she'd been tasked with investigating Reacher's background for a highly classified special assignment. But no one knew better than Mrs. Otto's daughter Kim that you never see the bullet that gets you.

She thought about the woman in the tub.

Kim had only seen one old profile photo of Jodie Jacob, the one on Brice's phone back at the restaurant. She might look entirely different now. Different hair. Heavier. Who knew?

But if Kim had to place a bet right this moment? Yeah, the odds were short that the woman in the tub was Jodie Jacob. The smart money was on her.

And if Brice was right about her relationship with Reacher, Jacob had been more important to him than the other women Kim had met so far. Maybe he'd even loved her at one time.

That simple thought opened up a whole batch of issues that Kim hadn't considered before. Reacher in love? What would that look like?

More specifically, how would Reacher's more human emotions impact her SPTF assignment?

That question was the last one that popped into her head before they reached the SUV. She filed it away for later.

They climbed inside, and Brice fired up the big engine. He executed a difficult three-point turn on the narrow road amid all the oversized vehicles parked on the shoulders and headed north on the twisty road toward Newburgh again. No new snow had fallen, and the road had been traveled enough tonight to improve driving conditions.

After a couple of miles, the engine had warmed up enough and Brice turned on the heat. The cabin began to thaw. Brice found his phone and made a call.

"We're on our way back. Couple hours' drive. Maybe more." He paused to listen. "Hard to say. No positive ID yet. But looks like her to me. Yeah. Same as the others."

He disconnected and gripped the steering wheel while peering into the unnatural darkness. "We've got a long drive back to the city. Keep me awake. Ask your questions."

Kim was a human lie detector. Like the machines, she needed a baseline. So far, Brice had been evasive, but he hadn't told any obvious whoppers. Since it was a crime to lie to an FBI agent, and since he was such a straight shooter, he probably would stick close to the truth, at least.

Might as well start with the easy ones. "Who did you call just now?"

"Deerfield. He was expecting us quite a while ago." Brice slowed and swerved around a tree limb in the road, brought down by the heavy snow.

Probably true. "What did you mean when you said same as the others?"

Brice shook his head. "Do you mind if we come back to that one?"

She shrugged, although he couldn't see her in the dark cabin. She said, "For what it's worth, I don't believe Reacher killed that woman."

He seemed surprised when he glanced at her and asked, "Why not?"

"Several reasons. Starting with his M.O. with women. But mainly, the murder's not his style."

"What does that mean?"

"You've read Reacher's Army files. You know what his skill sets are. If he'd wanted to kill her, he'd have used one of his usual methods. Guns and mayhem, usually."

Brice nodded slowly, soaking up her intel like a dry sponge. "Why do you think that?"

"Same reason you do. Because that's who he is. Straightforward. Honest, in his own way." She paused for a breath. "And because his methods work. They're fast, effective, and he's good at deploying them. One of the U.S. Army's best, by all accounts. Why would he change something that works for a convoluted kill like this one?"

Brice paused a beat too long before he nodded. "Makes sense. I guess."

Kim noticed the pause and let it go. For now. "You think that woman in the bathtub is Jodie Jacob, right?" Kim watched him as carefully as she could in the blue glow of the dashboard lights.

He breathed deeply, wiped his face with his palm, and snapped his grip to the wheel again. "I'm afraid so."

Kim nodded. Interesting phrasing. Not quite yes or no.

Although if he meant the phrase literally, he was smarter than she'd given him credit for. He should be afraid of Reacher. If he wasn't, then he was a fool. Good time to find out.

"And your theory is she was the great love of Reacher's life. The one who got away."

He hesitated as if he knew more, but she hadn't asked the right question yet. "Yes."

"Here's something to ponder, if you're right about that." She cocked her head and offered him a wry smile. She stretched like a cat, working the kinks out of her tired body. Giving him a little time and space to anticipate. Ramp up his anxiety level. "You allowed someone to kill her right under your nose."

Brice's wide-eyed glance came at the same time a deer dashed across the road.

"Look out!" Kim said, pointing ahead.

He whipped his eyes to the front and lifted his foot from the accelerator just in time to avoid a massacre. Deer could do a lot of damage to a vehicle. Not to mention the paperwork involved when a government vehicle hit one.

When the SUV was rolling smoothly north again, and Brice's breathing had returned to normal, Kim said, "What do you think Reacher will do to you when he finds out you watched the woman he loved go inside that house and you never even checked on her?"

"I'm not too worried about that," he said, easily.

Probably true. Which was also good to know. Her original assessment of his low mental acuity confirmed, she smiled.

He was a fool. He should be worried. Very worried.

# CHAPTER ELEVEN

*Saturday, January 29*
*1:05 a.m.*
*New York City, New York*

UNLIKE GASPAR, WHO COULD sleep through the detonation of a nuclear bomb at his elbow, Kim never slept in a moving vehicle of any kind. But Brice didn't know that. She closed her eyes and leaned her head back, and he spent the drive alone with whatever thoughts rattled around in his head.

They'd made good time once they reached the interstate and arrived in New York City shortly after one in the morning. Brice maneuvered through relatively light traffic like a pro, heading straight for their destination.

In Tribeca, he circled the block twice and finally found a parking spot not too far from Mostro's, a busy Italian restaurant abuzz with a late-night crowd.

Brice told her the place had struggled for a while until its reputation was made by a rave review from the food guy in the *New York Times* and all of a sudden, the owner looked like a genius for starting out with a building large enough to house an automobile showroom. The food guy said the portions were small, but the ravioli was to die for. After that, people flocked to the place around the clock.

They hurried along the sidewalk, which was sloppy with snow and slush, but easier to navigate than the roads, driveways, and parking lots upstate had been.

At the front entrance to Mostro's, Brice held the door while several upscale diners filed out, then he and Kim slipped inside. Brice gave his name to the tuxedoed man at the desk. A tuxedoed woman offered to take their coats and supplied a plastic tag in return.

"Right this way, Mr. Brice. Mr. Deerfield is waiting," the man said. He led them through two dimly lit dining rooms filled with prosperous New Yorkers enjoying the best food and drink the city had to offer. Toward the back of the restaurant, he opened a door that blended so well into the pale maple paneling Kim might have walked past it, even in broad daylight.

The private dining room held a single round table set for three. Only the center chair facing the door was occupied. An older man with a thatch of gray hair and calm but tired eyes behind thick glasses. Dark suit, red tie. He looked like what he was, a senior bureaucrat with one of the most important jobs in the country. He didn't stand up when they entered the room.

Brice moved to his seat on the man's right and gestured toward the opposite chair.

She joined the table and extended her hand. "Special Agent Kim L. Otto."

He hesitated and then shook hands. "I'm Alan Deerfield. Assistant Director, FBI. I run the New York Field Office."

Kim respected professionalism and competence, which no

man in Deerfield's position could operate without. Meaning he feigned that humble attitude to manipulate her. The interesting thing was that he'd bothered to make the effort. She wondered why.

She settled into the chair across from Brice. A discreet knock on the paneled door preceded a tuxedoed waiter with a tray. He delivered cookies arranged on a silver platter, coffee in a silver carafe, china cups, cream, and sugar. He withdrew as quietly as he'd entered and closed the door.

"Sorry for the late night after such a long day, Agent Otto," Deerfield said. "I won't keep you long. I'm headed out of town early tomorrow, so tonight is our only chance to talk for a few days."

"I appreciate your consideration, sir," Kim replied. She sipped her coffee and waited.

"Let me cut right to the meat of this thing. What I'm about to reveal is highly sensitive, classified information. You're authorized to discuss it only with the two agents sitting in this room. Understood?" He looked over his thick glasses, eyebrows raised as if this were a casual question instead of an order.

"I have a partner, sir. I don't feel comfortable withholding information from him."

Deerfield replied, "Agent Gaspar's on medical leave. We should have this wrapped up before he returns to work."

Kim nodded, mostly because she figured he wouldn't tell her anything if she rejected his terms. Besides, she didn't need his permission to talk to Gaspar. Her orders came from a higher authority.

Deerfield cleared his throat and leaned his forearms on the table. "A few years ago, a special task force worked an unusual serial killer case. Five victims, all women. They were found in their homes submerged in their bathtubs, each one containing twenty gallons or so of olive green camouflage paint."

He paused as if he wanted acknowledgment, so Kim nodded again, and he continued. "There were several other unusual features to the case. The murders were not clustered. The victims lived in various locations around the country. Which meant the killer was mobile, free to travel, and with the means to do so, as well as the means to commit the murders when he arrived. The case became a multi-office, cooperative effort. We had good forensics. Full autopsies were performed. But the cause of death couldn't be determined for any of them."

Kim nodded, acknowledging the likelihood of solving a series of murders under circumstances like that had to be close to zero. "How did you finally identify the killer?"

Deerfield shook his head. "The killing stopped, and the case went cold."

She shivered as the implications sunk in. "You think the body out in Garrison is the same guy, started up again."

"Possibly," Brice replied. "We don't know, but that's the obvious place to start. We need to rule it out."

"It's unusual for serial killers to stop for a long time and then restart. The compulsion that leads them to kill is powerful. They don't have a strong desire to resist those demons," Kim said.

"But it happens, unfortunately." Brice bowed his head. "I work Organized Crime, so I had to look this up. But the list of cold cases, where serial killings were interrupted but continued after a lengthy pause, is not something anybody in law enforcement likes to brag about."

Kim opened her mouth to request more facts, but she didn't get the chance.

"You two can cover all that later." Deerfield waved a hand in the air. "The reason we pulled you in on this, Otto, is because eventually, you'd have reached that old case anyway. Because Jack Reacher was a person of interest."

Kim felt her eyes widen in astonishment. "Are you kidding me?"

Brice shook his head. "Unfortunately, we are not."

"But—" Kim's objection was interrupted by Deerfield again.

"He knew all the victims. They were Army vets. When Reacher was an MP, he handled cases involving each of them. The connection to Reacher and his motive for murder were the only solid leads we had." Deerfield paused before he delivered the rest. "We scooped him up, he cooperated with us, and he was ruled out as a suspect. I made the call, after spending some time with him and reviewing the evidence we had available. I'm not pleased to know that I made the wrong decision, believe me."

Kim's head was swimming with the implications, whipsawed between incredulity, euphoria, and suspicion.

Reacher had been a suspect in a serial killer case handled by the FBI. He was interviewed. He was ruled out. The case wasn't closed.

At each step of that process, voluminous records would have been created. Multiple copies. Stored in various locations.

Several agents and other FBI personnel would have been involved.

A treasure trove of information about Reacher should be contained in those files.

*Files that did not exist. She knew because she'd looked. Thoroughly. More than once.*

*Which meant the files had been removed. By someone with way more juice than Alan Deerfield.*

She had so many questions, she didn't know where to start.

Before she had a chance to make a choice, Deerfield added even more outlandish details.

"Because Reacher knew all the victims, and because of his background as an MP, after we ruled him out as the killer, we read him in on the case."

*Say what?* Otto's mouth fell open. She snapped it shut, hoping Deerfield and Brice hadn't noticed.

"Reacher worked the case with us. He was an insider. He knew everything we knew. We trusted him. He attended meetings, worked directly in the field with our teams. Learned details we didn't release to the press or even to other agencies." Deerfield paused. He cleared his throat. "That may also have been a mistake."

*Had she joined Alice through the looking glass?*

Deerfield's admission was just as startling as his revelation of Reacher's involvement with the FBI. Assistant Directors admitting mistakes were rarer than the Star of India sapphire.

She cleared her throat and asked the blandest thing she could come up with. "How so?"

"The killings stopped after Reacher joined up with us." Deerfield looked down and fingered the tablecloth as if he was embarrassed to say what must be said. "Now we've got another murder. Similar MO. If the victim is Jodie Jacob, and we haven't been able to rule her out, she knew Reacher even better than the five women in the prior case."

Brice said, "The possibility we're considering is that maybe he was ruled out too soon back then. Reacher could have been the guy who killed those women. He might be active again now. And he's smart enough to change up his methods to make us believe we've got a copycat."

Kim's mouth dried up. She sipped cold coffee to wet her

vocal chords. "I'd like to see the old files. I might be able to identify something useful."

"Brice has already reviewed them. He's fully briefed. He'll work with you on this. Stay with you every step of the way," Deerfield said. "That'll be a lot faster. Save some time. We want this thing handled as quickly as possible."

The room fell silent, collectively holding its breath. Almost as if time stood still. She heard her own pulse pounding in her ears.

"Do you understand, Otto?" Deerfield asked.

She understood way more than he realized. But she was afraid to nod.

She actually believed her head might explode if she moved it.

Questions zipped through her mind faster than Usain Bolt sprinted a hundred meters.

What wasn't she being told? And why?

How did Deerfield know about the SPTF background check on Reacher? The assignment was off the books and had been from the beginning. Reacher's connection to Kim didn't exist in any records anywhere. Never had.

The SPTF assignment was deep black ops. Totally off the books. No eyes on the operation at all. Not even high-security clearance personnel knew.

She and Gaspar had been running the job independently, supervised only by the Boss, who was several levels above any Assistant Director in any FBI field office, including Deerfield.

The Boss would never have allowed Deerfield or anyone at that level into this particular operation. Not in a million years.

Who did Deerfield get his intel from?

*What the hell was his agenda here?*

Deerfield crossed his hands on the table as if the matter were settled. "Brice will work with you. Your assignment is simply stated but won't be easy to execute. You'll find Reacher, and either charge him or rule him out."

She nodded and breathed a little easier. She'd begun to see the possibilities.

These new ground rules could be better than fine. She could hunt for Reacher openly, using full FBI resources. Which was much better than hunting him off the books and without support.

But these two were up to something and whatever it was wouldn't be to her benefit.

She was nervous about Brice and Deerfield, all the way around. She didn't trust either of them two feet outside her range of vision. Her gut said at least eighty percent of what they'd just told her was total bullshit. The other twenty percent was disingenuous at best.

But for weeks, she'd been chasing Reacher's ghost on the down low using only her wits and whatever the Boss deigned to tell her. Putting her life on the line. Gaspar's too. Which was how he'd been shot. They had nothing to show for their efforts except a bunch of open questions and a lot of confusion.

Whatever these two were trying to do here, they'd presented an opportunity too good to refuse. Still, Deerfield didn't care about anything but his own agenda, whatever that was. Until she had a handle on him, the last thing she wanted was for Deerfield to get to Reacher before she did.

Which meant she needed some insurance, and there was only one place to get what she required.

# CHAPTER TWELVE

*Saturday, January 29*
*2:05 a.m.*
*New York City, New York*

DEERFIELD SIGNED FOR THE check, and they left Mostro's at the same time. A limo collected him at the curb outside the restaurant. Kim and Brice walked to the SUV.

"We made you a reservation at the Grand Hyatt. I'll drop you off." Brice said.

The plan jarred. She rarely came to New York, and she didn't have any particular hotel preferences. But she and Gaspar had stayed at the Grand Hyatt at Grand Central a couple of times on the Reacher SPTF assignment.

Brice's plan proved he knew that.

Which meant he had somehow acquired too much information about her and her assignment already.

She was way behind the curve here. She needed to catch up. Fast. But first, she had to understand exactly what she'd become caught up in.

Brice pulled up to the valet entrance, and a doorman approached her window.

"Checking in?" he asked.

She nodded. She opened the door. "Could you grab my bags from the back seat?"

"Sure thing." He collected her bags, closed the door, and moved to the sidewalk, waiting.

She collected her phone and her alligator clamp and slipped into her coat.

Brice said, "I'll pick you up in the morning. Late. I'll call first. Get some sleep."

She grabbed the handhold above the door and stepped onto the running board.

"Oh, hang on a second." He reached into the center console and pulled out a padded manila envelope. "Smithers was supposed to give you this at the Stewart airport. It slipped my mind until now, with all that's been going on. Sorry. And here's your room keys."

"Thanks." She didn't believe he'd forgotten anything, but she leaned in to take both items. She stepped off the running board onto the pavement and closed the door. He pulled the big SUV away from the hotel quickly and made the light at the next corner, where he turned north and kept going.

Kim recognized the envelope. It was exactly like the others she'd received from the Boss since she'd been assigned to complete Reacher's SPTF background check.

The envelope began to vibrate almost before she reached the sidewalk. The cell phone inside was receiving a call from the only man who knew its number. Which meant he knew precisely where she was standing. He'd been watching her, as expected. At the moment, she found that fact both comforting and annoying.

While the hotel porter was occupied with another guest, she unzipped an outside pocket of her travel bag and pulled out a new burner cell phone. She stuffed the vibrating envelope in the empty spot and zipped the pocket closed. She slipped her personal cell phone into a different pocket.

She gave one of the key cards to the porter when he asked, along with a twenty-dollar tip. "Can you put my bags in my room, please?"

"Of course," he replied. "I'll leave your extra key up there. You might need it later."

"Thanks." She stuffed her hands into her pockets and walked along the sidewalk toward Fifth Avenue.

She walked a couple of blocks before she found a Starbucks, crowded with late-nighters texting, talking on phones, and working on laptops. Many were using the free Wi-Fi, and others carried their personal connectivity everywhere with them. Multiple signals concentrated in one place meant that communications should be sufficiently muddled for her purposes for a short period of time.

Kim stood in line. She placed her order for a grande black coffee and waited for a fresh brew. When the barista called her name, she joined a table already in use by three others.

She set her coffee down and said she'd be right back.

"Sure," one guy replied. The others ignored her.

Kim ducked into the small corridor leading to the unisex restroom but instead walked through the exit to the alley out back. A couple of smokers stood nearby, working their phones while they puffed, either too busy to notice her or too disinterested to care.

She pulled the new burner phone from her pocket, broke it out of the blister pack and fired it up.

She dialed the memorized number. It rang twice before he picked up.

"It's a bit early in the day for cloak and dagger, isn't it?" Lamont Finlay's deep, resonant voice traveled well across the connection, as always.

"I need to see you about our mutual friend," she said. "It's important."

He sighed. "Give me a couple of hours, and I'll be done here."

Kim disconnected the call and went inside. She exited by the front door and returned to her hotel with the coffee, which was both good and still too hot to drink.

# CHAPTER THIRTEEN

*Saturday, January 29*
*3:05 a.m.*
*Center Line, New York*

THE CENTER LINE MULTIPLEX was busier than Reed expected for a late screening of *The Wednesday Night Massacre*, an infamous seven-year-old movie. He took it as a good sign. A crowded theater was more chaotic than a deserted one, which would work to his advantage.

Leonard had reserved his ticket online two days ago. The timing was unfortunate because of the Garrison house situation, but Reed had always been able to pivot between tasks effectively. At this hour, traffic was light, so he'd made it here in plenty of time.

He waited until he saw Leonard get off the bus alone and trudge toward the multiplex. Reed parked near the rear exit, turned up his collar, stuffed his hands into his pockets, and hustled around to the entrance.

Leonard stood in line at the will call window outside. As

always, he was alone. He seemed to have no friends or family at all. Served him right.

A group who had bought tickets earlier in the day skipped the line at the box office window and went inside. Reed fell in behind them, provided his ticket to the attendant when his turn came and passed through smoothly.

He stood behind an eight-foot poster illustrating coming attractions, waiting until Leonard handed over his ticket and entered the main lobby.

Leonard walked past the concession stand. He entered the men's room and a few moments later, emerged again. He glanced at the clock on the wall. The movie was scheduled to begin ten minutes ago, which meant the commercials for products had ended and the previews were running. The featured film would start in five minutes.

Leonard picked up his pace and moved toward theater number four. Two other groups were headed in the same direction. Leonard pulled the door open and ducked inside.

Reed watched two guys file in behind Leonard, and then he followed. He waited a moment after the door closed behind him allowing his eyes to adjust to the darkness. The sound system blared loud enough to cause floor vibrations and permanent hearing damage. Once the movie's non-stop gunfire began, nothing short of a nuclear explosion could be heard over the theater's surround sound.

Reed smiled in the dark. He spied his prey. He leaned against the wall to wait for his cue. Timing was always everything.

Leonard had climbed the stairs along the side wall toward the top. He always chose the last seat at the end of the top row because he'd been sitting there on the night of what the media had dubbed "The Center Line Theater Shooting."

Perhaps Leonard was reliving the glory, or maybe he was simply a creature of habit. Either way, finding Leonard inside the theater was never a problem. Reed always knew where to look.

Leonard rested his arm on top of the seat to his left to discourage anyone from sitting there. Seven years ago, on the night that changed so many lives forever, Leonard had saved the seat for his best friend. Walter Boyd and Leonard Kryl had walked into the Center Line Theater that night as a couple of nerdy nobodies, for the last time in their lives.

Boyd arrived late, ten minutes into the movie. He climbed the stairs and sat next to Leonard. They waited until the big finale, an eight-minute stretch of nothing but deafening weapons fire producing on-screen carnage worse than any actual battle ever fought in the history of warfare.

Boyd and Leonard pulled out their weapons and joined the firefight. Because of the film's overwhelming violence, the theater audience didn't immediately realize they were being attacked. When they finally accepted the unacceptable, panic and pandemonium reigned along with the bullets.

After six minutes of real gunfire, thirty-eight people were dead, thirty-seven shot and killed by Boyd, who soon became number thirty-eight.

Leonard Kryl, covered in blood, heart pounding with the thrill of it all, was arrested and charged with thirty-eight counts of felony murder.

Which was when the real perversion of justice began, as far as Reed was concerned. While he waited, he reviewed the situation one last time because the outcome of his mission would be irreversible. Measure twice, cut once, as his father used to say.

Leonard's wealthy parents hired a good lawyer, and the jury of their peers just did not want to believe the evidence or follow the law. Friends and neighbors raged against school bullies who hounded mercilessly. They blamed teachers who failed to protect and theater operators who failed to secure. They conducted all-night vigils and cried for the victims, now redefined to include Leonard and his family. They joined gun control groups and protested in marches on Albany and all the way to Washington DC.

Leonard's defense was that his gun had jammed and the bullets inside, even had they fired, were blanks. He had not actually killed anyone or planned to. All the killing was done by Walter Boyd, who lost a final gun battle with police at the scene.

Leonard claimed he didn't know about his best friend's plans to kill everyone in the theater that night. Even though the boys were inseparable. Even though they had planned the assault for weeks in advance. Even though Leonard brought his loaded gun to the theater.

During the trial, relatives of some victims requested compassion for Leonard and his family, instead of vengeance for their massacred loved ones.

Every minute of the sensationalized trial was covered by the media. Sympathy for Leonard and Boyd ran high. Law enforcement personnel were disbelieved, degraded, and ultimately, disregarded.

In the end, the matter's intolerable conclusion came down to one simple thing. The jury wanted to free Leonard, so they did.

When the verdict was read, a collective gasp from law-abiding citizens everywhere was heard around the country. Grieving parents were denied justice. After a while, the Center Line Theater shooting was consigned to bits and bytes in online encyclopedias as neither the first nor the worst nor the last of its kind.

Leonard was released from jail without so much as a slap on the wrist. He finished college and now worked as a software designer. He spent his working hours developing the violent video games he craved and his off-work hours attending the even more violent films that thrilled him, almost always at the late-night show. Probably because he was less likely to be noticed or identified.

Leonard never missed a repeated run of *The Wednesday Night Massacre*, which had become a cult classic. He always sat in the same seat and saved the seat next to him for Walter Boyd's ghost to join him later.

Reed's mental review of the case had revealed no reason to abort the mission. As always, when the film's final massacre sequence began, the full attention of every patron in the theater was glued to the screen.

Reed climbed the stairs and moved across the aisle toward Leonard, unnoticed. Leonard leaned forward in his chair, immersed in the bloody battle as if he'd never seen it before, transfixed.

Reed sat in the seat reserved for Boyd, which seemed particularly fitting tonight. Leonard didn't move a muscle, anticipating the point in the movie when the audience cheered because the bad guy gets riddled with bullet holes. When the scene began, Leonard leaned forward, eyes front, supremely focused.

Reed reached into his pocket and withdrew the untraceable gun. A nice, slow, soft-nose .22 with a silencer. In one, swift, practiced motion, he lifted the weapon and put two quick rounds into Leonard's temple at the height of the blasting noise on the screen.

Two small splintery entrance wounds and two big messy exit wounds on the other side of Leonard's head seemed worthy of those cheers to Reed.

Leonard's body slumped to the wall on his right. The look on his face could only be described as blissful. Which wasn't what Reed had hoped for. Not at all.

Reed left the theater before the final on-screen battle ended. He left by the theater's rear exit, found his car, and drove away. He tossed the gun into the Hudson River when he crossed the bridge.

He wondered how long it would take them to find Leonard's body. Hard to guess. It was well past four o'clock in the morning now. In the sleepy upscale town of Center Line, the cleaning crew might have left for the night before the movie ended. Maybe no one would find him before morning.

Reed shrugged. Seven years too late for Leonard Kryl's victims, but justice had finally been served. Better late than never.

# CHAPTER FOURTEEN

*Saturday, January 29*
*3:05 a.m.*
*New York City, New York*

KIM GLANCED AT HER watch. She'd burned more time than
she'd expected, but she had a few more minutes to kill. She
needed an internet connection that might not be noticed
immediately.

Her personal equipment had access to everything she
needed, but it was in her room. If she logged on from there, the
Boss could easily track her laptop and her cell phone. Which
meant he'd know she was awake and active. She wasn't ready
for that just yet. Nor did she want to talk to him at the moment.

She checked the hotel's directory in the elevator lobby. The
amenities listed on the conference floor included a business
center, which would only have access to public information. She
shrugged. Better than nothing.

She followed the map and found the room exactly where the
directory indicated. Travelers from all over the world stayed here

and might have been connecting across multiple time zones. But she got lucky. Through the glass wall, she saw the business center was unoccupied.

Two small desks and two chairs snugged against the far wall. Each desk was outfitted with a computer and a house phone. Mounted between the desks were two shelves. One contained a ream of paper, paperclips, a stapler, and a pair of scissors. The other held a multi-function printer, copier, scanner.

Her key card could be traced through the hotel's security system. At this hour of the morning, for this particular room that was made available twenty-four-seven for hotel guests to use, only an extremely dedicated security officer would bother to monitor it constantly. The other option was to break in, which was more likely to trigger an alarm. She crossed her fingers for luck and used her key card to enter.

Inside, she chose the chair at the first computer and touched the spacebar on the keyboard. The black screen came awake. The hotel logo floated around on the display until she hit the spacebar again. A familiar search engine came up.

She didn't expect to find much, but all she wanted was a place to start unraveling the mystery of Jodie Jacob. She began with a quick name search for Leon Garber because he had been a public figure, of sorts.

She found his obituary right away, which contained a long list of professional accomplishments. He'd died at the age of sixty-four. Survived by a daughter, Jodie Garber Jacob.

Followed by the first solid lead. Jodie Jacob worked as a lawyer with the Spencer Gutman firm in Manhattan. Brice hadn't mentioned that.

Kim grinned. She'd caught a break. Jodie Jacob was not only a J.D., but she was also a New York lawyer.

Lawyers were some of the most heavily regulated humans on the planet. For lawyers with an active legal practice, anonymity was not an option.

Jacob was admitted to the bar in New York. She should be listed in multiple databases.

Which meant at a minimum that basic information like business address and phone number, date of birth, law license number, and so forth, should be findable with a few keystrokes. With luck, she'd find some photos, too.

Her optimism was short-lived.

She tried two dozen different ways to locate anything current on Jodie Jacob without success. Every result her searches returned was at least five years old. For some reason, current information on Jodie Jacob was simply not where it should be.

The old entries were puff pieces, mostly. Circulated by her law firm to enhance the firm's reputation. Jacob's pro bono work on high profile criminal cases was one of the humble brags that popped up several times.

The most notorious client she defended was a young nurse accused of neglecting her patient. The baby died. The puff piece made it sound like Jacob was Clarence Darrow and Atticus Finch combined, working against the full power of the government on behalf of the wrongly accused. Jacob tried valiantly to win a not guilty verdict for the nurse, but the best she could do was a reduced sentence, which was touted as a miracle in itself.

Odd that nothing more recent popped, though. Kim tried a few esoteric searches in public tax records and real estate listings and the like. No luck.

She checked the time on the computer's clock and finally gave up. She'd need secure connections and better databases to do the job properly, and she couldn't reach those sources on a public computer with limited internet access.

She picked up her cold coffee and headed upstairs in the elevator. She turned off the burner cell and when she arrived on her floor, stashed the phone in the dirt behind a big plant in the elevator lobby.

Inside her room, she turned the lights down to interfere with any interior surveillance. It was a risk to come back here. But she needed a quick shower and clean clothes.

Her travel bag and laptop case were in the closet where the porter had left them.

She retrieved her personal cell phone and the padded manila envelope from her bag and tossed them onto the bed. The envelope wasn't vibrating yet, which could be a good sign. Maybe the Boss had assumed she was sleeping because both of those phones never left the room after the porter brought them up.

She glanced at the clock. Finlay would be free soon. She picked up the house phone, called room service, and ordered breakfast.

She hurried into the bathroom and turned on the shower and ducked into the steamy water. She dressed in jeans and a heavier sweater, and restyled her long, black hair into the usual neat, low chignon at the base of her neck.

She checked herself in the mirror. The dark circles under her eyes revealed her lack of sleep. She dabbed concealer to cover them as well as possible. Otherwise, she thought, she didn't look too bad, considering.

She donned the hotel robe over her clothes and tied the wrap belt in a loose square knot around her waist, just in case anyone could see her. She turned on the television to create background noise.

A solid knock on the door came ten minutes later. She peered through the peephole. A waiter dressed in a Grand Hyatt uniform, pushing a cart, stood in the hallway. She opened the door, and he came inside.

"Good morning, Ms. Otto. Here's your newspaper," he said quietly as if someone in the room might still be sleeping. He handed her a copy of the thin Saturday edition of *The New York Times*.

"Thanks," she whispered.

He set up the table and asked her to sign the delivery receipt. She added a generous tip.

She held the door open for him as he left.

When he turned the corner at the end of the hallway, Kim slipped out behind him and let the door close softly, but loud enough for listening ears to hear. For a while, at least, the breakfast and the television and the two phones emitting tracking signals should be enough to satisfy watchers that she was still in her room.

She dodged the hallway surveillance cameras, grabbed the burner phone from the planter, and rode down in the service elevator where she slipped out of the bathrobe and dropped it onto the floor.

In the kitchen, she slipped through the back door into the alley. She hurried to the street and flagged down a cab.

She gave the driver the address of Finlay's hotel and relaxed against the back seat for the short ride.

# CHAPTER FIFTEEN

*Saturday, January 29*
*5:30 a.m.*
*New York City, New York*

KIM WAITED LESS THAN five minutes in a small conference room inside the spacious midtown hotel's penthouse suite. She heard footsteps in the hallway. Lamont Finlay, Ph.D., Special Assistant to the President for Strategy, pushed the door open and crossed the threshold as if he owned the room and everything in it.

Even before six o'clock in the morning, his appearance was impeccably perfect. He stood tall and straight, solid as an oak tree. Clean-shaven. Well dressed. Everything polished to high gloss. She'd seen him several times on a moment's notice at all hours. Every time, he looked like royalty, and his vibe was intimidating as hell.

"Good morning, Agent Otto." His voice was deep and resonant. He'd been raised in Boston and educated at Harvard. The accent was faint after all these years, but she could hear it.

"Agent Gaspar still on medical leave, or is he unaware that you're here?"

She smiled. Both guesses were dead on. His information sources were always precise. Not for the first time, she wondered why he continued such close watch on her activities. He was a man who kept his own secrets. She hoped that meant he would keep hers. Gaspar disagreed.

After countless arguments, Gaspar remained wary of Finlay, and Kim remained undecided. Was he friend or foe? Wiser to assume the worst, even though he had proven helpful at several critical moments.

So far, he'd been willing to assist her when no one else would. For that alone, she took risks with Finlay that Gaspar regularly disapproved.

Bottom line? Finlay held power she couldn't otherwise access. His relationship with the Boss was as ambiguous as everything else about him, but her instincts said she was better served with Finlay in her corner. Until he did something to change her mind.

"You know Alan Deerfield?"

Finlay's face remained impassive. "Assistant Director, FBI New York Field Office. In the line of succession to become Director of the FBI."

Kim nodded. "He wants Reacher."

"Why?"

"I was hoping you'd know the answer to that question."

"Why would I?" Finlay poured coffee in a china cup from the carafe on the fully stocked sideboard and carried the saucer to the sofa.

Kim did the same and settled in a chair across from him. "Do you know anything about a woman named Jodie Jacob?"

"Should I?" Finlay shook his head slowly as if he might be thinking about Kim's question.

"How about Leon Garber? U.S. Army General. Five stars. Retired. Does that name mean anything to you?"

"Should it?"

Her internal lie detector accepted his benign non-answers, and she moved on.

"Jodie Jacob is Leon Garber's daughter. Apparently, Garber was a cross between a mentor and a role model for Reacher in the Army."

"I've never met Garber or Jacob as far as I know," Finlay said. "Remember, I only met Reacher in Margrave, six months after he left Uncle Sam's employ."

Kim believed him. Mainly because his eye didn't flick the way it did when he lied to her. "Garber died of a heart attack a few years ago. Deerfield says Reacher and Jodie were lovers after Garber died."

"Sounds like Reacher." Finlay shrugged.

"How so?"

"The officer and a gentleman thing." Finlay relaxed against the sofa, one arm resting across the back. "Reacher would have considered it disrespectful to date a superior officer's daughter. If he felt any kind of respect for Garber, he definitely wouldn't have made a move on Garber's kid."

Kim nodded. What he said made sense for the military culture. Whether those cultural norms had motivated Reacher back in the day was a whole different question.

"Deerfield says Reacher was in love with Jacob. He says Jacob left Reacher to take a job in Europe and Reacher wasn't okay with that. He says Reacher took the news badly."

"Sounds plausible." Finlay shrugged again. "Couples break

up. Happens all the time. I gather this is relevant to why you're here?"

She leaned forward to watch carefully for the telltale flick of his right eyelid she'd failed to see when she'd first met him. The flick that revealed his lies. Hadn't happened so far during this conversation.

She kept going. "It's possible that Jodie Jacob is dead. Murdered."

He nodded as if the possibility was reasonable. No flick. "What else?"

Kim took a deep breath. "Deerfield believes that Reacher killed her."

"What do you believe?" He never operated from mere curiosity. Finlay's habit was to ask questions with a purpose. The technique had the effect of suggesting that he knew everything relevant already, even when he didn't say so. Most of the time, he knew.

"The body resembles photographs I've seen of Jodie Jacob. Could be her. Also, Jacob is missing, Deerfield says. She's not where she should be, and he can't find her. But that doesn't mean this victim is her, or that she's dead, or that Reacher killed her." She paused in case he wanted to offer something brilliant. When he didn't, she said, "The first step is to identify the body, which could take a while."

"You're wondering why Deerfield can't simply wait for the ID." Finlay had followed her logic. She didn't know Reacher, though. Finlay did. "You're asking whether Deerfield could be right about Reacher killing her. Or, if Reacher loved this woman, and valued his relationship with her father, and she's been murdered, whether he may want to deal with the killer himself."

"Partially," Kim replied.

"What else?" Finlay asked.

"I know this might sound a little crazy." She took a deep breath and told him what she came here to say. "I suspect Reacher's being set up. I suspect we're all being set up. You, me, Gaspar. Maybe even Cooper. But I don't know why. Or how. Or what to do about it. I believe Reacher's at the center of this, though. Somehow."

Finlay said nothing for a good, long time. Kim couldn't guess where his mind was going, but she sensed she should let him work his own way through.

After a while, he finished his coffee and placed the cup and saucer on the low table. "What is it that you want from me?"

Good question. "Deerfield had me sent here. He's assigned me to find Reacher. He's given me the full resources of the Bureau to do the job. But it feels like he has a hidden agenda, like he's trying to lure Reacher back to New York."

Finlay smiled. "According to Gaspar, I have a hidden agenda where you are concerned. Cooper, too."

Kim smiled back. "And Gaspar's not wrong, is he?"

"Touché, Agent Otto." Finlay threw his head back and laughed. But he offered no answer to the question. "Again, what do you want me to do?"

Still a good question. What *could* he do?

The precise nature of Finlay's job was nowhere described. Which was more than enough to shove her internal threat-level against the top of the red zone and hold it there. But it made him more valuable to her, too.

He'd been selected by the highest-ranking civilian responsible for Homeland Security and Counterterrorism and placed one heartbeat away from the U.S. Commander in Chief. No watchdog kept tabs on him. He reported seldom and only through verbal briefings. No paper trail so much as named the missions he'd undertaken.

Everything she'd learned about Finlay marked him as dangerous. He deployed unspecified unique skills on unidentified matters with unacknowledged results.

All of which meant that he could do anything she needed. He could squash Deerfield like a bug, among a long list of possibilities. What did she *want* him to do?

No flashes of brilliance popped into her head. She didn't know how best to proceed, and that was the problem.

She went with her gut. "Contact Reacher. Tell him what's going on. Tell him not to take the bait. To stay out of New York until this gets resolved. Whatever it is."

Finlay's eyebrows shot up. "That's what you want? You've been digging around in Reacher's background for weeks. That's your one official job. If he shows up, you can ask him your questions. Wrap up your SPTF assignment and tie a bow around it and hand it to Cooper. You can move on. Why don't you want that to happen now when Deerfield is handing it to you on a silver platter?"

"That's not what *you* want to happen, is it?" Kim narrowed her eyes. "You don't want me to find Reacher, and you never have."

"We're not talking about me." Finlay shrugged, but not even the briefest flick of his right eyelid. "How is Reacher walking into Deerfield's lair a bad outcome for *you*?"

"Call it instinct or whatever you want. I know it sounds lame." Kim shook her head slowly. "But if Deerfield pulls this off, whatever his agenda is, things won't turn out well for you or me or Cooper. Probably won't go well for Reacher, either."

"Seems likely," Finlay said.

She nodded. "I need time to figure out what's really going on and deal with it. Before Reacher steps in and makes matters worse."

"You know I can't contact Reacher. I've told you that before." She gave him the side-eye, and Finlay mocked genuine hurt feelings. "You don't believe me?"

Kim said nothing. The truth was that she didn't know whether to believe him or not. The question and the answer were irrelevant. Finlay's brand of assistance was the only chance she had.

If the Boss wanted to stop Deerfield, he'd have done it already. He didn't. Which meant that even with the most powerful player in the FBI on her side, Finlay was her best weapon. He had resources well beyond anything she could muster quietly. Every other option she'd considered would raise all sorts of red flags in several quarters, particularly in the short term.

"Tell me something about the murder case that would make Reacher back off, assuming I can find him," Finlay said, clasping his hands together loosely. Still relaxed. Unruffled.

"Deerfield says Reacher helped the FBI on a serial killer case a few years back. The case had some unusual features, and it went cold after they brought Reacher in." She still couldn't believe that story. But she hadn't debunked it yet, either.

If Finlay felt any astonishment or even mild curiosity about Reacher working with the FBI, he didn't show it.

"Serial killer cases always have unusual features of one kind or another. Serial killers are sick puppies. That's why they do what they do," Finlay said with the kind of assurance every cop who's worked such cases knew. "What kind of twisted behaviors were involved in the old case?"

She listed the points Deerfield mentioned. The paint, the women, the mysterious cause of death, the far-flung crime scenes, the connection to the Army and to Reacher.

"A bathtub filled with green paint?" Finlay asked. "What was the significance of that?"

"I haven't seen the file yet, and Deerfield didn't say. Since the case wasn't closed, the original team probably never figured that out." Kim shrugged. "Deerfield says the killing stopped for a few years and has started up again. He says some of the features in the fresh case are not the same as the old one, but there's enough similarity that he thinks Reacher was the original serial killer. And still is."

"I see." Finlay cocked his head. "And what do you think?"

"Statistically, the new murder must be a copycat. Serial killers don't quit and then start up again. Like you said, they're sick, and they're driven to do what they do. They can't just stop." She paused and took a breath. "But someone's gone to a lot of trouble to kill this latest victim and stage the murder like the original ones. Which means the killer knows about the old cases. He's clever and strong and familiar with investigation procedures, too. Reacher possesses all those characteristics and more."

"But you're not sold on Deerfield's theory that Reacher's the killer. Why not?"

"Just doesn't feel like Reacher to me, you know?" She shook her head. "What possible motive could he have?"

Finlay shrugged. "Deerfield is probably planning to ask him, don't you think?"

"The body's been there for about ten days. Deerfield's theory is that Reacher killed Jodie Jacob because she left him. And then he left town."

Finlay nodded. "Common motive in about eighty-four percent of female homicides, unfortunately."

"But what about the previous victims? There was no evidence that he'd been in love with them all or that they'd walked out on him, I'm guessing. Because if Deerfield had facts like that, he'd have told me," Kim said.

"What else?" Finlay asked.

"Wouldn't he have killed the victims in a more Reacher-like way?"

"Dead is dead. What else are you thinking?" He frowned.

"Reacher's…well, let's call him an efficient killer. The Army trains them that way, and he was an excellent student. Minimal fanfare. Weapons of choice are guns, mayhem, and brute force, mainly." She paused. "None of which were employed to kill these victims."

Finlay grinned. "I see your point."

A brief knock at the door and Russell, Finlay's Secret Service assistant, looked in. "Dr. Finlay, your seven o'clock is here. I put him in the blue room."

Finlay nodded, and Russell backed out and closed the door.

"Send me the names of the victims. I'll dig up the old file. And I need to see the new crime scene and the body," Finlay said. "Do you have video or photos?"

"Yes," Kim replied. "I'll leave you the address, too. You've got access to satellite images of the area around the house. Look back at least a couple of weeks. Deerfield says Jodie Jacob walked into the house and never came out. You'll see why that's not likely. And while you're at it, look for Reacher, too. I doubt you'll find him sneaking around that house. That's not his style, either."

He frowned. "Why would we have surveillance satellites aimed at a private residence?"

"Because the house is located in Garrison, New York. Across the river from West Point." West Point, the Naval Academy, and other military-related schools were solid targets for terrorists and skilled killers of every kind. Every military installation around the country was watched constantly by various US agencies. Probably monitored by foreign actors and private industry, too.

"Ah. I see. What does Cooper say about all of this?" Finlay asked.

Kim paused long enough for him to guess that she hadn't discussed her theories with the Boss.

Finlay nodded, and his frown deepened. He stood and buttoned his jacket. "No promises. I don't know where Reacher is. I've told you that before. I can put the word out that I want to hear from him. Send me what you can on the murders. I'll let you know if I have anything useful to contribute."

When he left the room and closed the door behind him, her adrenaline plummeted. She fell back into the chair, exhausted. Finlay drained every ounce of energy she could muster, every time. She never let him see her sweat, but the truth was that he scared her beyond reason.

Gaspar would say she was an idiot to get Finlay involved in this thing, regardless of what was actually going on. Which was precisely why she didn't tell her partner she was coming here, either.

She couldn't linger, although she wanted to curl up on the sofa and sleep. She took the elevator to the lobby and a taxi back to her hotel. She stashed the burner phone in the planter by the elevator again.

When she reached her room, the manila envelope was still lying in the center of her bed next to her personal cell. The envelope was vibrating like crazy.

She shook her head. This time, the Boss probably didn't see her enter the hotel since he thought she was already in her room. He'd probably been calling since yesterday morning, at intervals, attempting to reach her. He wanted to talk, but she wasn't ready. Not yet.

She tossed the envelope and her personal cell onto a chair and collapsed on the bed. She closed her eyes and fell into a deep sleep in less than ten seconds.

# CHAPTER SIXTEEN

*Saturday, January 29*
*8:35 a.m.*
*New York City, New York*

HER BRAIN EVENTUALLY REGISTERED the nagging
intrusion through the fog of sleep. Once the fog was penetrated,
she subconsciously identified the noise. Her personal cell phone,
vibrating incessantly. Six long rings, and then automatically sent
to voicemail. Every time the unanswered call kicked over to
request a message, the caller hung up and tried again.

She ignored the sound for a while, but after two dozen
attempts, she caved.

Without opening her eyes, she fumbled until she found
the phone under the manila envelope in the chair where she'd
tossed them.

"Otto." She answered the call without looking at the
caller ID.

"Were you still sleeping? Sorry. I've been calling awhile.
Figured you were in the shower," Brice said. He sounded awake

and alert and annoying as hell. "I'm on my way to pick you up. We've got a full plate today. Be there in ten."

"No." Her voice croaked. She needed another couple of hours of shut-eye. At least. "Sorry. Can't."

"Can't what?" Brice sounded preoccupied, but not discouraged. "Turn your television on. Get up to speed on the media coverage. Someone did us a favor. Shooting at that theater out in Center Line. Where the big mass shooting was a few years ago. Lots of coverage for the new murder. Our case is already number two on the lineup in local news and moving down the list."

"What are you talking about?" She opened her eyes to find the remote and pressed the power button. The screen came to life on the hotel menu. She located the live TV button, muted the volume, and ran through channels until she found the all-news station.

The Center Line Theater shooting was front and center, as he'd said. She read the crawl along the bottom of the screen. One man shot. Shooter in the wind. She closed her eyes and flopped back on the bed.

"We've got a little space now. Let's make the most of it before the spotlight comes back. I'll detour and grab you a big coffee. Pick you up at the valet entrance in twenty." Brice disconnected before she could refuse again.

Kim groaned. She punched up the volume on the TV and headed to the shower. She wasn't dirty, but she needed to wake up. Coffee alone wouldn't do the job.

She caught headlines while she dressed. There were very few known facts about last night's shooting beyond what she'd read on the crawl.

One body, identity not public until next of kin could be

notified. Killed execution style with small caliber bullets to the left temple. They didn't mention the size of the exit wounds on the right temple or how those bullets mash up the brain on the way through. For Kim, they didn't need to explain.

The rest of the coverage was a rehash of the original case. The Center Line Theater shooting had been one of the worst mass shootings in the country at the time. She listened with half an ear.

Kim remembered the basic facts fairly well. Two seventeen-year-old boys were engaged in a role-playing game at the release of a popular movie. The film had been developed from an exceptionally violent video game. The climax scene was an epic gun battle. The teens joined in, using guns they'd stolen and smuggled into the theater.

One of the teens had loaded his weapon with blanks, which he said later was their plan.

The other teen had loaded his with live bullets.

The shooting had shocked and horrified the upscale community where the most noteworthy thing that ever happened was bad weather during tourist seasons.

When the shooter was killed by police a few minutes into the firefight, inevitable questions about his motives remained unanswered.

During the wee hours of this morning, Kim figured it was the second teen who had been executed. There was no more accurate way to say it, although the reporters did their best to avoid the word for understandable reasons. Speculation was rampant that the executioner had been a bereaved family member of one of the original victims.

For the twenty minutes Kim paid slight attention to the broadcast, nothing was mentioned about the body in the bathtub in Garrison. Brice was pleased, and so was she, but probably for different reasons.

Keeping the media off her back on a new homicide was a full-time project. Coverage made her job exponentially more difficult every time.

But Deerfield couldn't be happy. Delayed reporting could mean that Reacher wouldn't hear about the bathtub murder for a while. If Deerfield were still in town, he'd probably have already scheduled a press conference, she thought sourly.

Which made Brice's reaction even more curious. He'd been such a toady last night. Why the change of heart?

She kept the set on and left the room. She retrieved her burner phone from the planter before entering the elevator and made her way downstairs to the valet entrance.

True to his word, Brice was waiting out front behind the wheel of the black SUV. So predictable. Some women might find that comforting, Kim supposed. She climbed up and settled into the passenger seat. Two cups of coffee were waiting in the console's cup holders. Reliable, though, which was okay.

"Where are we going?" she asked.

"Meeting Detective Grassley first. Then the morgue. The autopsy on our vic could be finished this morning."

"I need to know what we're doing here, Brice. If we're not dealing with a serial killer, and we both know the odds are long this killer is the same one as the old cases, then we don't have any jurisdiction on a homicide. Grassley has made it clear she's not inviting the FBI into her case." She punched the plastic opening on the cup's lid and swigged her first coffee of the morning. "Later today, I'll read the old case files. For now, tell me what I need to know."

"Deerfield gave you all the highlights already. He worked

the original case because Reacher was living in New York when he was picked up. Five victims, various locations around the country. All the victims suffocated, but they never figured out why. All were found in a bathtub filled with Army green paint." He shrugged. "That's about it."

"And the killing simply stopped?" She stared at him a second or so until he noticed. "You're sure nothing happened to the guy? Like some not-so-friendly fire, maybe?"

Brice shrugged. "Our killer could have been arrested and sent away for something else. If he was military, and he could be since the victims were vets, he might have been deployed. Maybe he's been sick. Heart attack or a car wreck kept him off the playing field for a while. Could be a thousand explanations. Who knows?"

"How, specifically, was Reacher involved in the case?" Kim asked.

Brice glanced at her. "Investigators scooped him up in an alley near Mostro's. Saw him roughing up a couple of guys who were shaking down the owner. Our protection rackets unit had been watching these two and saw the whole thing. Reacher pounded the guy's head on the concrete a bit too vigorously, I guess."

Kim shuddered. "How was that related to the bathtub cases?"

Brice squirmed in his seat. "It, uh, wasn't. The Serial Crimes Unit was already looking for Reacher. They had him as a person of interest because he knew all the victims like we told you. When he ended up in custody, they hit the jackpot, I guess."

"So they flipped him? Pressured him into cooperating with the investigation?"

Brice shrugged. "The file's a little unclear on that. But he ended up working with our team on the case. Until the case fizzled. Then he moved on."

Kim thought about the story for a couple of minutes. "How'd he get out of the maimed mobster problem?"

"The file's vague about that, too."

"Figures." She wasn't the least bit surprised. Where Reacher was concerned, the patterns repeated. The guy was a trouble magnet. He attracted felons like rotten fruit attracts angry wasps. When he managed to get himself arrested, he never stayed in custody very long. "Was there a female agent on the team, by any chance?"

"I don't know. Why?"

Kim smirked. "I've got fifty bucks that says an attractive woman was on the investigative team. Wanna bet?"

"Uh, maybe, I guess. Dunno." Brice cocked his head. He pulled into a parking spot at the curb. "Grassley's waiting for us."

Kim scanned the busy Manhattan street. She saw nothing familiar. "Where are we?"

"Wall Street. Jodie Jacob's law firm, Spencer Gutman. Grassley's interviewing the partners."

"Grassley identified the body? It's definitely Jacob?"

"Not yet. But maybe we can rule Jacob out. Whether it's her or not, we need the interviews. Come on."

He walked around the front of the SUV and waited for Kim to climb out. They found the elevator and rode up into the rarified air of pricey Manhattan real estate.

The firm's reception area was quiet. After a couple of minutes, a woman returned to the front desk. Brice showed his badge and asked for Grassley. The woman led them down a corridor lined with law books on oak shelves. They came to a set of double doors.

She opened the door to a blinding wall of windows. "Detective Grassley, your colleagues have arrived."

Once her eyes adjusted, Kim saw Grassley at a long conference table, backlit by the rare winter sunshine. Across the table was a stocky man, about fifty, thinning brown hair. Dressed in a suit that cost more than the entire wardrobes of all three public servants combined.

The man looked up.

Brice flashed his badge again. "FBI Special Agents Brice and Otto."

The man nodded, "Charles Copeland."

Grassley said, "Mr. Copeland worked closely with Ms. Jacob. Until she left the New York office for Europe and later, she left the firm."

Kim cocked her head. "Wasn't Jodie Jacob a partner here? My friends who have partnerships in firms like this are serving a life sentence."

Copeland chuckled. "The golden handcuffs are very real, Agent Otto. Partners do usually stick with us until they retire or die. But no one is chained to the desk. Slavery's been illegal in this country for a century or so."

Brice swept his arm wide. "So you're saying Jodie Jacob simply walked away from all this?"

"We didn't fire her if that's what you're asking. Which is another thing that's hard to do with a partner, anyway," Copeland replied. "She did a stint in our European offices. We were very happy with her and with her work. No one wanted her to go."

Kim said, "But she wasn't all that happy with Spencer Gutman, I gather."

He shrugged. "I don't know why she left. I already explained that to Detective Grassley."

"When did she stop working with the firm?" Grassley asked.

Copeland shook his head. "Maybe a couple of years ago? I'm not sure. Spencer Gutman is a big firm. More than a thousand lawyers, all told. She was a member of my department, but we weren't working together directly. I was here in Manhattan, and she was in Brussels at that point, I think."

"Where did she go when she left Spencer Gutman?" Brice asked.

Copeland shrugged again. "I don't really know. By the time I found out she was gone, it was months later. Our paths haven't crossed again."

"Anybody here in the New York office who would know where she's working now?" Kim asked.

Grassley said, "The personnel department gave us her residential address. They said they didn't have a new professional address for her."

"That's unusual, isn't it Mr. Copeland?" Brice asked.

"I don't know. I don't handle personnel matters for the firm," Copeland replied.

"What is your area of expertise, exactly?" Kim asked since he seemed to know almost nothing about a partner in his own department, which she found hard to believe.

"Same as Jodie's. Mergers and acquisitions. But my clients are based on the East Coast, primarily. Like I said, Jodie worked with our European clients. Totally different continents."

"Yeah. Europe and the U.S. are on different continents. I'm aware." Kim held on to her patience, but barely. "When did you see Jodie Jacob the last time?"

"Maybe five or six years ago? She would have been here in New York." He cocked his head and pooched his lips to work in a way that could have meant he was seriously thinking about the question. Or not. He shrugged. "I remember the party when we celebrated her election to partner. I'm really not sure if I saw her again after that. I haven't been to our European offices for at least a decade, and like I said, that's where she was working. I'm sorry I'm not more help."

Grassley asked, "Did you know any of Jacob's friends or family?"

Copeland cocked his head again. "There was an ex-husband, I guess. And after that, a significant other. Do we still say 'boyfriend' anymore?"

Brice replied, "Boyfriend is fine. We know what you mean."

"He came to her partnership party, but he was late getting here. Big guy. Huge. Must have been six-five, two-fifty, at least. Hands the size of catcher's mitts. I remember he looked a mess. Like he'd been in a bar fight or something." Copeland paused and wrinkled his nose. "He wore dusty work boots, and his clothes were wrinkled and crusty with what he said was dried paint. Really strange. We don't see many guys like that in our offices. Not the kind of thing you forget."

Kim felt her breath catch in her throat. "What was his name?"

"Joe? Jim? Jack? John? Something short like that, I think. But she called him something like Teacher, as I recall. No clue why."

# CHAPTER SEVENTEEN

*Saturday, January 29*
*9:45 a.m.*
*New York City, New York*

COPELAND HAD ALREADY GIVEN up the only useful thing
he was likely to admit, so Kim tuned him out. Reacher was
Jacob's boyfriend. She'd been serious enough about him to
invite him to her partnership celebration, which no newly elected
partner would do with a casual date. That day, his work boots
and clothes were wrinkled, dusty, and stiff with dried paint.

First question, unless Copeland was lying, which seemed
unlikely, how could Reacher explain the paint? Jodie Jacob
might have asked him. Under those circumstances, a normal
girlfriend would have. If Reacher had been the original serial
killer, he'd probably have lied. If he wasn't the original killer,
then he might have told her something no one else would know.
Lovers shared stuff like that, or at least the normal ones did.

Kim wandered to the window wall and looked fifty stories
down to the almost deserted street below. Saturday wasn't a big

day on Wall Street for traders or tourists, either, when the temperatures were below freezing.

Grassley and Brice continued with the Copeland interview. When Grassley asked to speak to associates Jacob had worked with, Kim was ready to move on. She understood why Grassley needed to follow every possible lead, but she wasn't going to find Jacob here.

It was time to talk to the Boss. She'd put it off too long already. She had questions, and he had answers. Whether he'd tell her anything helpful was always a crapshoot, but he might.

She asked Brice for the keys, slipped out of the conference room, and returned to the SUV. She found the Boss's manila envelope, tore it open, and retrieved the burner phone inside. It wasn't set up for voicemail and he wouldn't have left any kind of recorded message anyway. But the list of recent calls were all from one unidentified number, as expected.

This area, like all New York City, was under constant surveillance. Everything was recorded. But monitoring all that data was a monumental task and on a Saturday wouldn't be a top priority. She closed the SUV and walked half a block along the sidewalk before she pushed the call back on the last one. After two rings, she wondered where he was.

He picked up on the fifth. "Making any progress?"

"Weren't you listening?" She swiped her palm over her face. The cold wind blowing through the street felt like standing in a wind tunnel. She hugged her coat tighter around her body.

He ignored the question. "I sent file materials to your partner."

She knew he meant Gaspar. "What kind of materials? The old serial killer file? I can get that from here."

"Remember where you are. Eyes and ears are always on. Not all are friendly." He said nothing more for a moment. "Talk to him."

She understood the surveillance risks but took a chance anyway. "How does Deerfield know about our assignment?"

Another long silence on his end of the connection. "I'm working on that."

"Did you redirect the media from this case?"

"No."

"Takes the spotlight off the bathtub murder, which is exactly the opposite of what Deerfield wants. Can't see why he'd be responsible for that particular misdirection."

"In that case, we'll give the shooter a medal when they find him," he snapped.

Kim grinned. She'd pushed him into showing his hand. That didn't happen often. His view of Deerfield was the same as hers. The Boss didn't like the guy. Good to know because it meant he could take care of Deerfield. Maybe he would.

"After you talk to your partner, call me back," he said.

Before he disconnected, Kim asked, "Is Jacob's body in the bathtub?"

This time, the long pause was eventually followed by a terse reply before he hung up. "Possibly."

She stood outside in the biting cold wind for another half a second. It was too cold to stay out here, but the cabin of the SUV was monitored more closely than the eyes and ears constantly surveilling the financial heartbeat of the country.

She glanced around the almost deserted street until she spied an open coffee shop up the block on the other side and a drugstore on the corner. She locked the SUV and hurried along the sidewalk, careful of the snow and ice along her path.

# CHAPTER EIGHTEEN

*Saturday, January 29*
*10:45 a.m.*
*New York City, New York*

KIM HURRIED INTO THE drugstore, found the small electronics aisle in the back, and bought four new burner phones and a package of gum. She paid with cash and stuffed the phones in her pockets and hurried out again. Two doors down, she entered the coffee shop.

She texted her location to Brice once she settled into a table in the back. The Boss and anyone else who could track her personal cell phone would know where she was. Who else would care enough to pay attention? Deerfield and Finlay, at least. Which was okay for now.

Brice replied to her text. They'd found a couple of associates to question about Jacob. He'd be another half hour, at least. She texted, "OK."

She pulled up a list of recent calls on her personal cell. Brice's number was repeatedly listed, covering about twenty minutes this morning before she'd finally picked up. Before that, the last call was the one she made yesterday from the airport in Detroit to tell her mother she wouldn't be there for Friday night dinner.

From her personal cell, she dialed Gaspar's home number. On the third ring, he declined the call, which was their signal that he was available.

She called again on one of the new burners she'd bought at the drugstore. A blocked number called back less than a minute later. She noticed it was one digit different from the number she'd dialed to reach the Boss. He wanted to talk on a phone the Boss gave him, which would make this new burner useless after the call.

"Good to hear from you," she said when she answered.

Gaspar replied, "You've got file materials to download. From both of us. As soon as you can."

"Will do. But it could be a while. I don't get much time to myself."

"Understood." Gaspar's words were clipped, but his tone was relaxed.

"I'll call again when I can," she said and waited for him to disconnect.

She'd worked with Gaspar for not quite ninety days and she'd never seen him lose his composure. Not once. No matter what happened.

She'd discovered that Gaspar and Reacher were wired very much alike. Both were exceptionally masculine men. Similar ages. Similar expertise. Ex-Army officers. Cops, more or less. Reacher had been a military policeman for thirteen years. Gaspar was an MP and afterward, had joined the FBI as a special agent. Both had stellar careers, for a while. Both had washed out early but in different ways.

Gaspar was unlike Reacher in a few other critical ways as well. Reacher was a loner, a drifter, no family, few friends, never around when needed. Gaspar was happily married and the father of five, including a new baby. He'd lived in Miami all his life, amid a very close extended family. He was about as anchored down as a man could get, and he loved it.

The differences between the two men made Gaspar a great partner and a good friend. The similarities made him her secret weapon. Simply put, Gaspar understood how Reacher thinks. When she used Gaspar's expertise appropriately, it gave her an edge she wouldn't otherwise have. An edge Reacher definitely did not have when he tried to anticipate her moves.

She walked back to the unisex restroom and went inside. She locked the door. The place was filthy, which wasn't okay, even though she didn't intend to touch anything. She removed the back from the burner phone she'd used to call Gaspar and dismantled it. She flushed those bits down the toilet. She stomped on the plastic case and flushed those pieces next.

Every conversation in this area of the city, including the coffee shop, was recorded and could have been monitored in real time. Her brief exchange with Gaspar, too. Nothing she could do to change those facts. But she could try to make them feel comfortable enough that they wouldn't bother paying attention to her. At least, not immediately.

She walked back to her table, pulled out her personal cell and placed another call to Gaspar, this time to his personal cell. When he picked up, she said, "I've got a little time to kill while I'm waiting for Agent Brice. You have a minute to talk, Chico?"

She could feel Gaspar's grin traveling all the way from Miami. "I got nothing but time, Susie Wong. My leg's improving. I'm going insane watching soaps all day."

"I'll bet you're driving your family nuts, too. When can you get back to work?"

"Monday. Marie will drive me. Desk duty only, for a while. But at least I'll be doing something useful."

Gaspar loved his kids like crazy, but he wasn't the kind of hands-on dad who coached soccer. His talents lay elsewhere. Even with his disability, he was a damn fine FBI Special Agent, and he'd saved Kim's butt more than once. He loved being in the field. Sitting at a desk would drive him nuts.

"I've caught a new case while you're basking in the sunshine by the pool. Detroit loaned me out to the New York Field Office," she said, choosing her words carefully to convey only what she wanted known. Since she was in a public place, discretion would be expected by civilians, anyway.

"Anything you can tell me about it?" Gaspar replied.

"Not much at the moment. Two reasons. One is we really don't know much yet. The other is that I'm in a coffee shop." She paused. "Tell me about the kids."

So he did. For about five minutes, until Brice's text interrupted. He was on his way back to the SUV. She casually left the coffee shop, chatting with Gaspar all the way back to the vehicle.

When Brice and Grassley walked out of the Spencer Gutman building together, Kim moved a bit quicker. She wrapped up the call, dropped the phone into her pocket, and met them at the SUV where they stood huddled against the wind on the sidewalk.

"What's next on the lineup?" Kim asked.

Brice said, "Looks like the coroner is running behind. She hasn't started on the autopsy yet. No use going to the morgue until she's got something to tell us."

"We've got a residential address for Jodie Jacob. I'm going to head over there," Grassley replied. "You coming?"

"Where is it?" Brice asked.

"Broadway. South of Canal, I think. I don't have the address handy," Grassley replied.

Kim could see that Brice was torn between seeing Jacob's apartment firsthand, and something else. She wondered what the other thing was because Jacob's apartment had probably been unoccupied for quite a while. Visiting her apartment was pro forma for Grassley, but nothing useful to Kim would come of it.

Brice said, "Have you interviewed her ex-husband? He's a lawyer, too, I guess."

Grassley replied, "Not yet. He's on the list. But they've been divorced for years. It's not likely he's got anything helpful to add."

Kim said, "Have you identified the body in the tub yet?"

Grassley shook her head. "Her DNA doesn't match any of our databases, which only means she wasn't convicted of a felony in New York since we started collecting DNA from prisoners. We've got a subpoena being prepared for the ancestry websites, which could turn something up next week."

"Doubtful." Kim stomped her feet to stay warm. "Fingerprints?"

"Because Jacob is a lawyer, her fingerprints are on file. But the fingerprints on the body were degraded by what we believe is the chemicals in that paint. The lab is working on it."

"Dental records?" Brice asked.

"Jacob left no family to give consent. We're working on a court order for the dental records." Grassley raised a hand to tame wisps of curly red hair that had escaped her scrunchie and bounced around her freckled face. "This case is less than twelve hours old, Brice. We're working on all of it. And it's not the only thing on our plate besides the gangbangers, as you no doubt heard."

"Right. Of course," Brice said, shivering. "Any leads on the latest Center Line Theater killer?"

"That's not my case." Grassley grimaced. "But nothing, as far as I know. It was a professional hit. That's all we know so far."

Brice nodded. "We've got a meeting with another agent on a different case. Let's touch base in a couple of hours. How's that?"

"Fine. I'm friggin' freezing my ass off out here. Call me whenever you feel like it," Grassley growled and stomped off toward her unmarked sedan parked at the curb down the block.

"What's wrong with her?" Brice's quizzical expression reminded Kim of a puppy who doesn't understand potty training.

Kim pushed the button on the key fob to unlock the SUV and handed Brice the keys. She climbed into the cabin. She managed to stifle her laughter while he started the engine and buckled up. Her empty stomach reminded her that she hadn't eaten anything since that dry toast in Newburgh last night, and for a long while before that because of the plane flight. She glanced at the clock on the dashboard. Almost noon. Her stomach growled.

Brice glanced over. "Don't worry. I'm planning to feed you."

"Glad to hear it. When?"

"Half an hour or less. Traffic's light."

"It takes that long to get to FBI headquarters from Wall Street on a Saturday?"

"We're not meeting at headquarters." Brice took a quick left.

Something about his tone was odd. "Who are we meeting? If I don't need to be there, I brought a ton of work with me. I can get room service."

"One of the agents who worked on the original bathtub cases with Reacher is in town for meetings. She's leaving later today, so this is our only chance to connect with her before she goes back to Portland."

A dark red blush started at his collar and flooded his face all the way to his hairline.

Uh, huh. Just as Kim figured. "What's her name?"

"Harper, I think."

"You think?"

"Well, I mean, I-I haven't met her before. But the caller ID on the message said L. Harper." He was perspiring now, and he looked thoroughly miserable.

"You've seen her picture. She's attractive. Right?"

"I swear, I would have mentioned her name when you asked me about female agents on the cold case. I didn't know she was in town. I hadn't seen her photo when you asked me about attractive women yesterday." His apoplectic complexion and the pulsing vein in his right temple attested to his stress levels. Maybe he had high blood pressure, too. The guy was a walking stroke waiting to happen.

"Of course not," Kim replied, sarcasm thick as peanut butter on bread.

Her cell phone rang before she had the chance to let him off the hook. She fished it out of her pocket and saw the caller ID. It was the hot Treasury Agent she'd met a couple of weeks ago. They'd been talking regularly, but that's as far as things had progressed because they were both busy and he lived too far away for casual drinks after work.

She put the smile into her voice when she connected the call. "Hello."

"Kim? It's John Lawton."

"Good to hear from you. Guess where I am?" she said, warmly.

"Detroit, I hope. I just landed. Still on the ground at the Delta terminal. I'm only here for a couple of nights. Any chance we can have dinner while I'm in town?"

She shook her head. No wonder she never had a date. Not that she'd been looking when Lawton showed up. Maybe her mother was right. Maybe she really was married to the FBI.

# CHAPTER NINETEEN

*Saturday, January 29*
*10:45 a.m.*
*New York City, New York*

REED HAD FOLLOWED BRICE from Otto's hotel to the
building that housed Jacob's Wall Street office. When they went
inside, he moved the stolen car he'd borrowed from a parking lot
to a better location, one with a clear sight line to Brice's
unmarked SUV. He'd recognized Grassley's unmarked sedan
parked a few spaces farther up.

Otto came outside alone. She'd made a phone call, but she
hadn't used her personal cell phone. She was using burners. He
slammed the flat of his hand on the steering wheel in frustration.
Who was she talking to? Reacher? No way to tell using the
equipment he had with him.

He'd watched her walk along the sidewalk, doing more
talking than listening. The call was fairly short. She returned to
the SUV and locked it. Then she trotted across the street to the
drug store, went in and came out with no shopping bags in her

hands. She moved into the coffee shop. He had a clear view of both from his new vantage point.

She moved deeper into the coffee shop where he couldn't see her. She had her personal cell on her so he could track her. After a while, she made a call. She moved even deeper into the shop, stayed a short time, then returned and made another call, this time on her personal cell.

The phone number she called was her partner, Gaspar. Reed listened to the conversation, which was nothing but inane chatter. When Brice and Grassley came out of Jacob's office tower, Otto joined them at the SUV. The three split up.

Grassley stomped off toward her car. Brice and Otto entered the SUV. Briefly, Reed considered following Grassley. But Otto was more important to Reacher, so Reed stuck to his original plan.

Eventually, Brice dropped Otto off at a restaurant, and she went inside. Brice parked down the street and walked back. The restaurant was crowded and too noisy. Reed couldn't hear any of the conversation.

He figured they'd be inside for at least an hour. Which would give him time to change vehicles and come back before they moved on. If they left early for any reason, he could track both phones and Brice's SUV without difficulty.

He needed a sedan. One he was reasonably sure wouldn't be reported stolen for a few days, at least. And he knew precisely where to get it.

# CHAPTER TWENTY

*Saturday, January 29*
*12:30 p.m.*
*New York City, New York*

THEY REACHED THE RESTAURANT ten minutes late. Brice dropped her off at the curb. While he parked the SUV, Kim went inside to find Harper. Locating her only took a nanosecond because she was waiting just inside the door, hand extended to shake.

"Agent Otto? I recognized you from your FBI profile photo. I'm FBI Special Agent Lisa Harper. NSB. Please call me Lisa."

They shook hands and Kim tried not to stare, but it wasn't easy.

Harper wasn't simply attractive or merely stunning. She was spectacular. And so far out of Houston Brice's league that he couldn't even hope to find the ballpark with a GPS.

She had long, straight, blonde hair pulled back in a low ponytail. Her face was tanned and her teeth so brightly white a toothpaste company should have snapped her up as an international ambassador. Wide blue eyes were rimmed with lush black lashes. No makeup other than a touch of lip gloss that reinforced her youthful appearance. She had to be mid-thirties, but she looked a decade younger.

She was also more than six feet tall, in ballet flats. Long-limbed. Very slender. Wearing an extensively tailored man's suit that showed off her body. White shirt, loosely knotted tie. If she'd meant to convey how seriously androgynous she was, she'd failed totally.

"I've requested a table. I'm sorry that my time is so short because I know you've probably got a ton of stuff to cover. Is Agent Brice on his way?" Harper's look was frank, guileless. Kim figured that look was an asset to her National Security Branch job every day.

"Let's get settled. He's just parking the car, which seems to be a never-ending battle in this city," Kim replied. Two seconds later, they were trailing the hostess to a corner table.

"I'm starving," Harper said. "Would you mind if we ordered right away?"

Harper could be that rarest of females. Astonishingly stunning, and also genuine, inside and out. If so, she'd be the first such bird Kim had ever met.

They took a quick look at the menu and placed their orders. Brice arrived and did the same.

"Okay," Harper said, folding her hands and resting her forearms on the table. "How can I help?"

Brice seemed to have lost his capacity for speech in Lisa Harper's presence, so Kim took the lead. "You worked on a serial killer case a few years back. Female victims, all found in a bathtub filled with green paint."

Some of Harper's brightness dimmed. She lowered her eyes. "Hard to forget a case like that."

"Brice's team believes the killer is active again," Kim said.

Harper looked up, and her eyes widened with bald astonishment. The best question she could ask immediately was, "Really?"

"They found a new body. A bathtub filled with olive green paint in Garrison, New York. That's a tiny place across the river from West Point. You know it?" Kim asked.

Harper shook her head. "I've never been anywhere in New York except the city."

"You had to be a new agent back then," Kim said.

Even seated, Harper still had to lower her chin to look Kim in the eye. "I'd been at Quantico two years at the time. Assigned to operations, not the serial crimes unit. So, yeah. Low agent on the totem pole, for sure."

"What was your role during the original investigation?"

"I was assigned to a guy classified as SU, status unknown, maybe hostile, maybe friendly. Usually, that meant some lower-level organized crime dude willing to testify against his bosses in exchange for a better sentence. Sometimes witness protection was the carrot." She shrugged and offered a weak smile. "Sometimes, it was me. You might be surprised how many tough guys lose their heads around a woman, even if she's obviously a cop. And even more obviously not interested."

Kim dipped her head toward Brice, still star-struck by Harper's sex appeal, and replied dryly, "No. I wouldn't be surprised at all."

The waitress brought the food and Harper fell on her pasta like a starving wolf. Brice seemed to have misplaced his appetite. Kim had ordered soup, which was too steaming hot to eat.

"So who was the guy?" Kim asked although she suspected she knew the answer already.

Harper's eyebrows rose, and she raised a finger. Kim waited while she swallowed ravioli. "What guy?"

"The SU you were assigned to during the bathtub murders."

"Former Army MP who fit the profile. His name was Jack Reacher."

"What profile?"

"The one the Behavioral Science Unit team had worked up."

"How so?" Kim cocked her head and paid close attention because she didn't see Reacher remotely close to what she figured the profile of the serial killer must have been.

"There were several elements to it." Harper paused. "But as I recall, it was a smart guy, a loner, Army, knew the victims… movements unaccounted for… Seems like there was one more."

Kim tried a bit of the soup while she waited for Harper to stop pretending she didn't remember the last thing. The soup was excellent.

When she figured she'd waited long enough, she said, "What was the last thing? The first elements are facts. The last one is usually some kind of psychobabble bullshit conclusion the profilers tack on to justify their existence."

"That's why I couldn't remember. It wasn't an official diagnosis." Harper flashed another megawatter, like she'd had an epiphany. "A brutal, vigilante personality. That's how they put it."

Kim nodded. Actually, all those elements seemed to fit Reacher like a bespoke suit. Which was probably the precise reason they were chosen.

She asked, "Which status was he? Your SU. Hostile or friendly?"

"Both, I guess you'd say. He cooperated with us under pressure."

"What kind of pressure?"

"Threats, mostly. Conviction, prison time, and so on. The usual." Harper lowered her eyes and paid attention to her food.

Harper seemed guileless, but she wasn't. Not at all. No straightforward cop, FBI agent or otherwise, could survive as long as she had without a capacity for deception. She didn't say what she meant. But what coercive methods did they use to flip Reacher?

For starters, he would never respond favorably to personal threats. Kim didn't. Gaspar certainly didn't. Threats had the exact opposite effect on Gaspar, and he was a lot more civilized than Reacher. Gaspar would dig his heels in to the extreme simply to resist the pressure. She'd seen him do it.

Reacher had to be a hundred times worse.

Because of his size and skills, guys who threatened Reacher during his Army years were few and far between. They generally didn't live to brag about it, either.

So would threats of conviction and prison time have persuaded Reacher to move from hostile to friendly? Not a chance.

FBI agents, including the behavioral profilers, were attuned to human motivations and reactions. The serial crimes unit wouldn't have wasted their resources on techniques destined to fail. They'd have deployed threats expected to succeed.

Which, in Reacher's case, was what?

The answer flooded her senses instantly, like a fire hose floods a bucket. Deerfield wasn't playing the odds here. He wasn't a betting man. Not at all. He was a con artist. Kim spent a few moments on her soup while she walked through the logic.

Deerfield *knew* the new bathtub murder would lure Reacher out of the shadows.

He was absolutely certain.

Because he'd used the same strategy on Reacher before.

He'd threatened. Reacher had reacted.

The tactic was easy. Elegant. Effective.

Threats of conviction and prison time against Reacher failed. Deerfield must have moved on to threatening someone Reacher cared about enough to get Reacher on Deerfield's side.

Deerfield had discovered Reacher's Achilles heel back then, and he applied the same leverage again now.

The person Reacher had cared about most in the world was not himself, but Jodie Jacob.

If Jacob was the woman in the tub, Reacher was coming for her killer.

No force on earth would be sufficient to stop him.

# CHAPTER TWENTY-ONE

*Saturday, January 29*
*2:05 p.m.*
*New York City, New York*

KIM'S HOT SOUP WAS barely touched when Lisa Harper
finished the last of her lunch and sat back in her chair. Kim
picked up her spoon.

Harper looked at Brice, who had contributed nothing useful
to the interview yet. "So you've got a copycat killer?"

He shrugged. "Like Otto said, we think it's the original
killer. We think he's been dormant for a while and now he's
back."

Harper nodded slowly, but she didn't agree. Which wasn't
surprising, if she agreed with Kim's guess about the copycat.
"Tell me about your crime scene. Naked woman in a bathtub in
her own home, right?"

"Same as the earlier cases, according to the files," Brice
replied.

"Yeah, all that was covered by the media at the time. If your copycat's a local guy, he might not have heard any of the details because we didn't have any victims in New York. Media here might not have covered it. But it's pretty easy for a copycat to find those facts with a quick online search." Harper paused. "You found her yesterday?"

"Local cops on the scene late in the afternoon. Autopsy's pending."

"You don't know who she is?" Harper's eyes widened. From her reaction, Kim figured this was a new bit the copycat had added, too.

Brice replied, "Not yet."

"How was her body posed?" Harper asked.

"Leaning against the back of the tub. Paint up to her neck. Hands folded across her abdomen," Brice replied.

Harper cocked her head. "How much paint?"

"I'm not exactly sure. The tech took it out of the tub in a fifty-five-gallon shop vac. So something less than that."

"What color?" Harper asked, still not confirming that any of Brice's answers matched the original cases.

If Brice noticed, he didn't follow up. "Army camo green. Same as always."

Harper nodded. "What kind of paint? That's another detail we didn't release to the press at the time."

"We think it's oil-based because there were no visible signs of freezing and it's been damned cold here. We're waiting on lab results for that, too," Brice replied.

Harper glanced at her watch. "I'm sorry, but I've only got about ten more minutes."

"Where's your meeting?" Kim asked.

"Here. Private room in the back." She reached into her jacket

pocket and pulled out a couple of business cards. She put one
near Kim and the other near Brice. They reciprocated. "You can
call me, of course. But let's make the most of our time. What did
you want to know?"

"You were the agent responsible for watching Reacher on
the original case. Did he talk to you about Jodie Jacob?" Brice
asked.

Harper's eyebrows arched. "His lawyer? Sure. He'd known
her since she was a kid. I think I remember they were having an
affair at the time."

"Are lawyers supposed to sleep with their clients?" Brice
said.

Harper smiled. "I'm not a lawyer. But you've got your
timing mixed up. The way I understood it, they were lovers first.
She only became his lawyer after he was arrested."

Brice said, "Originally, the team believed Reacher was the
killer. He was ruled out because he had an alibi for one of the
murders. We believe now that his alibi was false."

All the color drained from Harper's face. Her blue eyes grew
larger than quarters. She lifted her water glass with a slightly
unsteady hand and sipped.

She cleared her throat. "I'm not sure what I can say about
that. If you have new evidence against Reacher, you could solve
a very cold case."

"We have to find him first. Which is proving difficult to do.
Have you heard from him?" Brice asked.

She shook her head. "Never. Not since the case fizzled when
we were out west. He had a travel voucher, and he went back to
New York. Something about Jodie Jacob's partnership party,
maybe?"

Brice leaned in and lowered his voice. "You spent a lot of

time with the guy. More than anyone else we've located so far. If you wanted to find him now, how would you do it?"

The blank look on her face said it all, but she replied, "I have no earthly idea. The usual missing persons protocols, I guess? Maybe starting with Jodie Jacob. She knew him a lot better and a lot longer than I did."

"Tell me something about Reacher that I can't find in his files. Something I can follow up, maybe locate him, bring him back in for questioning." Brice was probably mindful of the rapidly ticking clock and simply throwing a Hail Mary with a blanket request like that.

Kim thought Harper might volunteer that Reacher was a good kisser, just to mess with him. But she didn't.

"That was years ago." Harper shrugged and to her credit, seemed to think about it. She glanced at her watch. "I've really got to run. But quickly, let's see if anything I can remember might help. He knew a lot about the victims, which is always good in any kind of investigation, but that was the thing that made him especially helpful to us. Not sure that's useful unless your victim was in the Army, too. The only other thing—and I'm not a behavioral scientist so I can't put a label on it—but something about Reacher rubbed people the wrong way. Nobody on the team liked him at all."

*Except for you. Imagine that.* Kim hid her smile behind a spoonful of soup as she wondered once again why women had such a fondness for Reacher.

"Was that unusual down at Quantico for suspects classified as Status Unknown? Because it's pretty common here in our New York office. We don't make friends with the suspects," Brice said, lip curled as if the very concept was repulsive.

"Honestly, everything about the case was unusual, including Reacher. He was both terrifying and intriguing, all at once. I've never met another guy quite like him, inside or outside a prison cell. But I'll say this. I don't for a second believe he killed those women back then. I'd say you're barking up the wrong tree on that score. You might want to focus on a better suspect." She grabbed her briefcase and the check and was three steps toward the door when she looked back briefly at Kim and said, "Call me if you need anything else. My cell phone number is on the back of those cards."

Brice watched her go like a defeated boxer mixed with a lovesick teenager.

Kim smiled and finished the last spoonful of soup. "So? What's your opinion of Lisa Harper?"

"She's a star at the NSB, I'm told. She pretended to be helpful. But her opinion of Reacher doesn't match what we know about him. Not even close. So I guess it doesn't mean much. She didn't actually tell us anything anyway, did she?" Brice frowned like he'd just now figured that out.

"No, she didn't," Kim said. "If there's nothing you need me to do right now, I'm heading back to my hotel for a few hours to get some work done. And a nap."

Still focused on Harper, Brice nodded absently. "I'll drop you off. You'll never get a cab in this neighborhood today."

Twenty minutes later, Kim climbed down from the SUV's cabin outside her hotel and watched Brice drive away. Once again, he turned north at the first opportunity and continued out of sight.

# CHAPTER TWENTY-TWO

*Saturday, January 29*
*3:55 p.m.*
*New York City, New York*

THE DOORMAN STOOD CLOSE to the entrance, out of the biting wind. Kim figured he was entitled to the break. She looked around for a cab, usually as thick as weeds on 42nd Street at this hour. After a couple of minutes, her nose was as red as Santa, and her toes were practically frozen inside her boots.

The doorman took pity on her. "Can I get you a ride?"

"Would you? You're a lifesaver." She stuffed her hands into her coat pockets.

"Cabs are scarce, but is a car service okay?"

She nodded.

He raised his hand, and a white Audi sedan appeared like magic. He palmed the folded twenty-dollar bill she handed him expertly and held the door open while she slipped quickly into the warm back seat. He closed the door and tapped the Audi's roof.

"Where to, Miss?" The back seat was separated from the front by a thick opaque partition. The driver used a handset in the front seat, and his voice came from a speaker in the rear deck.

She gave him the address of the restaurant where she'd met Lisa Harper earlier. Harper's meetings were being held there, she'd said. Kim planned to track her down for a more private conversation. Harper knew a lot more about the old bathtub murders than she'd let on. Kim suspected Harper also believed the Garrison murder was a copycat. She wanted to know precisely why.

The driver traveled the New York City streets expertly without fanfare and pulled up in front of the restaurant in fifteen minutes.

"What do I owe you?" She looked for a credit card terminal or a way to slide cash through the partition but found neither.

"We have payment arrangements with your hotel, Miss. Charges will be added to your hotel bill." He spoke into the handset, which she'd rapidly appreciated the first time he'd employed it. No incessant chatter to deal with.

He pointed over his right shoulder. "If you'd like me to pick you up later, just call the cell number on my license posted on the partition behind my seat."

She noted the number, thanked him, and let herself out. The temperature had dropped a few degrees, and the wind speed had picked up. She dashed inside.

The restaurant was no longer busy, but a few diners remained. Once she was seated at an isolated table away from the cold wind that blew inside every time the door opened, Kim found Harper's card.

She texted, "Otto here. In the dining room. Alone. Join me?"

After that, she ordered coffee and settled in to wait. Before the coffee arrived, she received two texts. The first one was from an unknown number. Short and to the point. "Say hello to Harper for me. R."

Her spinal nerves jumped to attention. She'd told no one she was meeting Lisa Harper. Hell, she'd only made the decision after Brice dropped her off at the hotel. She looked up from her phone and scanned the restaurant for watchers. If he was inside, she didn't spot him. *Outside then. Or electronics. Stay alert, Otto.*

She looked at her phone again.

The second text was from Harper. "Fifteen minutes."

She arrived in ten, every bit as stunning as she'd looked earlier. She had luggage with her this time. She leaned it against the wall near her chair and took her seat. "My flight leaves JFK at 7:05. Traffic shouldn't be a big issue tonight. But I don't want to get stuck here, with the snow coming in. I can give you thirty minutes."

"If we have more to talk about, I'll ride out with you, and we can talk in the car," Kim said.

Harper shrugged. "Totally up to you. How can I help you? Have you read the old files? Everything should be in there. The cases were extensively documented at the time."

"I haven't received the files yet. But I know generally what was going on. What I'm really interested in is Reacher." Kim expected some pushback but didn't get any. "You said he didn't kill those women. How do you know?"

Harper leaned in, forearms on the table, hands clasped, and lowered her voice. "Have you ever met Reacher?"

"No," she replied. True enough. She felt no need to explain the various ways she'd experienced Reacher, though.

"Well, if you had, you'd understand. He's not a guy who's going to lug a bunch of paint to a bunch of houses so that he can drown some naked women. Not even if he didn't like them very much." Harper's opinion on that was emphatic. Arguing would be futile, but also unnecessary. Kim already agreed with her.

Kim spent a few minutes exploring Harper's general knowledge of Reacher's Army career, which was limited. They discussed Reacher's behavior inside and outside the rules laid down by the military police. Harper seemed to have less information about Reacher's career history than Kim did.

Then she returned to the material Harper knew much better. "What about the Behavioral Science Unit profile? Didn't you say it fit Reacher perfectly?"

"A little too perfectly, if you ask me." Harper cocked her head. "What's a brutal, vigilante personality, anyway? I mean, that's not a technical term for any kind of mental defect or disease."

"If all you knew about him came from what you saw in his Army files, the term pretty well describes Reacher, though, doesn't it? I've seen those records and interviewed people who knew him. The brutal part is a common thread. He wasn't one to avoid confrontation, that's for sure. There's plenty of the vigilante in what I've been told, too," Kim said.

"I didn't know him back then." Harper shrugged. "He wasn't like that with me."

She didn't claim that Reacher failed to display such behavior, though. So Kim pressed her. "You said earlier that he was terrifying. What did you mean by that?"

"He was huge, for one thing. As petite as you are, he could knock you over with a flip of his big paw." She smiled a little, and when Kim did not, she continued. "His combat skills were very well-honed, too. All of that made him terrifying to the wrong people."

"Who were the wrong people?"

"I guess I don't know." Harper shrugged again. "And before you even think it, no. We didn't have sex. I don't sleep with co-workers or suspects, for one thing. But he didn't even try. He had a girlfriend. Like I told you."

"How about the rest of the BSU profile? Definitely a fit for him?"

"Almost, but not quite." Harper nodded. "He was a smart guy and a loner. He was ex-Army. All that was true. Probably still is. But the part about his movements being unaccounted for wasn't true."

Kim arched her eyebrows. "Really? I've been looking for the guy for weeks, and I can't find him. We live in the most heavily monitored country on earth, and he has no digital footprint we've been able to locate. I'd say his movements are unaccounted for, for sure."

"That could be how it is now, I don't know," Harper replied, perfectly tweezed eyebrows arched. "But back then, he was out of the Army for three years. He had a house and a girlfriend and a car and taxes to pay like everybody does. He'd been living in New York for a while when they picked him up. At his home, mind you. So I'd say he was pretty well accounted for, wouldn't you?"

"Sounds like you're right." She nodded, thinking about what she'd been told by others. "Deerfield said Reacher was cleared because he had an alibi for one of the murders. Is that how it worked back then? One element of the profile doesn't fit, and they just give up on their best suspect?"

Harper took a deep breath. "Not just any element, I guess. I already told you that his whereabouts were the farthest thing from unknown. But having an alibi for the time and place of a murder is a pretty compelling defense, as you know."

Hard to be in two places at once. Even for Reacher.

Kim said, "Deerfield was the one who flipped him, right?"

Harper nodded. "And you've guessed already that he used threats against Jodie Jacob to do it. Reacher was really gone on her. He would never allow anything bad to happen to her. You can ask her. She'll tell you all about it, I'm sure."

"When I find her, I will," Kim said. "At the moment, we're not sure where she is."

"She's missing?" Harper's eyes widened and then her mouth formed a perfect O as she gasped. "You think she's the murder victim? And you think Reacher killed her?"

Kim paused a bit, waffling before she took another risk with Harper. "Actually, I don't think so. But Deerfield does. Brice, too."

"That's crazy," Harper said, emphatically, shaking her head.

Once again, Kim agreed. But she wanted to hear Harper's reasons. "Why?"

"Well, not only for all the other reasons I'd never like Reacher for this but also because he *really* loved her. He just wouldn't do that," Harper declared.

Kim replied, "That's exactly why Deerfield thinks he killed her. Because he loved her and she left him. Happens all the time, as we all know."

"Deerfield is wrong. Sorry." Harper fell back in her chair, shaking her head. "I don't believe that. Something else is going on here. You can take that to the bank."

"As it happens, I agree with you," Kim said. "What do you think is really going on?"

"I have no idea," Harper replied. "None at all."

"Do you trust Deerfield?" Kim asked.

"Pfft!" A little puff of air escaped her lips. She shook her head. "Not even a little bit. And you shouldn't either if you know what's good for you."

Harper glanced at the darkness outside and seemed to notice the time. "I've got to run. Do you want to come along? Change of plans for me came up during my meetings after lunch. I'm not going back to Portland. You won't be able to reach me for a few days if you want to talk again."

Kim shook her head. "I think we're okay for now. And I need to get into those old files tonight."

"You can always text me. If I can, I'll get back to you." Harper gathered her bags and used her phone to call a ride. "Can I give you a lift? It's not easy to get a cab here. You might freeze to death before an empty one comes along."

"Thanks. That'd be great." Kim followed her out, still feeling dwarfed while standing next to her.

When they were settled into the private car, Kim said, "Deerfield's a little old to be sitting in the New York Field Office. Guy his age, with his experience, should be closer to the top of the food chain. You know anything about why he's not?"

Harper glanced around uneasily. "The driver's one of ours, but it's generally not safe to discuss sensitive intel inside vehicles in the city. Could be a career killer, you know?"

"Understood." Kim nodded. "I wouldn't ask, but you're going quiet tonight, and it's important."

"You know how it is, Kim." Harper inhaled loudly and exhaled slowly. "Rarified air up at the top of any pyramid scheme, which is what all government agencies and just about every other kind of organization is. You worked as an accountant in one of the big firms. And you're a lawyer by training. Surely, you understand how few people reach the status he has now, even."

"True. He's in the number nine position, though. He's not down here with the rest of us, swimming upstream." She paused. "Once a guy gets to where he is, going higher shouldn't be a matter of qualifications or expertise."

"Exactly. Advancement decisions are made by people above you. The criteria are subjective more than objective. You've passed all the tests, you've put in your time." Harper glanced out the window and said quietly, "At that point, it's just a question of how well you get along with the top cop, isn't it?"

She nodded. "When did he stop moving up?"

Harper looked pointedly at her and said nothing.

She nodded again. Understood.

With her hand on the door, Kim turned and asked her last question. "Lisa, when you worked with Reacher, what did he call you?"

"You know, you asked me before how he was with me? Well, he was the first man at Quantico to treat me like a professional instead of trying to get into my bed. It was a refreshing change." Lisa frowned a moment, and then a dazzling smile brightened her whole face as if she'd remembered something long forgotten that had touched her heart. "Most people call me Lisa, and men always do. Men think using my first name will warm me up, make me like them better. Usually, it's the opposite. I don't like men using my first name without permission. It's too familiar. Reacher understood the dynamics of communication. He called me Harper."

"Good to know. Thanks again for all your help." Kim's stomach churned as she stepped out on shaky legs. Reacher was a low-tech guy. He'd probably do his watching the old-fashioned way. As she closed the door, she scanned the street, sidewalks, doorways, and nearby vehicles for a big man paying too much attention.

# CHAPTER TWENTY-THREE

*Saturday, January 29*
*3:55 p.m.*
*New York City, New York*

FROM BEHIND THE WHEEL of the stolen Toyota sedan he'd removed from the impound lot, Reed had watched Brice pull away from the valet entrance at Otto's hotel. She stood on the sidewalk and waited until Brice turned north and could no longer see her in his rearview mirror. Then she asked the doorman to flag a cab.

The vehicle she stepped into a couple minutes later was actually a white Audi sedan from one of the car services, which were common in the city these days. Tourists liked the services better than taxis, so the drivers hung around the better hotels and paid off the doormen to get better fares. The vehicles were unmarked, usually foreign models on the higher end of the price range, and a lot cleaner than an average New York taxi. Payment was handled in various ways, but passengers weren't required to have cash on hand, which they found more convenient.

If Otto hadn't known about the car services before, she did now.

The Audi went around the block and headed back in the direction Brice and Otto had arrived from. Reed followed, hanging back in the light traffic to avoid being spotted. He was tracking Otto's personal cell phone. He wasn't worried about losing her. After they'd traveled a few blocks, he was sure he knew where she was headed, anyway.

When the Audi stopped in front of the restaurant where Brice and Otto had had lunch, Reed circled the block looking for a place to park. On the third pass, he gave up on finding a spot with an unobstructed view from the Toyota's front seat and parked a couple of blocks down.

He glanced at his watch. He still had time to kill. Reed wasn't dressed appropriately for the restaurant, and his abdominal pain had returned with a vengeance, but he walked back and went inside.

He looked around the mostly empty dining area until he saw Otto's back. She was dwarfed by the striking blonde woman seated across the table. At first, Reed guessed the woman was a model or maybe a TV reporter. But then he recognized her as the woman in the photos his brother had shared. Lisa Harper. No doubt.

*Well, well, well.*

They were deeply engrossed in their conversation. Neither noticed him, and he wanted to keep it that way. He turned his back and found a partially obscured table. He ordered to avoid suspicion, although his stomach wouldn't accept solid food today.

Reed put the earpiece into his left ear and found Otto's encrypted cell phone easily enough. He couldn't hear very well.

Their voices were hushed, and the phone was inside Otto's pocket. He raised the volume, but still caught only snippets of the conversation. Garrison. Bathtub. Serial killer. Jodie Jacob. Deerfield.

And then he heard the only name that mattered to him. Reacher.

After a while, he noticed the noise level rising in the restaurant. Streetlights came on outside and splashed a glow across his table. He looked through the window, surprised by the encroaching twilight.

Time to go. He'd pick up with Otto later.

Reed tossed a few bills on the table and returned to the Toyota.

# CHAPTER TWENTY-FOUR

*Saturday, January 29*
*5:45 p.m.*
*New York City, New York*

HARPER'S DRIVER LEFT KIM at the entrance to her hotel, which was bustling with guests headed to and from Saturday night activities. She stood on the sidewalk, shivering in the cold.

She needed to move. She'd been sitting too much, and she felt restless. It was too damn cold to walk anywhere, but she didn't want to hang out alone in her room and she had no energy for the hotel gym tonight. Her options were limited.

People were everywhere along with bumper-to-bumper traffic. On the sidewalks, pedestrians moved quickly like salmon swimming upstream in both directions. At various establishments, doors opened, and patrons entered and exited in bursts. A sizeable knot pushed through the double doors leading from Grand Central Terminal just ahead.

She had been there several times before. Inside were shops,

restaurants, open corridors, and best of all, heat. She hurried to the entrance and went inside.

The terminal was crowded, too. People scurried to board the trains as inbound passengers emerged. The stores were filled with last-minute shoppers headed home. Even the restaurants were busy. It seemed that everyone in New York wanted to be inside tonight.

She walked the corridors, end to end simply for the exercise. She felt like a caged animal in winter. Always had, since she was a kid growing up in Michigan. Simply moving her limbs for a while was a welcome change.

Walking also helped her think, as one thing led to another, one step at a time. At the end of the first corridor, she turned to walk back, focused on Alan Deerfield. There was something not right going on with him.

She had checked the basic facts about Deerfield on the FBI's public website. The first thing she noticed? Deerfield was long overdue for a promotion. He was number nine in the direct line of succession to become Director of the FBI, with eight others ahead of him. As an Assistant Director already, only four titles above his separated him from the Director position.

The problem was, Deerfield had not moved an inch in years. The timing was suspicious, too. He came to the Bureau later in his career after a stint with Phoenix PD. He'd had a stellar trajectory up the ranks before the bathtub murders case ended without an arrest or conviction. At that point, his career had stalled like an airplane engine choked for fuel. He'd been gliding along at the same level all this time. He hadn't crashed and burned yet, but he was on his way down for sure.

The timing didn't make sense. Could be an unlucky coincidence.

The bathtub murders case, on its own, wasn't the kind of screwup that should have stalled any career at Deerfield's level. His office handled much more significant matters with alarming frequency. Some didn't end well, which was to be expected. The good guys didn't always win, and the bureau was realistic about the odds.

Which probably meant that the bathtub murders case wasn't Deerfield's first or only failure. Maybe he'd had a string of flameouts, and this one was the final straw. She'd seen that sort of thing happen before.

The possible reasons he'd been stuck in place were limited, though. An Assistant Director in charge of an office like New York would have been thoroughly vetted long before he got to that position.

She quickly ruled out the easy ones, like Deerfield's personal choice.

He didn't strike her as the kind of guy who craved a steady nine-to-five for thirty and out. Gaspar was that guy. Deerfield wasn't. He was more like her, looking for the top spot someday. Certainly, he'd have wanted to move up at least once in the past ten years.

The way things worked, he must have been passed over a few times. Some organizations had a three-strike rule, up or out. The FBI didn't. So they didn't toss him out like last week's fish.

What they did was worse. They parked him in a very public place for the whole world to see. Every day. For years. Must have been a bitter pill. He might be tempted to even the score and was looking for the right chance. She would have been, under the same circumstances.

She'd also checked those above Deerfield on the organizational chart. All were names she recognized. One, in particular, required no research because she already knew him too well.

Charles Cooper, the Boss. He controlled everything and everyone inside the bureau along with a lot of stuff outside it. He wasn't the Director, but he didn't need to be. Bottom line, if the Boss wanted Deerfield promoted, he would've been. The opposite was also true.

Which meant the Boss had effectively ended Deerfield's career and held him up to ridicule for a very long time. Not surprising. The Boss called his actions principled, but it was really just plain stubbornness. She came from a long line of stubborn Germans, but she'd known the Boss to hold grudges way beyond the point when she and every member of her family would have surrendered.

So Deerfield's stalled advancement could have been caused by almost any actual or suspected performance failure. Three connected things told her Reacher was at the center of Deerfield's dispute with the Boss. Jodie Jacob, the green paint copycat murder, and her own presence here.

She'd reached the end of another corridor inside the terminal and turned to walk back. The crowd had thinned. It was well after seven o'clock. She'd been walking for more than an hour. She planned to sleep well tonight and read Gaspar's files in the morning. Dinner and a couple of glasses of expensive wine she could add to the Boss's tab should help.

Standing in the Grand Central Concourse, located in the center of the terminal, she spied Cipriani Dolci in the balcony. A perfect spot for what she had in mind.

She gave her name to the host and climbed onto a comfortable stool at the balcony bar to wait for her table. She ordered a glass of Cabernet and found her phone.

Kim tapped a knuckle against her lips. She needed better intel on Deerfield. Insights and gossip would be helpful, too. The kind of stuff one of the local agents on the Garrison house murder should know. Subordinates always knew more about the boss than bosses knew about them. Brice was an annoying waste of time. She'd only met Poulton once and had no idea what he was about yet. For straight answers, she figured the most likely place to get them was Reggie Smithers.

# CHAPTER TWENTY-FIVE

*Saturday, January 29*
*7:25 p.m.*
*New York City, New York*

THE BARTENDER POURED HER wine while she called one
of her colleagues back in Detroit. When he answered the phone,
she spent less than two minutes on hold while he located
Smithers' personal cell phone.

She dialed the number. He picked up immediately.

"Smithers," he said, in the best resonant bass voice since
James Earl Jones. Background noise sounded like a subway
train.

"It's Kim Otto. Are you anywhere near Forty-Second and
Lexington? I'd like to buy you a cup of coffee." She sipped the
wine.

He chuckled. "Coffee keeps me awake. Make it a good
Scotch, and I can be at Grand Central in twenty minutes. I'm on
my way already. Meeting the wife later for dinner."

Kim figured his wife must be amazing. "I'm at the balcony bar near Cipriani Dolci. How's that?"

"See you there," he replied.

While she waited, she used the browser on her phone to search Deerfield's name to locate news stories. Some were mere mentions, and others were longer pieces. The FBI's New York Field Office was one of the most important in the country, even before 9/11. After the World Trade Center bombing, the Assistant Director of the New York office was frequently in the spotlight's glare.

Deerfield's office had handled dozens of high-profile matters since the bathtub murders ended. One of the most visible included a thwarted terrorist attack on the President during an official state visit with world dignitaries at the UN.

No doubt about it. Deerfield had enjoyed the kind of high profile career that should have led him much further up the ladder, his reputation as a jerk notwithstanding. He had to be mad as hell. The kind of deep anger that ended one of two ways. Imploding, causing a massive stroke or heart attack and instant death. Or exploding without further provocation into deadly violence. Deerfield seemed like an exploder to her.

If Deerfield held Reacher responsible for his career problems, would he have killed Reacher's girlfriend and stuffed her in that bathtub in Garrison? The house that Reacher's beloved mentor had owned and given to him? The lawman's equivalent of a horse head in the bed for a treacherous Mafioso?

She nodded. Men had gone off the rails for a lot less.

An involuntary shudder ran through her. She slipped the phone into her pocket and lifted the wine glass to her lips. She glanced across the concourse where the crowd parted like a wave as Smithers moved through.

She figured Reacher could do the same through any crowd anywhere. He wasn't quite as big as Smithers, which probably made no difference at all.

Smithers swiftly covered the stairs to join her at the bar. "It's Saturday night in the city that never sleeps, Otto. Couldn't you find a better date than me?"

She smiled and replied, "The normal-sized guys on the list were all babysitting."

"My kids are at grandma's and my wife is with her sister for another hour. So you lucked out." He moved the stool aside, leaned onto the bar, and ordered an expensive Scotch. "How may I be of service to you this evening?"

"I'm interested in Alan Deerfield."

Smithers raised his eyebrows. "Why? No one else is. Except for Brice."

"Yeah, I thought Brice might be his son-in-law or something."

Smithers laughed. "You Asians are very astute."

"I'm no more Asian than you are. Born in Michigan, right smack in the middle of the U.S. of A.," she replied pleasantly. "And I was joking. Brice is actually his son-in-law?"

"I stand corrected," Smithers replied with mock formality. "Deerfield's daughter divorced Brice last year. Poor bastard walks around on eggshells worried about getting the ax from his ex-father-in-law. Not a good way to live."

"No kidding," Kim frowned. "How long have you been working directly for Deerfield?"

"Since never. Technically we all report to Deerfield, I guess. But that's like saying we all report to the Director or the president. Deerfield's in charge of the whole office and everybody in it. But I'm in the Organized Crime Unit and don't report directly to him at all." He paused to thank the bartender for the Scotch and raised his glass toward her. "Garrison is Brice's operation, even if he has to get permission to go to the bathroom from Deerfield first."

"I'm trying to figure out Deerfield's play here, and I just don't know him well enough." She raised her glass in response to Smithers's mock toast. "Deerfield called me in, claiming he wanted me to see the body in the bathtub. But he knew I never worked the old case. There were no victims in Detroit, and Detroit is the only field office I've ever worked from. Which is something he could have learned in a nanosecond."

Smithers nodded slowly but said nothing.

"A few hours after I arrived in New York, Deerfield left. Haven't seen or heard from him since. I haven't been briefed on the current case or the old ones." She shrugged. "Nothing more has happened, and I don't get why I'm here."

Smithers said, "It's odd that Deerfield didn't tell you what he wanted you to do. He's usually the opposite of vague. You never need to guess where you stand with the guy if you know what I mean."

Kim nodded. "I've heard he can be bombastic, demanding, and quite the bully."

"Among other things," Smithers replied. "Let's give him the benefit of the doubt. It's the weekend. We're government workers. Not much is gonna happen on a case like this until Monday. Gotta be the same in Detroit, right?"

She nodded and sipped the wine. "What do you think will happen on Monday?"

"I imagine we'll get an ID on the body. Probably not much else unless you know something I don't," Smithers said.

"Grassley, the NYPD detective, is conducting the

investigation into the bathtub murder as far as I know. I haven't heard anything from her or from Brice since lunch. I'm assuming no one has found Jodie Jacob."

Smithers cocked his head. "I guess I feel like we did find her. She's the one in the tub, don't you think?"

"I hope not." She ordered another pricey Scotch for Smithers and a second glass of wine. He nodded his appreciation. "Do you have any idea why Deerfield hasn't moved upstairs long before now?"

Smithers warmed the Scotch in his hands. One big paw was all he needed for the job. "He's certainly qualified. Better than some of the guys above him, actually. It's too bad. Rumor mill says he pissed off one of the big dudes a while back."

"You believe that?"

Smithers nodded. "Seems likely to me."

"Why?"

"Were you in the military, Otto?"

She shook her head.

He thumped his chest. "Once a Marine, always a Marine. But I've been FBI for a long time now, which is not so different. When guys like Deerfield stall out like he has, it's always one of two causes. Either bureaucratic bullshit or somebody higher up with a grudge."

"For Deerfield, it could be mere bureaucracy, couldn't it? He's getting pretty old for the job. Maybe it's that."

"Anything's possible."

"You don't think so, though."

"Like you said yesterday, the guy's an asshole." Smithers frowned. "It's not hard to read the tea leaves."

"What do the tea leaves tell you?"

"Deerfield pissed somebody off. Big time. So big, he can't

get past it." Smithers paused as if he might not continue, so she waited. He lowered his voice. "Some of us suspect things could be changing. He's seemed cockier than usual lately. Like he expects some really great news, you know?"

"Yeah, I know." She nodded. He'd confirmed her theory. "What kind of news you think he'd be so pleased about?"

"Hard to say. A guy like Deerfield, it's usually all about power."

"He's got plenty of power now, doesn't he?"

"Does he? Think about it." Smithers gave her a knowing look. "Guy's well qualified. He's got skills. Runs one of the most important law enforcement agencies in the world a long time, right?"

She nodded.

"He looks around and sees all of the people higher up than him with less expertise. Makes him doubt himself, maybe." Smithers steady gaze never wavered. "So he bulks up his résumé. He gets passed over time and again. He starts to feel disrespected. Then he gets angry. What does the guy do next?"

She shrugged.

Smithers said, "He gets even, right?"

"How does he do that?" she asked quietly.

"He can't fight Goliath with a slingshot." Smithers grinned, but she didn't. "Okay, there's plenty of retaliatory options to choose from. But nothing subtle. That kind of payback calls for shock and awe, as they say."

"Within the confines of the FBI, the options are limited, though. He wants to move up, not get himself killed or sent to prison," she replied.

"True. But trust me. You don't want to be in the line of fire when he does whatever he plans to do. Neither do I." Smithers looked across the concourse and drained the rest of his Scotch in one gulp. "Sorry. Gotta go. That's my brother-in-law down there. We're meeting our wives over on Broadway for dinner after the play."

"Have a great evening. My table's ready, too." She handed the bartender her credit card and said, "Thanks for coming."

He waved on his way down the stairs and hurried toward another man she couldn't see well from this distance. She watched as they headed toward the exit, wondering about Deerfield's attitude change and what might have caused it.

Because she was watching Smithers, she didn't notice the big man walking across the concourse at first. When he snagged her attention, she only saw him from behind. Work boots. Jeans. Leather jacket. Fair hair cut close. No hat. Hands as big as frozen turkeys.

*Reacher?* She slid off the bar stool and dashed down the stairs. She lost sight of him when he rounded the corner toward one of the subways. She picked up the pace.

There he was, up ahead, standing alone on the outside of the group of waiting passengers. The train was pulling into the station. She hurried to catch up.

The train stopped, the doors slid open, and passengers piled out. She ran the last few feet and touched his arm as travelers were starting to board.

"Reacher?" she said.

He turned his body halfway to face her. A smile lit his features when he looked down at her hand on his arm. "Can I help you?"

She released her hold and shook her head. "I'm sorry. I thought you were someone else."

"Who did you want me to be?" he said, with a broad Southern accent. "Tell me, and I'll give it my best shot."

"Sorry. You'd better catch your train."

He shrugged and climbed aboard. The doors closed, and the train pulled away while she watched. Then she turned and walked back to collect her credit card from the bartender.

Her phone vibrated with an incoming text message on the way to her table. "Better luck next time. R."

She shook her head and dropped the phone into her pocket.

Through her solitary dinner, she considered what Deerfield might be planning to do. And what the Boss would do in response. And where the hell Reacher had been watching her from and for how long. And more importantly, why?

# CHAPTER TWENTY-SIX

*Sunday, January 30*
*9:30 a.m.*
*New York City, New York*

KIM HAD SLEPT WELL, awakened without a barrage of phone calls and been to the gym for a three-mile run. She'd ordered coffee after her shower and was dressed when she heard the heavy knock on the door. "Room service," he called out.

She unlocked the door and, without checking through the peephole, opened it and simultaneously stepped aside. Gaspar, leaning on a cane, limped across the threshold and pointed his thumb over his shoulder at the fellow standing behind him. "Brought your breakfast, Sunshine."

"Excellent." She grinned. "Nice to see you vertical, Zorro."

"You're not surprised, are you?"

"Not at all."

Gaspar looked good. Better than good. For a while there, he'd been in critical condition at the hospital in West Palm Beach. But he was a determined patient, as stubborn about his health as he was everything else. Intractability was one of his most infuriating qualities. He'd been released after a few days and had been recuperating at home.

"Why are you here?" she asked him after the waiter left and the door closed behind him.

"The Boss is worried. He says Deerfield is dangerous and he doesn't trust Brice or their whole team. He didn't want you here on your own. Especially after your clandestine trip to Finlay's place." He grinned, although she saw the strain of travel etched into the lines on his face. "I told him I could babysit and keep you out of oncoming traffic."

"You're too kind." She wrinkled her nose and gave him a glare. But she was glad to see him, and he knew it.

"Are you staying here?" she asked.

He replied by tilting his head toward the room next door before he leaned against the wall and closed his eyes. Even with the Boss smoothing his way, the travel had exhausted him.

"Why don't you grab some rest while I download and read the files. I'll catch you up afterward. We'll be on the same page a lot faster that way." The plan made sense, but she expected objections. He never admitted he needed to rest.

Instead of his usual bristle, he nodded. "Call when you're ready."

Kim spent twenty minutes dealing with the surveillance equipment in her room. She located the cameras and microphones and set up looping feeds to keep them occupied. For more sophisticated watchers, she deployed the jamming devices she always brought along.

Not perfect, but nothing was. Determined snoops couldn't be stopped in any surveillance nation.

Next, she poured coffee and downloaded the voluminous

files from the secure satellite, which took a while. A glowing coal of anger, kindled by the sheer volume of data relating to Reacher that had been withheld from her smoldered in her gut and burned hotter with every new file she extracted.

Before she could begin to read anything, she jumped up and paced the room, talking herself down, before anger grew to all-consuming rage.

Everything about the SPTF background investigation on Reacher had felt wrong from the start. Why hadn't she trusted her instincts? Because the assignment came directly from the Boss, that's why. She'd trusted him.

*What a fool.* She kicked the bed, hard enough to hurt her foot. She yelped and glared at the bed, which was undamaged. That thought made her laugh. But it didn't douse the smoldering heat within her.

The very first Jack Reacher file the Boss gave her was too stale and too thin to be credible. No human could be as invisible as Reacher appeared to be, whether he was currently above the ground or under it. There was always a camera and a microphone somewhere. *Always.*

Even then. She *knew*, dammit.

*Knew* the file the Boss supplied had been sanitized.

Otherwise, Reacher was the most off-the-grid paranoid she'd ever heard of. Which she hadn't truly believed, even as the evidence stared her in the face.

No one could live in the twenty-first century without leaving data footprints, and plenty of them. Very few people could pull that off. Even fewer actually tried.

Reacher hadn't tried either. Hell, he'd owned a *house*. Aside from death and taxes, nothing required more paperwork than real estate. Harper said he'd owned a car, too. *None* of those documents were provided to her. Over and over again, she was told they didn't exist.

Sure, Reacher was smart and clever. He moved around. He was careful. He had certain skills. A guy like that could stay out of the spotlight, maybe.

But Reacher could never have managed the level of invisibility she'd noticed in that very first file. She was mostly outraged that she'd allowed herself to be persuaded otherwise. She felt duped. Betrayed.

Nothing could be done about that now, of course. History was always water under the bridge, over the waterfall, and every other damn place. She paused. She took several deep breaths.

Going forward? Trust but verify. In the future, she'd also follow her own lead and to hell with protocol.

She disconnected her laptop from the secure satellite and moved from the uncomfortable desk to the king-sized bed to read. She had a lot of catching up to do.

Gaspar had summarized the main points of the original bathtub murders. He'd included more detail, but in the main, Gaspar's summary dovetailed with the highlights Deerfield and Brice had already told her.

Gaspar included a few new details that were not released to the media at that time.

When the victims were found, their clothes were gone. At the Garrison house, the victim's clothes were piled on the floor at the end of the tub.

In the original cases, the tubs were filled right to the rim with paint, estimated at twenty to thirty gallons. At the Garrison house, the victim's neck and head were not covered, and the tub was about half-filled.

The only similarity between the original paint and the

Garrison house paint was the color, which wasn't an exact match, either.

The original paint's chemistry was completely different. Identified as army camouflage base coat, flat green, manufactured in Illinois. It skinned over in a couple of hours. Below the surface, it jellified. Left long enough, the whole tub of paint might have dried solid with the bodies encased inside, she supposed. Not so at the Garrison house.

Gaspar's notes repeated that the cause of death for each victim was suffocation, but the mechanism was never identified. He included a laundry list of methods that were *not* used. The victims were not stabbed, bludgeoned, beaten, strangled, or shot. Definitely not death by natural causes or accidental death. No evidence of suicide.

After that, he listed the evidence that didn't exist. No trace evidence left at the scenes by the killer. No hair, fibers, blood, saliva, prints, skin cells, or DNA.

The original victims were found in their homes in California, Florida, Idaho, Oregon, and New Hampshire. As Harper had said, none of the original victims were killed in New York. All were easily identified.

They were all Army vets, and their Army careers varied. Different roles, different locations. The new Garrison victim, assuming she was Jodie Jacob, never served in the Army, but her father had. She was an Army brat. Close enough, maybe. But not the same.

There seemed to be only one thing all the victims had in common. The original victims all knew Reacher. If Jodie Jacob was the Garrison victim, then she'd known Reacher, too. Of course, they might all have had more colleagues and friends in common, and they probably had. Because they were all involved with the Army in or around the same time frame, other connections between them were impossible to rule out.

Gaspar's conclusion was plainly stated. The Garrison victim could have been murdered by a copycat killer. Or the original killer could have changed a few details for a variety of reasons and started up again. Either or both killers could have been Reacher. Or not.

"Thanks a lot for that extremely helpful analysis," Kim said sarcastically.

She glanced at the digital clock on the bedside table. She'd been reading for two hours. She rubbed her sore neck and climbed off the bed, muscles stiff and complaining about the inactivity.

She picked up the phone and ordered more coffee, this time with extra cream and sugar for Gaspar, and a few snacks. She included pastries and cookies because Gaspar's sweet tooth was insatiable. Delivery was promised for less than thirty minutes.

After room service, she called next door. He answered on the third ring. The phone woke him. She could tell. "Yeah."

"Coffee and snacks are on the way up," she said. "Come on over."

"Let me get a quick shower. Be there in ten."

# CHAPTER TWENTY-SEVEN

*Sunday, January 30*
*11:45 a.m.*
*New York City, New York*

HER STOMACH GROWLED. SHE rummaged through the mini-bar and located a small can of mixed nuts and a bottle of water. She munched thoughtfully, considering the facts she knew and the impressions she'd formed of all the players.

The biggest question was still the same. Why was she here?

She'd been requested. Deerfield had called his counterpart in the Detroit Field Office, and the Agent in Charge had put her on the next plane.

The Boss hadn't interfered with her assignment. At least, not at first. Maybe because he didn't know about it. He might have planned to send her to Garrison anyway, and the official request made it easier to get her embedded. Either way, she'd had no reason or means to connect to him for several hours because Brice hadn't given her the envelope with the cell phone in it.

Maybe Brice had withheld the envelope intentionally.

Maybe on orders from Deerfield. Or maybe not. But initially, she'd been without the intel she needed to do her job. Which didn't feel like an oversight. It felt intentional. Deerfield was pulling the strings. Brice didn't have the nerve or the smarts to try something like that on his own.

She heard a knock on the door.

"Room service," a male voice said.

This time she checked through the peephole to confirm before she opened the door.

He set up the order in her room, requested her signature, and left. As he walked out, Gaspar came in and closed the door behind him.

His hair was still wet from his shower, and he'd changed clothes. He looked loads better. He poured a half-cup of coffee and filled the rest with cream, and then he added enough sugar to rot his teeth in one sip.

Gaspar fueled up by mainlining sugar. He claimed his sweet tooth was essential to his Cuban DNA. Kim figured he'd eaten too many frosted cereals as a kid.

"I read your notes, but I haven't reviewed the original files," she said, still pacing. If she stopped now, her muscles might petrify after her grueling uphill run on the treadmill earlier.

"You know everything you need to know. All the relevant facts are in my notes. The files contain the blow-by-blow, but most of it's useless," he replied, refilling his coffee cup and this time, snagging one of the pastries, too.

"Good to have you back, Chico," Kim said, somewhat surprised to realize how true her sentiment was. "But really, why are you here? You're obviously not ready to return to work yet. What's the rush?"

"I'm a highly paid courier. I've got some video to show you.

The Boss didn't want to risk getting it to you any other way. You're behind enemy lines here or something, I guess." He left his coffee on the tray and held the pastry in his teeth. He fished an unfamiliar phone out of his pocket and pushed a few buttons. He handed the phone to her.

Loaded on the screen was a video ready to play when she pushed the start icon. "What am I looking at here?"

"I don't know how he got it, but it's surveillance footage from Brice's team. The date is thirteen days ago. Monday, January 17. No sound, but the quality's pretty good, under the circumstances," Gaspar said, scarfing down sweets.

The video began with an establishing shot of the Garrison house. The driveway was clear of snow, as was the sidewalk leading to the front door, probably because the snow had thawed. There was no snow lining the edges like she'd expect if the driveway had been plowed.

A sporty red sedan pulled into the driveway and parked close to the garage door. A tall, thin woman with blonde hair, dressed in black, and wearing sunglasses, got out. She walked up the sidewalk to the front door. She bent over the doorknob for a second or so. She opened the door and went inside.

The video zoomed in on the sedan's New York license plate, which was too dirty to read.

"Let me guess," Kim said. "This is Jodie Jacob arriving at the Garrison house."

Gaspar replied, "We think so. She owns a red Lexus IS F Sport with a New York plate. Traffic cams show the car coming in from Manhattan. The woman looks like her."

"Brice said she went into the house and never came out. Can we confirm? Did you see FBI surveillance video for every single minute after this until I arrived to view the body?" Kim asked.

"I did. More than once. Nothing noteworthy on it. In fact, nothing else ever happens except snowfall. I ran through every second for the two weeks before she arrived, too. Nothing on that video, either." Gaspar refilled his sweet coffee again. "She never comes out of the front entrance, which is the only video we have. It's possible there's a back exit. But then we'd have seen her walk around to the front and get into the car."

"You didn't see anything like that, I gather? And you didn't see Reacher, either, right?"

He shook his head. "But later that day, the car is gone."

Kim raised her eyebrows. "What do you mean, gone? Someone drove it away somewhere?"

Gaspar shook his head. "Nope. I watched every single second of that video, several times. No one ever drove the vehicle away. But it's gone later that same day. Did you see the sedan in the driveway when you were there?"

"No. When we arrived, there was an unmarked FBI black SUV parked in that spot. Later, I learned it was Brice's. No other vehicles unless they were in the garage," Kim said.

Gaspar nodded. "Right. That's the next vehicle that shows up on the video. The SUV pulled into the driveway about six hours before you arrived on Friday. Brice and another agent, Terry Poulton, went inside. After half an hour, Poulton came out, and Brice stayed inside."

"So that's when Brice and Poulton discovered the body? Brice called Deerfield, who called Detroit, and I was ordered to take a non-stop flight immediately."

"Seems like it," Gaspar said, finishing up the pastry and choosing a cherry Danish next. "I checked the files. Brice is a nebbish. He's been in the Organized Crime Unit for a few years. Mostly, he handles office work. Rarely gets into the field."

"Figures."

"Poulton is a little more interesting. He started out NYPD, worked up to detective, and then moved over to FBI's Organized Crime Unit. By all accounts, a good cop and a better agent." Gaspar paused to gobble another half a Danish. "What's interesting is that Terry Poulton's brother was FBI Special Agent Tony Poulton, Serial Crimes Unit. Tony worked the original bathtub murders. A couple of years later, he was killed in the line of duty down Alabama. He was shot during a raid on a human trafficking ring, apparently."

She carried the water bottle in her right hand and munched a cheese cube in her left while she thought about the video. "So what do we think happened here? Jodie Jacob walked into that house on her own two feet. We don't know why. We don't know what happened once she got inside. That it?"

Gaspar shrugged. "We don't have interior surveillance, unfortunately. The Boss is looking. So far, no luck."

"We still don't know for certain if the woman in the red sedan is Jodie Jacob," Kim said.

"We don't. Not for sure. But we have no reason to believe otherwise. Do you?"

Kim shook her head and sipped the water and munched the cheese. "Jodie Jacob resigned from her firm a while back, according to the head of her department. He didn't know when or where she went. Could have been something personal or maybe she just changed jobs, he said."

"You're the lawyer here." Gaspar cocked his head. "But that's odd, isn't it?"

"Yes. But it's not illegal. Adults are free to move around if they want to. Nothing requires her to leave a forwarding address, either, as far as I know." Kim paced the room, just to move a little. Her muscles were still tight. Walking felt good, even though the room wasn't large enough to rack up any mileage. "But she still has a residential address in Manhattan, NYPD Detective Grassley said."

"You saw the body. Is it Jacob? In the tub?" Gaspar popped the last of the cherry Danish into his mouth.

"It could be. The victim looks like Jacob." Kim stopped pacing. "The killer might have left her head out so the paint wouldn't damage her face too much. So she'd be recognized. And Jacob is missing. It could be her."

"But?"

"But it doesn't feel right."

"Why?" Gaspar snagged the apricot turnover next and refilled his coffee.

"I've been thinking about that." She laid out her reasoning. "The house belonged to her father, who left it to Reacher. He lived there for a while, which was about three years after he left the Army. Jacob was having an affair with Reacher when he lived there. So she was tenuously connected to the house in at least three different ways."

"But?" he said, licking the sugar from his fingers, one at a time.

"All of that was a while back. It's not likely to be a motivating factor now." Kim paused and turned at the end of her short track "Why would she go to the house thirteen days ago? Why would someone kill her and leave her body there? What happened to her car?"

Gaspar said, "What we need is satellite surveillance of the house, including the back and the whole lot, as well as the front. With West Point across the river, there's gotta be satellites aimed all around that area constantly. I asked the Boss to get the video.

For some reason, he hasn't found it yet."

"I agree." She nodded. "That's why I went to see Finlay."

"And?" Gaspar tensed at the mention of Finlay's name. Kim could feel the hostile vibes all the way across the room.

"I haven't heard back from him yet. Give him a chance." She shrugged. "I don't know what went on inside that house. I don't know why Jodie Jacob went there if she did. I don't know why she didn't come out unless that's her body in the tub. But none of this makes sense. And when things don't make sense, it means we're missing something."

Gaspar said, "I've been over every word of those old bathtub killer files. Thousands of pages. But nothing in them seems like a reason to kill Jodie Jacob now when the killer didn't target her back then."

"Other than her relationship to Reacher, you mean."

"Not even that. She and Reacher broke up years ago. She moved to Europe, and he moved on to wherever he goes. The house was sold. Twice." Gaspar shook his head. "Humans are motivated to action. What caused Jacob to go back? Who objected to her being there?"

Kim considered the question for a few seconds. Maybe there was another angle. "Who owns the house now? Could the owner be one of her clients? Or a witness in a case that Jacob was working?"

Gaspar said, "Reacher gave the house to Jacob, and she sold it. A year later, a guy named Petrosian bought it. Not the chess champion. I checked."

Kim cocked her head. "How old a guy is he?"

"Mid-thirties. Married. Two kids. His old man was a Syrian mobster, Almar Petrosian. And he isn't involved in the family business, according to the New York Field Office," Gaspar said.

"Here's the interesting part. The current owner of the house is missing."

"Son of a mobster gone missing. Now there's an original story," Kim said dryly. "You believe that he's not involved in the family business?"

"Wanna buy some swamp land in the Everglades?" Gaspar grinned. "Of course, I don't believe that. Crime families tend to include all the generations. Petrosian, the father, is dead. Gang war. Happened unexpectedly around the time Reacher was living in the Garrison house. Back when Jodie Jacob was Reacher's lawyer."

"Given the timing, any chance Reacher killed the father? Maybe the son is carrying a grudge? Against Jacob and Reacher?" Kim drained her water bottle and shrugged. "I suppose that's possible. But he could have dumped Jacob's body in the river or a construction site or something. Presents the same question as Reacher doing this. Why abandon his own house and then use it for a crime scene?"

Gaspar shrugged.

Kim took another pass around the small track she'd created. "Here's something else. This Petrosian guy? He's spent a lot of money on that house. It's a real showpiece. Market value's well over five million, according to the real estate listing. When Reacher owned the house, it was what? Maybe half a million?"

Gaspar nodded. "I looked deeper on Petrosian. Turns out Almar had three sons. Two older ones are living here in New York. Oldest is Samir. Second is Tariq. Business as usual with those two. They picked up where their old man left off. The sons have expanded the protection rackets in Tribeca the old man controlled to a much broader territory. Like I said, the third son, Farid Petrosian, owns the Garrison house. Maybe he's a gangster, and maybe he's not. Hasn't been seen in several weeks."

"What about his family? Wife, kids?"

"Again, interesting. Farid's wife and kids are in witness protection. Deerfield set it up. Before you ask, no, we don't know why. Yet."

"Feels like there's way too many missing persons in this case, don't you think?" Kim asked. "With Deerfield at the center of everything."

"He wants Reacher." Gaspar shrugged. "He should get in line behind the rest of us."

"Seems that way, doesn't it?" Kim replied.

Gaspar raised one eyebrow. "Meaning you're willing to let him have Reacher?"

"Meaning the whole damn thing seems too contrived, doesn't it? Your summaries of the old files show that Deerfield handled Reacher back then. They flipped Reacher somehow, according to Lisa Harper. Who, by the way, is more disingenuous than she seems." Kim gave him the side-eye. "Don't let yourself get distracted when she turns that megawatt smile your way."

"Noted." He grinned. "I've seen her photos. Brought my sunglasses."

"Ha, ha. So Deerfield knew Reacher's pressure points, which he learned by trial and error on the original case. Figures out Reacher will do whatever it takes to protect Jacob, according to Harper. Now, he deploys the same strategy—using Jacob—and Reacher falls in line again?" Kim cocked her head.

Gaspar shrugged. "That's one theory."

Kim replied, "Fifty bucks says that when he had Reacher confined and as controlled as Reacher can be, he couldn't make Reacher do what he wanted, even when he threatened Jacob."

Gaspar nodded slowly, following her logic, moving to the next issue. "So why repeat a failed strategy now?"

"Exactly." She paused. "What makes sense is that Deerfield is using Reacher as a tool. He's after something else."

"Which would be what?"

"Dunno." Kim shook her head slowly as her mind searched for the missing piece. No luck.

Gaspar stretched his legs out and seemed to be thinking things through.

After a while, she grabbed another bottle of water and said, "Let's back up. Why did Deerfield have eyes on that house to begin with? Petrosian?"

"Yet another excellent question." Gaspar scarfed down the last pastry and shrugged, which was his all-purpose response. "Everything about the Petrosian operation is being held pretty tight."

# CHAPTER TWENTY-EIGHT

*Sunday, January 30*
*1:35 p.m.*
*Gowanus, New York*

REAL ESTATE AGENTS CLAIMED Gowanus was an up-and-coming neighborhood in transition, and it probably was. Legend was that the old Mafia families had dumped bodies in the canal, which was later filled with toxic chemicals and who knew what else. The legend was probably true. But Reed noticed signs of gentrification as he drove through in the unusual mix of old-school Brooklyn pride and active industrial areas.

Reed parked the Toyota in one of the locations that remained heavily industrial and mostly deserted on Sunday when the facilities were closed.

Across the street, near the infamous canal, was Donovan's favorite after-hours club. The club sold booze around the clock, even during the hours when alcohol sales were illegal. No doubt he'd spent the night alternately drinking and sleeping it off before he began drinking again, as he'd done most nights for the past eight years.

Reed would wait until six-year-old Lacey Arndt's killer staggered out of the illegal club.

Donovan was drunk the day he murdered Lacey. Donovan had been drunk almost every day since he was fourteen years old. The only difference between every day before he killed Lacey and every day after was his mode of transportation.

After he murdered Lacey Arndt, Donovan had finally surrendered his vehicle keys. Which was all the proof of guilt Reed needed.

Reed's memory of the videos he'd seen haunted his days and nights. Lacey at four, at five, at six. Brunette ringlets bouncing as she laughed. Dimpled cheeks as precious as Shirley Temple's.

Lacey would have become an exceptional adult if she'd been given a chance. Donovan stole her childhood and her life. Reed knew it. Donovan knew it. Everyone knew it.

Knowing was not enough.

Lacey was dead, and Donovan wasn't. The injustice demanded Reed's attention.

Lacey Arndt had begged her parents to visit New York for months. She wanted to see *Disney on Ice* at Rockefeller Center. Finally, the Arndts had packed up the family van and driven two days from Indiana.

Drunk as usual on his way home from a different bar, Donovan had driven his heavy SUV off the road and onto the sidewalk, striking Lacey down and dragging her lifeless, broken body more than a hundred feet before he managed to shake her free from the chassis.

Donovan sped away from the scene. He took the SUV to the closest car wash and destroyed the forensic evidence of his

monstrous crime. No bystanders could identify his vehicle or his
license plate, which had been covered with mud at the time.

The SUV had been borrowed from a friend in Connecticut.
Donovan denied that he'd been driving.

After months of investigation, forensics, and hundreds of
man-hours for witness interviews, no evidence was found that
put Donovan behind the wheel when Lacey was murdered.

No prosecutor would charge Donovan without that evidence.
He walked.

Reed was outraged.

Reed had attempted to console Lacey's devastated family
with the certainty that Donovan would make another mistake,
one that would finally give them justice, although not for
Lacey's murder.

Lacey's family made peace with Reed's promises. They
prayed. They offered forgiveness. The beautiful, bubbly Lacey
was gone. Nothing could bring her back. The trip had been worth
the sacrifices, her mom said because Lacey had never been
happier. The last memories her parents had of their bubbly
daughter alive were joyful ones. They were grateful for that
much, they said, but Reed didn't believe them.

He waited for Donovan to leave the bar. On a Sunday,
Donovan might stay until tomorrow. He usually did. Sometimes,
he'd fall asleep in the corner. After an hour or two, he'd wake up
and order another pint. Donovan had nowhere else to go.

Reed resolved to wait as long as he could. Once again, he
got lucky.

Donovan emerged from the club. He staggered along the
broken sidewalk. When he reached a deserted stretch of concrete
halfway down the second block, Reed revved his engine, popped
the transmission into first gear, and floored the accelerator.

The sedan's wheels spun in the slushy snow-covered street, faster and faster. Reed moved his foot off the brake pedal, and the vehicle leaped forward.

He took aim for Donovan, who seemed oblivious to the charging sedan. Or maybe he was tired of living. Reed was happy to oblige.

In mere moments, the sedan's front bumper slammed into Donovan's emaciated body. When 3,200 pounds of moving steel collided with softer tissues of the human body at a high rate of speed, the outcome was assured. Vehicle slams human. Human dies. As simple as that.

Donovan went down, flat on his stomach, face smashed into the pavement. Bright red blood bloomed on the filthy snow.

The sedan's right front tire ran over Donovan's body. The rear tire followed as day follows night.

The full weight of the vehicle crushed Donovan from head to toes, but he never knew. Like Lacey, he was already dead when his head first collided with the sidewalk.

Reed drove away, leaving Donovan like road kill. Just like Donovan had done to Lacey. No one was around to notice.

Another one off the list. Now he could focus all his attention on Reacher.

# CHAPTER TWENTY-NINE

*Sunday, January 30*
*2:15 p.m.*
*New York City, New York*

"WHAT DO WE KNOW about it so far?" Kim cocked her head, trying to fit the pieces together as Gaspar shared intel on the Petrosian situation.

"No one mourned much when Papa Petrosian was murdered by a rival gang. He was not only a ruthless killer, but he also had a very short fuse. Flew off the handle at the slightest provocation. He was also amazingly expert with a knife."

"Lovely," Kim murmured sarcastically.

"Scary as hell, by all accounts. He was a depraved sexual deviant, too. Not something his family wanted people to know, but not exactly a secret, either. His executions involved a sexual element, and the corpses were bizarrely displayed, always naked, often mutilated. Both males and females. I've seen a few of the pictures." Gaspar's lip curled with distaste. "And the three son apples didn't fall too far from the papa tree.

Samir and Tariq, particularly. Farid seems a little more civilized, but who knows?"

Kim took a long drink of water and then replied, "The body in the tub in Garrison wasn't mutilated. She's naked, and I guess the display is bizarre. But from what you're saying, this one is fairly tame compared to the old guy's methods."

"It seems that way," Gaspar agreed. "But the oldest son, in particular, learned his techniques at the knee of the master, from what I hear."

"Don't show me any photos. My imagination is vivid enough." Kim shuddered. "Farid Petrosian's wife and kids are in witness protection, you said. I've placed witnesses in WITSEC. You probably have, too."

Gaspar nodded.

Kim said, "Placements take a while to organize. The whole process, plus the paperwork, is a hassle and a half. Do we know if she's being protected *from* her husband or *because* her husband is important to the case?"

"I'll reach out to some colleagues and see what I can find." Gaspar shook his head. "Lot of gaps in my research. It's not clear who the actual target of the Petrosian investigation is. Or for that matter, who the witness is. Targets could be both brothers, Samir and Tariq. Farid may be planning to join his family in WITSEC. Or maybe he already has."

"Let's see if we can nail that down. And back to my earlier question," Kim said. She drained the water bottle and tossed it into the trash can ten feet away. "Deerfield had a team watching the Garrison house for quite a while. Had to be related to the Petrosian case, right?"

Gaspar shrugged. "That's as good a guess as any."

"When we first viewed the body in the tub, I asked Brice whether the victim was the owner's wife. He seemed surprised by the question, but he said no. Emphatically."

"Understandable," Gaspar nodded. "Evana Petrosian is a dark haired, brown-eyed beauty. Her two kids are exotically attractive, too, from the photos taken at Papa Petrosian's funeral. Evana's definitely not the blonde in the tub."

Kim nodded slowly, paced the room, thinking through the intel, the unanswered questions, trying to make sense of everything.

"I can see the wheels turning in your head. Talk it out to me, Suzy Wong," Gaspar said. "Maybe I can help."

"I'm thinking this is not all one thing. We have three things going on here. Maybe more."

"Which are?"

"Thing one is something involving Reacher. I'm not sure what, exactly, but my gut says it's not really about Jodie Jacob, although she seems to be at the center of it." She paused. "Whatever the Reacher thing is, that's why you and I are here."

"Agreed," Gaspar replied. "Which means Cooper is worried about it."

"Right. Thing two is something involving that house." Kim felt herself frowning. She used her fingers to smooth the vertical furrows between her eyes. "Deerfield authorizing that surveillance is just odd. If our New York colleagues are up in Garrison on a legitimate case, then why have an off the books operation going on at the same time? They'd be stepping all over themselves. And if the FBI surveillance team is working through channels, what evidence supports a long-term plan like that?"

"Not to mention the budget required. I've tried to get surveillance budgets approved. The bean counters kill them more often than not." Gaspar nodded. "And the third thing is Farid Petrosian?"

"Yes. WITSEC for Evana and her kids, maybe Farid Petrosian, too. More pricey stuff. Suggests one or more of them will be testifying. About what? Against whom? Where? When?" Kim looked at Gaspar as if he should have the answers. The blank look on his face proved he didn't. "And somehow, all of it ties back to the Garrison house. Everything begins and ends there."

Gaspar shifted in the chair, trying to get comfortable, which he could never do even before this latest gunshot injury.

Guilt stabbed Kim's conscience. He hadn't been cleared to return to desk duty in Miami until tomorrow, and here he was in the field in New York, solely because he thought she needed him.

"Don't look so mortified, Sunshine." He grinned as he settled into another awkward position. "Nobody held a gun to my head. I came here of my own free will. I'm fine."

"Marie must want to kill me."

"Yeah, you probably shouldn't show your face in Miami for a few weeks." He ducked his head and easily avoided the daggers shooting from her eyes. He paused as if he might say something else, but then he moved on. "As long as you don't let me get killed while I'm here, Marie will get over it. She was tired of having me hanging around, anyway. You've got plenty of other things to worry about. How do you figure Reacher fits into all of this?"

Kim took a deep breath and stared at the carpet. "Honestly, I don't know what to think about Reacher these days."

"Don't get all sentimental on me now, Suzy Wong." He frowned. "Reacher's still the same psycho he's always been.

You believe he might have saved your life in Palm Beach. First, that's just a guess. And second, so what?"

"Why would he do that? He knows we've been sticking our noses in his business. He knows Cooper's behind everything. He had a chance to let me die, and he didn't."

"So what?"

"So maybe we've got the wrong idea about him." She was thinking about the stuff Lisa Harper said about Reacher. Could Harper be right?

"Oh, for the love of God." Gaspar's exasperation all but exploded. He swiped a palm over his face. "Look, Kim. Don't delude yourself here. Reacher is still who he is. And what he is. If he fished you out of the Atlantic before you drowned—and that's a big if—he's not some kind of misunderstood hero. He did it for reasons of his own. He never does anything he doesn't want to do. Simple as that, and you know it."

"How can you be so sure?"

"Because I am. Because leopards don't change their spots. Because he's demonstrated time and time again that he's willing to do whatever it takes to get what he wants. Including murder." Gaspar paused and throttled down his frustration. "Reacher's a violent, ruthless, vigilante who does exactly whatever he pleases, regardless of the law. He's judge, jury, and executioner. He'll kill either one of us in a hot New York second if it serves his purposes. Don't think he won't. Don't romanticize him. It's dangerous for all of us."

Kim said nothing.

# CHAPTER THIRTY

*Sunday, January 30*
*4:15 p.m.*
*New York City, New York*

"KEEP YOUR EYE ON the ball here. If you don't, you'll risk not only your career but your *life* and mine, too." Gaspar grinned. "And then you'll never be able to return to Miami because Marie really will kill you."

Kim smiled weakly. "I know, I know. You've got twenty years to go and five kids to put through college."

"Damn straight. College is pricey." Gaspar said, nodding forcefully. He paused again as if he might say more, but then he simply finished up with a lame, "And don't you forget it."

"Okay." She took another deep breath, unconvinced, but moved on. She already had plenty to worry about. She'd come back to whatever was going on with Gaspar later. "So now what?"

"I'm sorry to say it, but I think there's only one choice, Mata Hari." The sour expression on his face suggested he'd swallowed a moldy key lime.

"Me? An exotic double agent?" He looked so ridiculous, Kim burst out laughing, but she knew exactly what he meant.

Gaspar didn't like Finlay and dealing with Finlay was a necessary evil that fell to Kim. Gaspar made clear that she was consorting with the enemy, even when Finlay was the only real choice.

Kim gave him a droll look. "Well, okay then. Lamont Finlay it is. You coming with?"

"God, no." He struck a pose filled with mock horror, which made her laugh. "Honestly? I'd only slow you down. My walking isn't what it should be yet. I'll find the answers we need on the Petrosian situation. Call in some favors. Maybe figure this out by the time you get back."

Kim was already rooting around in her pockets for the burner phone that connected her to Finlay. She found it, fired it up, and was surprised to see a voicemail icon on the screen indicating she had two messages. She punched the little envelope button on the keypad and put the phone to her ear.

The first was from Finlay. He'd called a couple of hours ago. "Call me." That was the whole message. Typical. He didn't waste many words.

The second call came from another number. One Kim didn't recognize. She pulled the message up and played it. She felt the color drain from her face.

The voice was definitely male. Tenor, not bass. Speech clipped. Accent sort of non-descript Midwest American. If she'd been pressed to describe it, she'd have said he sounded harmless enough. He looked dangerous, but he didn't speak the same way. Gaspar figured the voice helped him get close to his targets.

She'd heard his voice twice before. Once, on a tape-recorded interrogation, he'd conducted in Tampa while he was still an Army MP.

The second time, a couple of brief phone conversations were captured by an agency wiretap listening to unrelated targets.

This message was from Reacher. No doubt in her mind.

There was only one reasonable way Reacher could have obtained the burner's number. Finlay.

Which meant that Finlay had lied about his ability to contact Reacher.

Finlay couldn't be trusted, and Gaspar's opinion of Finlay was vindicated.

Which didn't mean he was no longer useful. Only that Finlay's usefulness was motivated by his own agenda. No surprise there.

Gaspar had been thumbing through his contacts, searching for a colleague's number. He glanced up and noticed her expression. "What is it?"

"You tell me." Kim pushed the speaker button on the phone and played the message aloud.

*Thanks for the warning, Agent Otto. Go with your gut. Deerfield can't be trusted. Harper's solid. Petrosian's the problem. Finlay has details. Watch your back.*

A short pause.

*Don't go swimming alone.*

The end. Call disconnected.

"That's Reacher," Gaspar said.

She replied, "Sounds like him. But it seems unlikely, doesn't it?"

"Doesn't matter how likely it is. I recognize his voice, and so do you. And Reacher's calling you now? We've got Finlay to thank for that, no doubt." Gaspar scowled. "What the hell does all that mean?"

"Means someone's feeding him intel or he's following me. I think he sent me a text yesterday while I was waiting for Harper." Kim plopped down on the bed. "Sounds like he's saying we're on the right track, though. We can get voice analysis on the message. Get a positive ID. But he says the Petrosian case is where we should be concentrating."

"We're taking orders from Reacher?" Gaspar's scowl deepened. "Where the hell is he?"

"The number he called from has a New York area code, and it's different from the one he used to text me on my other phone, which is why I didn't recognize it. This could be a pay phone, and there aren't too many of those left in existence. We can chase it down, I guess," Kim replied.

"No point to that. He's miles away by now," Gaspar replied, still annoyed. "If it was a pay phone, he might have made other calls, though. I can find out. See who he's connecting with now that we know he's here. Maybe I can get some CCTV from somewhere near the phone."

"Sounds good." She gave him the phone number Reacher had used and then she pushed the call back button for Finlay. He picked up. "On my way."

She disconnected before he could object. She pulled two new burner cell phones from her bag, fired them up, and walked into the hallway to test them. She'd done what she could to keep listeners at bay inside the hotel room, but a determined snoop couldn't be thwarted. The best she could manage was slowing the high-tech types down and keeping the amateurs working hard to figure things out.

She tossed one of the new burners to Gaspar. He glanced at the exchanged texts and nodded. She pulled her personal cell from her pocket and tossed it on the bed, along with the Boss's burner.

As Kim donned her coat, Gaspar said, "I'll check in with the Boss while you're gone. See what I can find out about Deerfield and Petrosian."

"See what he'll admit to knowing about the Garrison house, too. I'll be back as soon as I can. Finlay never has that much time, so not more than a couple of hours, max." She left the room, took the elevator down.

Even in January, weekend visitors filled the lobby in the middle of the day. Couples, families, tour groups, and more mingled as they came and went.

Kim rode the down escalator from the main lobby past the perpetual fountain and joined the line waiting for a taxi. Two doormen choreographed the arrivals and departures efficiently. At the valet entrance, a variety of cabs and car service vehicles pulled up. Passengers paid fares and climbed out, and hotel guests heading to New York City's weekend entertainment venues filled the vehicles again.

Kim worried about Gaspar while she waited her turn. Twice, she'd expected him to tell her something, and he'd backed off. She selfishly hoped he wouldn't take disability retirement. But she could see how difficult the job had become for him, although he refused to discuss his condition.

The line moved quickly. After about five minutes, the doorman blew his whistle to call the next car and waved Kim outside. She walked into the cold and stepped through the open passenger door into a warm taxi. She gave the driver Finlay's address and sat back in the seat for the short trip.

# CHAPTER THIRTY-ONE

*Sunday, January 30*
*5:05 p.m.*
*New York City, New York*

THE SECRET SERVICE AGENT, Russell, opened the door to Finlay's suite, as he'd done every time she came here. "Good evening, Agent Otto."

She nodded. "Russell. Seems like we just did this dance, doesn't it?"

"Indeed. We have you set up in the same room as before." He waved her into the open doorway on the left. "Make yourself comfortable. I'll let Dr. Finlay know you've arrived."

"Thanks." She slipped her coat off her shoulders and dropped it into a chair. Refreshments were arranged on the buffet table, as always. She grabbed a bottle of sparkling water and walked around the room to stretch. She felt like her muscles had, indeed, solidified. If required to run for her life, she'd be in trouble.

Finlay arrived with the usual level of pomp. Which was to say that he came in and closed the door acting like he owned the place. She was starting to think that maybe he did. If he had a home or a more formal base of operations, she'd never heard about it. Not that she would have. They weren't friends or colleagues. Theirs was a relationship of necessity.

"Let's not waste our time." He waved her to a chair and took his seat on the sofa. "You've located and reviewed the old bathtub murder files, I assume?"

The mere mention of those files raised her blood pressure ten points. "Cooper sent them. I've read Gaspar's summaries."

"You know the details of the murder cases, then. We can move on to Petrosian," Finlay said. "Did Cooper provide the Organized Crime files on Almar Petrosian?"

"No."

He nodded and launched right into the meat of the matter.

"Back then, Reacher was picked up, and they flipped him, as Deerfield said. But both cases were going on at the same time. Reacher was scooped up in the Petrosian matter, not the bathtub murders."

She raised her eyebrows. "You're sure?"

"He was a person of interest in the bathtub murders, but the Serial Crimes Unit hadn't made a move on him yet. They piled on after he was already in custody. Serial Crimes wouldn't have been able to get a warrant on the evidence they had." He paused, probably to give her a chance to catch up. "Here's the important part. Reacher was never charged in either case."

Kim cocked her head. "If he wasn't charged, why didn't he just walk away?"

Finlay shook his head. "I'm not a mind reader. My guess is Deerfield had dodgy leverage that kept Reacher on the hook. The leverage is not explained in the files. We can probably guess what it was."

"Of course, it's not in the files," Kim sneered. If Deerfield had threatened Jodie Jacob or allowed his subordinates to threaten her to coerce Reacher, no one would have been stupid enough to make a record of illegal activity like that.

"Now here's the problem." Finlay paused, perhaps to be sure she was paying attention. "*Both* of Deerfield's cases terminated prematurely. A double loss. Petrosian, the father, died in a gang war, which effectively ended the organized crime case. And the bathtub killer stopped killing before they caught him."

"So Deerfield's office spent a lot of time and money and plenty of attention, but not a single arrest or conviction," Kim said slowly. "Which probably didn't make Cooper very happy, right?"

"Bingo." Finlay smiled. "Cooper considered the lack of results a colossal failure. Which effectively ended Deerfield's career. Assistant Director of the New York Field Office was as high as he'd ever go."

"Cooper didn't demand his resignation? That's what I'd expect him to do." Kim said.

"He did. Deerfield refused." Finlay's lips twitched. "Deerfield has bigger balls than I imagined."

Kim made no effort to conceal her grin. The Boss was old school, in every sense of the word. Deerfield failed publicly, spectacularly, and simultaneously, in two high profile matters that embarrassed and ridiculed the bureau. He should have done the honorable thing. When he didn't slink away with his tail between his legs, the Boss would have been furious.

Without question, the Boss would still be holding that grudge and looking for every opportunity to humiliate Deerfield until he resigned.

"So what we have now, I suspect, is payback." Finlay smiled. "By a twist of fate, both the Petrosians and the bathtub murders are active again. It's not often we get a do-over in this business. Deerfield knows that. He doesn't intend to let this particular crisis go to waste. No way will Cooper allow Deerfield a chance to redeem himself. Cooper wouldn't piss on Deerfield if he was on fire, and he'd shoot the first man who tried to help."

Kim nodded. Everything Finlay said rang true. In every law enforcement agency, there was plenty of testosterone to go around. It was no stretch to believe that Cooper and Deerfield played together about as well as Patton and Rommel.

Made perfect sense.

"Tell me about the Petrosians," she said.

"There's a lot to tell, and you'll hear most of it since Gaspar's already asking around." He paused as if she might disavow Gaspar's actions, but she didn't bother.

She nodded.

"Modern fiction notwithstanding, there is no honor among thieves. Bottom line: Farid Petrosian approached the FBI with an offer. Deerfield accepted," Finlay said.

"What was the offer?" Kim replied, although she already knew it included WITSEC for Farid's wife and kids.

Finlay said, "Farid provided records detailing the Petrosians' criminal enterprise, along with promised testimony, in exchange for immunity and protection for himself and his family."

"What kind of criminal enterprise?"

"Are you familiar with the Family Secrets case in Chicago?"

"Of course. Every federal agent not living under a rock is aware of that case." Kim said. "One of the biggest and most successful FBI investigations of organized crime ever conducted. Racketeering, murder, money laundering. A long list.

Indictments of fourteen defendants charged with eighteen murders and at least one attempted murder."

Finlay nodded. "The Petrosians aren't anywhere near the Chicago Outfit level, but they've been operating long enough to build up impressive criminal résumés. If Deerfield's office sews this one up, he'll do the bureau and the country a service and redeem himself to just about everyone."

"You said 'if' Deerfield can make the case. He's got an insider witness and written records. What more does he need?" Kim asked.

"He probably doesn't *need* anything else. But he *wants* a couple of bodies and forensics tying the murders to Samir and Tariq Petrosian, which, to mix our metaphors, would make the case a touchdown." Finlay paused to grin again. "And Deerfield could spike the ball in Cooper's face where everybody can see him do it, too."

Kim shook her head. "I can see why that might appeal to Deerfield."

"You're Team Cooper, I know." Finlay folded his hands around his knee and spoke quietly. "But can you also see the lengths to which Cooper might go to prevent Deerfield from succeeding?"

She wanted to issue a hot denial, but she felt her face flush and her stomach start churning, so she said nothing.

Kim must have looked a little green because Finlay turned his back and walked to the buffet table to give her a moment. "Can I bring you something? Coffee? Water?"

"Coffee, please." She cleared her throat. "So why hasn't Deerfield arrested Samir and Tariq Petrosian?"

"Deerfield's problem is both evidence and timing." He brought the coffee and returned to the sofa.

"He doesn't have the bodies and the forensics settled yet, so he can't make a big splashy announcement in front of the whole world," she said.

"Exactly. He's working on obtaining enough evidence for a search warrant," Finlay replied.

"Farid's testimony and documents should be enough for a warrant to search Samir and Tariq's homes, offices, vehicles," Kim said. "What's the holdup?"

Finlay gazed directly into her eyes. "My source is impeccable and entirely off the record. Which means you and Gaspar agree not to inform Cooper directly or indirectly. Do I have your word on that?"

Kim didn't reply.

"Cooper's got plenty of resources. He may know already. But I won't be the one to tilt the playing field in his favor. If you can't agree to my terms, that's fine. You'll figure things out eventually," Finlay said. "You want time to talk it over with Gaspar?"

"Gaspar's number two. I'm the lead agent. My decisions are final." She paused. "You're effectively asking us not to discuss a crucial piece of the case with anyone at all."

He nodded. "Those are my terms. Totally up to you, of course."

"There's a whole team working on the Petrosian case. If Farid told Deerfield, then he's probably told others." She paused and then nodded agreement. "Intel doesn't do me much good if I can't use it for anything. If we get the information another way, we're free to use it as we wish."

"That's reasonable." Finlay nodded. "Farid Petrosian claims that Samir and Tariq killed two members of the Petrosian gang who were skimming money. These guys were shot while the renovations were being made to the Garrison house. Farid says the bodies were dumped with the guns used to kill them. The next day, the foundation was poured on top of them, and the master suite was added to the house."

"So Deerfield wants a warrant for LIDAR or X-rays or something to confirm that the bodies are down there before they tear the house down." Kim nodded. "He doesn't want to come up empty. Especially on a five-million-dollar house."

"And if he's wrong, it's definitely a career killer this time," Finlay said. "Cooper will make damn sure Deerfield is fired. No pension, even."

"Meanwhile, Deerfield has pushed the WITSEC process through the system for Farid and his family. Where is Farid now? Federal custody, I assume?" Kim asked, and Finlay shrugged, which she took as affirmative. "Samir and Tariq must be getting antsy. They don't know where Farid is. They do know where those bodies are. Which explains why Deerfield had eyes on that house until he could get his warrant."

What it didn't explain was why Brice and Deerfield failed to tell her the truth about the original surveillance. Or why Smithers wasn't straight with her last night. She understood the need for secrecy. But they officially added her to the team, and then purposely omitted essential information needed to do the job. Which meant none of them could be trusted.

"Deerfield is sitting on an extremely volatile situation," Finlay said. "Or at least, he was. Until the body in the tub was discovered."

"So he got lucky," Kim nodded. "At that point, they turned the crime scene over to NYPD. Now they've got cops and techs and media all over that place like white on rice. Samir and Tariq can't possibly start digging up the bodies."

"Which solves the mystery of the victim identification delay neatly, too. Deerfield doesn't want the victim identified too soon. While she's a Jane Doe, she's a lot more useful to his personal agenda, which is to screw Cooper and get the hell out of New York." Finlay drained his coffee. "Another cup?"

Kim stared. "You don't believe Deerfield killed that woman and staged the copycat crime, do you? Everything else you've said makes sense. But that's definitely a bridge too far."

"I considered it. But I don't believe he's completely lost his mind. In fact, I think it's precisely the opposite. He's being careful. Taking precautions. He doesn't want this Petrosian thing to blow up in his face again. Not when he's so close." Finlay shook his head. He glanced at the sliver-thin platinum watch on his wrist.

Kim said, "Deerfield didn't kill her, and he didn't stage the body. But I suspect he knows who did. This reads like an opportunity that dropped into his lap."

"That's how I read it, too," Finlay nodded. "I've got another meeting. You can call me if you need to, of course."

He was already out the door before she remembered she'd planned to ask about Reacher's phone message. She'd ask him next time. She already had plenty to deal with.

She headed downstairs.

The crowd lined up for rides at Finlay's hotel was longer now than when she arrived, but three doormen worked the line and Kim was soon seated and on her way. Two blocks later, traffic had slowed more than expected. Up ahead, a night crew was working on underground utilities, and traffic was detoured. Kim's driver turned at the first opportunity and headed north around the roadblock.

She had left her personal cell in her room to limit the Boss's efforts to track her or listen to her conversations. The burner cells in her pocket didn't have internet connectivity for research on the go, so she called Gaspar. After ten rings, he didn't answer. Maybe he'd call back.

She had nothing to discuss with anyone else at this point. All of which meant she was captive in the back of a New York City car service sedan, alone with her thoughts. Never a good thing.

# CHAPTER THIRTY-TWO

*Sunday, January 30*
*7:25 p.m.*
*New York, New York*

GASPAR RUBBED THE BACK of his neck and stretched the kinks out. He'd been hunched over his secure laptop and on the phone with confidential sources since Otto had left the room. She should be finishing up with Finlay anytime now.

He couldn't talk with her from the room. What he'd learned was too sensitive to risk it. The Boss was definitely listening, and Deerfield probably was, too. With time, diligence, and the right equipment, both of them could isolate and listen to every spoken word. The military grade scrambler she'd installed was good, but not perfect. No technology was.

Gaspar wouldn't be surprised if the Petrosians had ears on, too, and perhaps a few others. Their equipment was not as sophisticated, but their determination could make up for low tech.

Everywhere in the hotel would present the same problems, although sorting his communications from all the others might slow the amateurs down a bit.

Simply put, he didn't want to worry about it. He was feeling claustrophobic anyway. A bit of exercise couldn't hurt.

He located the dedicated burner Kim had given him and left everything else with a tracking beacon in the room. He left the cane, too. A few minutes later, he was on his way downstairs. He moved as quickly as he could, which was to say not very fast. He'd already swallowed too many Tylenol today, and they didn't make a dent in the pain anyway. The only thing to do was press forward.

At the bottom of the escalator, the line for rides was too long. On a cold night in January, no one wanted to walk. He shrugged, turned up his collar, and took the plunge. The Starbucks he wanted wasn't too far. Damn, it was cold out here, though. His Miami overcoat wasn't heavy enough for this weather.

A number of pedestrians wandered the sidewalks along with him. Many were talking on cell phones, and the others probably had at least one phone in their pockets. Lots of tracking beacons lighting up the scanning screens, which was good.

He pulled the burner cell out and fired it up. After a few seconds, the phone connected to a cell tower. He saw a voicemail notification and figured it had to be from Otto, probably not too long ago. Instead of listening, he called her back. Her phone rang several times and kicked over to voice mail. He waited for the tone.

"Call me when you get this message. I'm headed for coffee. You know the place. We need to talk. Important stuff. I'll wait for you there."

He disconnected and then opened Otto's earlier voice mail. The recorded message was less than one second of silence. She must have hung up when the call kicked over.

Gaspar kept the phone in his hand so he could feel the vibration when it rang. He stuffed his hands into his pockets and struggled to cover the distance while he waited for her to call back.

He'd stopped to rest several times. Hypothermia threatened constantly. Eventually, he arrived at the crowded coffee shop, chilled to his bones.

Dozens of New Yorkers had piled into the warmth. Few were actually talking to each other or talking on cell phones. Instead, they were connecting in cyberspace using numerous devices, exactly as he'd expected. This particular shop reliably confounded surveillance when he wanted to be a needle in a haystack. The effect was temporary but lasted long enough.

He made his way to the coffee line and ordered the largest espresso breve with heavy cream. He added a few cookies and a couple of pastries to his order. After he picked up the food and coffee, he stopped to collect a handful of sugar packets. A couple of guys were packing up to leave and offered him their small table.

After an hour of waiting for Otto's call, he began to worry. After the second hour, he forced himself to call Finlay's private number.

On the fourth ring, Finlay picked up. "Yes."

"It's Gaspar. Is Otto with you?"

"She left a couple of hours ago. Where are you?"

Gaspar ignored the question. He clenched his jaw and felt the muscles tense. "Did she go to meet Reacher?"

Finlay paused too long. Gaspar's grip on the phone tightened.

He felt the cheap plastic flex and eased off. This phone was his lifeline to Otto. Crushing it would be counterproductive.

"She didn't say where she was going, and I didn't ask," Finlay replied. "I assumed she was headed back to her hotel. If you're calling here, that must mean you can't find her."

Gaspar pressed his lips into a firm hard line to suppress the anger Finlay ignited without trying. "You have access to CCTV in your hotel, I assume?"

"Let me get that started," Finlay spoke without covering the phone's speaker. "Russell, please check the video and locate Agent Otto."

Gaspar had met Russell. As a species, Secret Service agents were adept. Russell was exceptional. Gaspar breathed a bit easier, confident Russell would produce the expected results swiftly.

Finlay said, "Why did you ask me if she went to meet Reacher?"

Gaspar cocked his head. A satisfied smile lifted the corner of his mouth. So she hadn't told him about Reacher's phone call. She wasn't quite as certain that Reacher was some kind of white knight as she'd argued back in the hotel. Ambivalence was good news, as far as Gaspar was concerned. There was a better chance that she'd remain wary of Reacher that way.

He enjoyed Finlay's discomfort for a couple of moments before he said, "He called her tonight. Left a voice message. She thought he got the number from you."

Finlay breathed heavily into the phone. "Why did she think I gave Reacher her number?"

Gaspar smiled. Too bad he wasn't in the same room with Finlay now. He'd love to see that bastard sweat. Just once. He didn't trust the guy at all. He was way too slick. Guys like Finlay always had things to hide. Sooner or later Gaspar would learn

Finlay's secrets. Until then, keeping Finlay at arm's length was the best strategy.

Russell returned, and Gaspar overheard snatches of his report. Enough to understand that Otto had joined the line of people waiting for cabs. She'd left Finley's hotel in a black Mercedes. Pretty high-end vehicle for a New York cabbie. But a lot of the private car services lined up at the better hotels hoping to pick up longer, more expensive fares. The Mercedes was probably one of those.

"Thanks, Russell. Find out where the Mercedes dropped her off." Finlay exhaled loud enough to be heard on the cheap burner cell in the crowded coffee shop. "She entered a Mercedes about two hours ago. Russell's chasing it down now. He'll trace the sedan on the traffic cam videos. We'll find her. I'll call back on this number."

"One more thing. Otto asked you for satellite surveillance of Farid Petrosian's Garrison house. Did you show it to her?"

Finley paused for a couple extra beats. "We discussed the Petrosian situation. At that time, I did not have the video."

Gaspar didn't believe that for a minute, which raised his blood pressure again. "But you've seen it now."

"Yes. Most disturbing."

"That's one way to put it. The guy who altered the FBI surveillance video to delete the woman leaving the house in Jacob's car will pay for it with a long stay in federal prison. I don't suppose you know who it was?"

"We're looking into that."

"Have you identified the woman?"

"It's probably Jacob. Looks like her. And that's most likely her car. She owns one like it." Finlay paused. "Which doesn't necessarily mean the bathtub victim is Jacob."

"Doesn't prove the victim ID either way. But the FBI's operating theory that Jacob went into the house and never came out is patently false. Which the FBI would have known." Gaspar paused. "Meaning Deerfield would have known."

Finlay breathed into the phone for a moment. "Are you *sure* the false intel is unknown higher up the food chain?"

Gaspar clenched his jaw as his temper flared again. Finlay knew damn well that Cooper had seen the satellite video. Gaspar and Otto were deliberately being kept in the dark. Which were only two of the things that pissed him off about the whole situation.

Finlay said nothing more. They understood each other. People inside the FBI couldn't be trusted. Who were the bad guys here?

Gaspar asked, "Have you identified the driver who reversed the black SUV into the garage two days after the woman's visit? Do you know what he did for the sixty-three minutes he was inside?"

"Again, not yet. But the same uncertainties apply, do they not?"

Had Finlay been in the room, Gaspar would have decked the pompous ass. Wrestling his Latin temper was like wrangling a swamp gator. The only thing that kept him on the leash was that he couldn't reach through the cheap cell phone and choke the life out of the bastard.

After a few deep breaths made it possible for him to speak without expletives, Gaspar said, "If you call me back within the next twenty minutes, it won't be necessary for me to ask the same questions of Cooper. We both know how well he'll respond."

"We are on the same page here, Gaspar," Finlay replied as calmly as ever. "Reacher has not abducted Otto if that's what you're thinking. He wasn't driving the Mercedes."

"I was not thinking that. But it's interesting that you're trying to rule it out." Gaspar all but sneered. He didn't know exactly what game Finlay was playing with Cooper, but he damn sure wasn't going to let Otto get killed in the middle of it. "So you know she's Cooper's bait. Deployed to lure Reacher. If that worked tonight, Cooper would be delighted. But when Reacher comes in from the cold, you won't be pleased at all, will you?"

Finlay remained quiet for a moment. "I'll get back to you as soon as I have something to share, Agent Gaspar."

Gaspar's nostrils flared. His voice hammered hard. "You do that. But don't forget what I said. Twenty minutes. If anything happens to Otto, that's on you. You'll pay the price. Count on it."

"Plenty of blame to share here, Gaspar. You're her partner. Where were you?" Finlay disconnected without another word.

Gaspar spent two full minutes tamping his white-hot anger down to a controllable blaze. He'd wait twenty minutes. No more.

He stretched his legs in front of the chair to relieve the constant pain and crossed his hands over his stomach to watch the clock.

# CHAPTER THIRTY-THREE

*Sunday, January 30*
*7:45 p.m.*
*New York City, New York*

SHE NOTICED THE TRANSPORT license posted behind the driver's seat on the thick partition separating the front from the back of the Mercedes sedan. His photo showed an attractive young black man with long dreadlocks. The back of the driver's neck made him a middle-aged white guy with red hair.

Kim looked through the partition into the rearview mirror mounted on the windshield. The driver's freckled forehead and blue eyes were looking back at her in the reflection. Sandy red eyebrows matched the hair poking beneath his cap and teased her memory somehow.

Maybe the regular driver was sick. Maybe he was an extra in a big Broadway production and he got a chance to perform tonight. A dozen innocent explanations were possible.

But the tiny hairs on the back of Kim's neck stood straight up, and her stomach churned like a blender.

Something was wrong here. She reached into her pocket for a bill to pay the fare and prepared to jump out the next time he stopped the car. As the driver slowed for the next red light, she reached for the door handle.

He stopped behind two cars already waiting.

She pulled the handle to open the door.

The handle moved easily, but the door was still locked.

She pushed the unlock button on the armrest, and nothing happened.

The manual lock was recessed, flush with the top of the door panel. She couldn't grab it.

She glanced at the manual lock on the door behind the driver, which was also recessed too far.

She slapped her palm on the thick partition between the seats and raised her voice to be heard through it. "Let me out here! Let me out!"

The light changed to green, and the driver rolled forward with the flow of traffic. She looked into the rearview mirror again. His blue eyes crinkled at the corners as if he was laughing at her puny efforts to escape. Which he probably was.

She pulled one of the burner phones from her pocket and punched 911 without looking at the screen. The call failed to connect. She hit the end call button and waited a second for the connection to establish. She tried again with the second phone and got the same result.

After another block, she made another attempt. She tried three more times after that. Both phones failed to pick up a signal at each location. In a city where everyone was connected every waking moment, the only way both phones could be offline was a blocked signal.

She scanned the city as the cab passed, looking for a landmark she recognized, but identified nothing familiar. Most street signs were outside her line of vision. Because the driver hadn't turned again, they must still be traveling north.

The cab had been making slow progress. They couldn't have traveled more than a couple of miles. But the traffic ahead was thinning out as the driver increased their distance from midtown Manhattan.

Her slim margin of opportunity to escape narrowed every second. What were her options?

The phones didn't work. The doors couldn't be opened.

Only one remaining choice. Her weapon rested snugly in her shoulder holster. She assumed he had a gun, too.

She couldn't disarm the driver from her position in the back seat, but she could shoot through the rear windows. Standard vehicle windows were both laminated and tinted. Which meant that when she shot through, they wouldn't send razor-sharp shards back to cut her.

Frigid temperatures discouraged sidewalk strollers but shooting into any pedestrian area was extremely dangerous. To limit the risks, she could damage the glass enough with two rounds, and then knock the pieces to the ground and climb out.

The driver might try to stop her, but if he came out of the cab, she'd have a clear shot at him. Which was sounding pretty damn good at the moment.

Before they reached the next red light, a speaker mounted on the back deck crackled. The driver had picked up a handset and held it close to his mouth. She could hear his breathing.

As if he'd read her mind, he said, "This vehicle has been modified in several respects. The body, including windows and the partition between us, are Type III and Type IV Ballistic

Resistant Protective Materials. Type IV prevents penetration from armor-piercing rifles. Type III stops shots from a .44 Magnum."

He paused, watching her in the rearview mirror for two full seconds.

"I'm sure you understand, Agent Otto?" When she didn't reply, he said, "Discharging your 9mm weapon inside this vehicle will definitely cause more harm to you than to anything you might aim for. But feel free to test my prediction for yourself, if you must."

Kim looked as closely as the variable ambient light entering intermittently from the city's streets permitted. The partition was significantly thicker and more opaque than the windows. She was able to confirm that each of the four windows, the rear window, and front windshield were also distorted.

The driver was right. Demonstrations in the field proved multiple 9mm rounds wouldn't penetrate or destroy this glass. Bullets would deflect into the cabin unpredictably. Thick particle dust would spray everywhere. The noise of gunshots in the small, enclosed space would be deafening.

In short, shooting inside the car was a spectacularly bad idea. She was more likely to end up dead or maimed than the driver. And the vehicle itself would be practically unscathed.

Reluctantly, she accepted that she couldn't escape from confinement by brute force, which didn't leave many options. "Abducting a federal agent will send you to prison."

He smiled. "You weren't abducted. You entered my cab voluntarily. Dozens of witnesses saw you do it."

"I've been abducted since the moment you refused to let me out of this vehicle," she replied.

He cupped his hand to his ear. "What? I can't hear you."

She said nothing.

"You have only one choice at the moment, Agent Otto. Relax and enjoy the ride." He returned the handset to its cradle and focused on his driving.

Kim fell back against the seat and remained alert for an opportunity to escape.

The chance never came.

The taxi left the city along a route that took them from New York to Connecticut. He'd transported a kidnapped federal agent across state lines. He wouldn't get the death penalty for that, but his maximum sentence could last the rest of his natural life. She vowed to make sure it did.

Farther north, he returned from Connecticut to cross into New York again. After a while, he drove through a suburban community. Large, upscale houses on spacious lots were set back from the roads on both sides.

He drove for another hour. Each mile away from Manhattan seemed more rural than the last. In the distance, she heard a train approaching. She watched the freight train running parallel to the road, and when it passed, the light on the last car faded into the distance.

Under the snow, Kim imagined rolling hills and agricultural fields, like she'd find if she drove so far from downtown Detroit.

She had no idea where she was. She hadn't seen a comprehensible sign for miles. The running rail fences along the roadside suggested they'd entered an equestrian area, but no visible horses or horse barns. Just the fences establishing pastures and property lines.

Up ahead, she saw a wide gap in the fence on the right side of the road. A driveway. They turned in and traveled half a mile across open land toward a mansion posed at the opposite end. The headlights illuminated the magnificent colonial farmhouse, which was probably more than two hundred years old. Rows of windows across the front suggested two stories and a loft or attic room in the center at the gable. A wraparound porch and double front door gave the place a homey, welcoming feel, even in the darkness.

The driver pulled up at the circular front entrance and stopped parallel to the steps leading to the porch. The handset crackled when he used it to relay her orders. "Field strip your gun and leave the components on the back seat."

She looked at his eyes in the rearview mirror. "No."

"You think you're a real firecracker, don't you? That wasn't a request, and you're in no position to refuse." He shook his head, but his eyes crinkled a bit as if he might be smiling. His voice was harsher the second time. "Disassemble your weapon and leave it on the seat."

She said nothing, and she made no move to follow directions.

"Use your head, Otto. You can't shoot me through the armor. We've been over all that. I'm dropping you off. Not sticking around. You won't have a chance to kill me anyway." His eyes watched her reflection as steadily as she watched his.

She remained seated, wary, alert to an opening.

He sighed and shook his head again. "Let me be clear. You're not leaving this vehicle while in possession of your firearm. I'm prepared to sleep in this seat. So we can stay here all night if you like. Or you can be out of the vehicle in less than ten seconds, where you'll have room to do whatever it is you think you can do. Your choice."

She said nothing. He slid the transmission into Park and turned off the lights. Kim waited for her eyes to adjust to the near total darkness.

# CHAPTER THIRTY-FOUR

*Sunday, January 30*
*9:55 p.m.*
*New York, New York*

NINETEEN MINUTES AFTER HANGING up with Finlay, Gaspar's burner phone rang. Which meant two things. Finlay took his threat to call the Boss seriously. And Finlay didn't want Gaspar to make that call. Both good to know.

He raised the phone to his ear. "Yeah."

Finlay sighed. "We're working on the same side, Gaspar. When are you going to accept that I'm not your enemy?"

"When you start acting like it."

Silence. Static on the line was the only clue that Finlay hadn't hung up. Gaspar watched the big clock on the wall as its second hand ticked around toward the twenty-minute deadline. Fifteen seconds left. He was tempted to hang up.

Finlay flinched first. "We tracked the Mercedes on traffic cams until it exited the I-95 expressway in Darien, Connecticut. After that, it seems to have disappeared."

"Which means the driver knew how to avoid traffic cams," Gaspar said.

"So it seems," Finlay replied. "We checked various CCTV systems in the area where he went dark. We also checked the satellites and all known tracking devices and systems. No luck so far."

"You're saying an FBI agent has been abducted and you can't find her?"

Finlay said, "We're continuing to work on this, but for the moment, yes. That's exactly what I'm saying."

Gaspar understood all too well. There were only two reasonable explanations. Otto could be deliberately avoiding all monitoring. She'd done it before. Or her abductors were uncommonly savvy about government surveillance systems. In this case, he feared the latter.

"Suggestions," Gaspar said through clenched teeth and only because Finlay's resources were vast. He could actually have options that were unavailable to Gaspar.

"Not yet. Stay on the grid. Keep me posted. I'll call you when we know more." Finlay disconnected.

Gaspar donned his coat and gloves and limped back to the hotel. He was tired and hurting, and several times he thought he might not make it. But he didn't stop to rest until he leaned against the wall inside the elevator as it rushed upward. When it reached his floor, he hurried out and down the hallway.

He used Otto's key card to enter her room. Personal devices were exactly where he'd left them. He located the Boss's burner cell phone and placed the call.

"We don't know where she is. We're working on it," Cooper said when he picked up the call. Which meant he'd heard something from Finlay or he'd been monitoring another way.

Gaspar didn't inquire or object. Questions and objections were irrelevant and would be ignored. He didn't have the energy.

He asked, "Where's Deerfield? He's responsible."

The Boss replied, "He was here. Claims he doesn't know where she is."

"You believe that?"

"No."

"What's his objective?"

"Blackmail."

"Why?"

"Career advancement."

Gaspar blinked. Had he heard correctly? "He wants what?"

"My job, apparently. Or so he says. Came here personally to demand it."

The Boss would have had him hauled out of his DC office in cuffs, at the very least. Deerfield was smarter than that. He'd have chosen a neutral location. "Where are you?"

"Phoenix."

Phoenix to New York City was more than a four-hour flight and if he flew into Stewart to be closer to Garrison, the travel time was closer to seven hours. Deerfield was due back in the morning.

"Where is he now?"

"Thirty thousand feet above New Mexico, probably."

From Cooper's tone, Gaspar figured Deerfield was lucky he'd booked a commercial flight. A private jet might have tempted the Boss to take him down with a surface-to-air missile.

"What did you tell him about the job?"

"To kiss my ass."

Gaspar chuckled quietly, which became a cough that caused the pain in his right side to grab his breath and hold it way too long. He pressed his side and took several shallow breaths, pushing the pain down to a tolerable level before he could speak again.

"He's abducted Otto to use her for blackmail?" Gaspar asked weakly.

"Close."

The Boss's silence lasted a couple of beats before Gaspar puzzled out that the leverage Deerfield had applied must have been related to Reacher. Otto was merely the disposable tool he'd applied.

"I see."

The terse reply came swiftly. "Good."

Gaspar considered whether to mention Reacher's phone and text messages. The Boss probably already knew about them. He might not know Reacher had called from a pay phone in Upstate New York, near Garrison.

The Boss made the decision easy. He said, "Order room service."

Then, Gaspar heard nothing but dead air. He used the hotel phone to order coffee and an assortment of desserts. After that, he gave in and swallowed two extra strength Tylenol, and stretched out on the bed to wait.

# CHAPTER THIRTY-FIVE

*Sunday, January 30*
*10:15 p.m.*
*Upstate New York*

THE LAND AROUND THE house had seemed to stretch endlessly in all directions. Probably an optical illusion, since this was not Wyoming. They'd only traveled maybe three hours from Manhattan, at the most. Which meant the house probably had electricity and other modern conveniences.

She'd been trained to escape likely dangers and survive the aftermath. Locked doors, restraining devices, vaults, elevators, moving vehicles of all kinds, abductors, hostage takers, firearms and other weapons, as well as animal and human predators. The list of lethal threats to petite women like Kim was seemingly endless.

The driver, or maybe his boss, must have known her qualifications because he'd devised a confinement she couldn't escape. Defeating Type III and Type IV ballistic resistant materials was beyond brute force or human ingenuity. She knew because she'd been trained there, too.

Heavy clouds blocked every hint of celestial light and sunrise was at least eight hours away. She could sit here until daylight, but then what?

Reluctantly, she concluded that she'd have a better chance of defeating the situation if she acquiesced to his demand. The decision infuriated her, but that wasn't helping, either.

She removed her gun from the holster and field stripped it in the dark in less than six seconds. She placed the parts on the seat, as instructed.

He turned the lights on and pushed the button to unlock her door. Wisely, he didn't say anything more. If he thought he'd won this war, he was an idiot. Perhaps he knew enough about her to understand that, too.

She opened the door and stepped outside, and shoved it closed. She'd already memorized the license name and number posted on the partition. Now that she could see it, she memorized the gold and blue New York state license plate.

She pulled the two burner phones from her pocket. Still no signal.

*Great. Now what?*

Standing on the driveway, darkness as far as the eye could see under a cloudy night sky, Kim wondered where in the hell she was. Manhattan was a long way to walk from here. She'd seen no traffic of any kind on the roads for quite a while. Hitchhiking wasn't an option.

A splash of light spilled from the top of the steps behind her when a large, swarthy man opened the front door.

The driver noticed the light. As if he'd handed her off and could now be gone, he rolled the Mercedes along the driveway toward the back of the house out of sight.

The man at the top of the stairs said, "Agent Otto. We've been expecting you. Please come in."

Kim briefly considered refusing, but what purpose would that serve? She trudged up the stairs, walked inside, and he closed the door behind her.

The front door opened into a central hallway. On the right and left, double doors led to dining and living rooms. Beyond the dining room, on the left side, a carpeted stairway led to the second floor. Framed photographs accompanied the treads along the left wall, and an elaborate dark oak handrail atop dark spindles marched up the right.

"This way." He turned his back and moved deeper into the house.

She shrugged and walked behind him. He stopped to open a doorway on the right and stood aside.

She entered a small library. Fully loaded bookshelves lined one wall. Floor to ceiling windows filled another. A working fireplace warmed the room and cast a pleasant glow over the traditional furnishings.

Four comfortable reading chairs were grouped to face the fire. A slender blonde Kim recognized occupied one of the chairs.

"Jodie Jacob, right?" She asked as she entered the room.

The woman looked up from her book as if she'd just noticed her visitor. Her eyebrows dipped into a concerned frown. "Do I know you?"

Kim heard the door close, and the lock click into place.

"I'm FBI Agent Kim Otto." She showed her badge to comfort the woman.

"I'd almost concluded no one even noticed I was missing." Jodie's mouth quivered, but she was remarkably composed under the circumstances. Whatever they were. The fire's shadows played over her skin, giving her an unearthly appearance.

Kim pressed her lips into a hard line. She was in no mood for waifish women jerking her around. She'd had more than enough of that for one night.

She moved to stand near the fire where she could see Jodie's face clearly. "Actually, we thought you'd been murdered. Assistant Director Alan Deerfield has custody of a body. He believes it's you."

Jodie barely blinked. The news seemed not to faze her at all. Perhaps her murder wasn't news to her, though. The story had been reported by several news outlets. She could have learned about the murder somehow. But her composure was surreal, even if she already knew.

"We found the victim in your father's house in Garrison."

No gasps or blinks or reactions of any kind, voluntary or involuntary, to this, either. As if she hadn't comprehended the words. Was something wrong with her? Did she lack mental capacity or something?

Kim tried stabbing her with the blunt truth, as a test. "Deerfield thinks Jack Reacher murdered you and left your body in a bathtub filled with green paint."

Jodie's weird composure cracked. Her breath caught. Her already translucent skin blanched to stark white, and her fingers lost their grip on her book, and it dropped heavily onto the rug. She didn't speak at all.

What had evoked her reaction? Reacher's name? The green paint murders?

Kim's curiosity temporarily trumped everything else. She softened her tone. "Tell me what's going on here, Jodie."

Her eyes rounded. She shook her head. "I wish I knew. I left my apartment late on a Tuesday morning, thirteen days ago. It was too cold and blustery to walk. I was in a hurry. I ordered a car from the service I've used a thousand times." She paused. Shrugged. "When I saw he was abducting me, I tried to get out of the car, but I couldn't. The driver brought me here."

"Could you identify the driver if you saw him again?" Kim asked.

"I never saw his face, and I figured the car was stolen." Jodie closed her eyes and cocked her head. "He was a redhead, I think. He wore a cap that covered his hair, but his eyebrows were sandy-colored, and his skin was freckled. He had blue eyes."

"What happened after he dropped you off here?" Kim asked.

"Not much. I tried to escape several times. Once, I made it a couple of miles down the road before they chased me down. After half a dozen failed attempts, I gave up. Since then, nothing really. I've been comfortable. I have a lovely room. I'm free to use the house or the grounds. They feed me regularly. There's a gym." She looked at Kim as if the story was too bizarre for her to believe. "But I'm a prisoner. I've had no contact with anyone outside of this house since I arrived."

"Do you have any idea who's responsible for holding you here or why they won't allow you to leave?" Kim asked.

Jodie shook her head. "At first, I thought I'd been kidnapped for ransom. That's a rampant problem, as you probably know. I've handled such cases for clients over the years. My old firm has insurance policies to pay the ransom, although those policies wouldn't cover me now. I haven't worked there for a while."

"Where have you been working, anyway?"

"The high pressured corporate lawyer life wasn't for me. I've been doing volunteer legal work for Army vets. I'll get another kind of job at some point. I told all of that to Agent Brice, Deerfield's right-hand guy when he came around to my apartment to ask me about the Petrosians last month."

Kim nodded. "I guess no one would assume a volunteer lawyer would have kidnap insurance, then?"

"Maybe not. The situation hasn't progressed normally at all. No request for a proof of life has come through to me. No ransom demands that I've been told about. No one has tried to harm me." She paused and took a breath. "Except that I can't contact anyone and can't leave here, once I stopped trying to escape this has been very civilized."

"Why can't you contact anyone?"

"My cell phone doesn't get a signal. There are no landline telephones. And we don't have internet access."

Kim nodded. "Why didn't your escape attempts work?"

"Mostly because it's so damn cold and there's nowhere to go. Getting out of the house is easy. But then what?" Jodie shook her head, and a wry grin lifted one side of her mouth. "After sunrise, look outside. You'll see why I gave up. Meanwhile, tell me, why you're here."

"I have no idea. I was abducted in the same way you were. Probably by the same person," Kim replied. "I'm not even sure where we are. Do you know?"

"Upstate New York. The driver took a long time to get here, and it seemed like he was trying to confuse me. But this is Orange County, I think. Maybe less than fifty miles west of Garrison, if I was asked to guess." Jodie said. "I'm not much of a horsewoman myself, but there are a lot of equestrian areas when you get away from the city. So I could be wrong."

The room was probably being monitored. Someone could be both watching and listening. More than one someone, for that matter. But Kim had no idea whether she'd have another chance to ask, so she took the gamble and added a white lie. "Reacher called me tonight. He's worried about you."

"Really? I haven't seen Reacher in years." Kim interpreted Jodie's expression as a truthful mix of curiosity, amusement, and concern. "Haven't talked to him or emailed him or anything else, either. If it's information about Reacher that you want, Agent Otto, you've come to the wrong place."

"You knew Reacher very well at one time, though, didn't you? Deerfield says you were the love of his life. The one that got away," Kim smiled. She couldn't help it. The mere idea of Reacher being that smitten by any woman was amusing.

"My father was very fond of Reacher, and I was a daddy's girl. So of course, I fell in love with Reacher when I was fifteen years old. He didn't know I was alive back then. We reconnected very intensely for a short period after my father died. We were both grieving. I suspect that had something to do with how we felt." Jodie cocked her head. "I'll probably always love Reacher. But don't imagine that he was heartbroken when I moved to Europe."

"So Deerfield is wrong about that?"

"Completely wrong," Jodie nodded emphatically. "Reacher has extreme wanderlust. Always will. The desire within him to travel and explore and be a free man is massive. Reacher will never settle down. It's simply not an option."

"Weren't you sad about that? When you broke up?"

"Sure. He was, too. But it was the only decision we could make, really." Jodie shook her head and wrapped her arms around herself. "I was excited about my promotion, the move to Europe. Every moment of my life was spoken for already. I didn't have time to mope about Reacher or anything else."

"He gave you the Garrison house, though. The one your father bequeathed him."

Jodie smiled again. "Dad thought Reacher might need a home, or he could use the money it would bring. But he wasn't interested in either. He's the least encumbered person I've ever met. Real estate is for people who want to put down roots. That was the last thing Reacher wanted."

Kim nodded. "So you sold the house. When was the last time you were out there?"

Jodie cocked her head and thought about it for a few seconds. Which Kim figured she wouldn't have had to do if she'd been there a few days ago.

"I don't believe I've been back to that house since Reacher moved out." Jodie grinned with genuine mirth this time. "The truth is that he never moved in. He didn't have anything to move. And he wasn't interested in acquiring anything that had to be moved, either. He just left one day. And then there was no reason for me to go back there."

"You didn't drive your car to the Garrison house fourteen days ago?"

"Agent Otto, I told you. No, I didn't go out to the Garrison house. As far as I know, my car's in the garage at my apartment, where I left it before I was abducted." She folded her hands and sat stiffly in the chair. Her body language and her questions became more formal. "What's this all about?"

"Once again, I wish I knew."

"I'm pretty good at what I do. Tell me what's going on. I know all the players and the history of this thing better than you do. Maybe we can figure it out together."

Kim considered the woman many believed had been found dead in a bathtub of olive green paint on Friday. By all accounts,

Jodie Jacob was a brilliant lawyer. Not all lawyers were good at problem-solving, but very few of the ones Kim knew totally sucked at the skill.

"Maybe you're right. Let's see if we can help each other. Are you representing the Petrosian gang?"

"No," Jodie mouthed without sound like she'd swallowed a bale of cotton. She raised her water glass with a shaky hand and tried again. "How are the Petrosians involved in all of this?"

"Farid Petrosian owns the Garrison house now. That's where Deerfield found the woman's body in the tub filled with olive green paint. The woman Deerfield believes is you."

The hand she raised to push her blonde hair behind her ears shook. She seemed incapable of speech.

Kim glanced around before she asked, "Is there any chance that Samir or Tariq Petrosian owns this house?"

Jodie's face blanched whiter than the new snow falling outside.

"What we need to do now is get away from here, Jodie. We need to do it before daylight. Are you up for that?"

Jodie didn't move a muscle. She looked like a beautiful, frail statue, frozen in her chair.

# CHAPTER THIRTY-SIX

*Sunday, January 30*
*10:35 p.m.*
*Upstate New York*

AFTER OTTO HAD TRUDGED up the stairs into the house, Terry "Reed" Poulton pulled off his cap and ruffled the red hair responsible for his nickname. None of those names were accurate, but he'd used them all his life.

His first name was Terrence, not Terry, and the last name, Poulton, was complete fiction. Family lore claimed that an ancestor broke out of prison in England and acquired the surname when he misunderstood the U.S. immigration agent's request for his birthplace. Once the surname was erroneously recorded, it couldn't be changed, he was told. A long line of Poulton progeny followed, amused by their fictional small village heritage where the Saxons had declared "reed" the appropriate nickname for a redheaded boy.

Reed drove the Mercedes around the house to the garage, jockeyed the vehicles around, and backed the Mercedes into place.

He reached into the back seat, grabbed the magazine and two essential parts of Otto's gun, and dropped them into his pocket.

Without another glance toward the Mercedes or the house, he started his FBI vehicle and pulled it onto the driveway to warm up while he punched the code into the keypad to lower the big garage door.

Sure, it would have been easier to kill both women. He could have dumped the bodies somewhere, and they'd have kept until spring, at least. He had no love for lawyers in general or these two in particular, but neither Otto nor Jacob had crossed the line between righteous and scumbag. Not yet. Not that he knew about, anyway. And Terry "Reed" Poulton was not a guy who killed for his own convenience. Those guys were the Petrosians and others like them.

Ten minutes after he'd dropped Otto at the farmhouse, he was on his way back to Garrison. He was due at the surveillance house to relieve Brice at 0100 hours. He checked the clock on the dash. Plenty of time for a bite of dinner first. He'd find an eatery closer to the interstate.

Reed settled into the quiet drive. His thoughts returned to the bathtub victim, the one who started him down this path. He shook his head. Almost two weeks and no one had been asking official questions about her yet.

Valerie Vance, formerly known as Valerie Webb, had been due to report to work after a week's vacation seven days ago. That idiot CEO or another colleague should have reported her missing by now. Somebody would put two and two together eventually.

Webb and her pro bono lawyer actually looked a bit alike. He remembered thinking at the original trial that Webb and Jodie Jacob could have been cousins. Blonde, thin, single. Both married to their work, apparently. So far as he knew, that's where the similarities ended. Jacob was a law-abiding citizen. Webb? Not so much.

He'd long wondered how an angelic looking creature like Webb could be so evil. It no longer mattered. Webb had escaped justice for at least ten murders originally and seven more over the past six months. Justice might have caught up with her someday, but Reed was almost out of time. Which meant Webb was out of time, too.

Lady Luck had helped him find Webb again by pure serendipity. Which was only fitting since a tragedy of errors had allowed her to kill again.

Which was a crime in itself, as far as Reed was concerned. A different kind of guy would have made her lawyer pay. But Jacob wasn't the only one to blame, and Reed was not that kind of guy, either.

He fumed every time he thought about the prosecutors who said Reed's team hadn't collected enough solid evidence to support multiple convictions. One count of criminal negligence was all they could prove, they said. But they promised one count would be enough to keep her in prison. They were wrong.

Reed had been swamped with work and his divorce at the time. After the trial, Reed lost track of Webb. Lost track of her lawyer, too.

When overcrowded prison conditions and Webb's "good behavior" resulted in her unbelievably early release, Reed had not heard about it. Webb served fewer than five years. She changed her surname to Vance and moved to a new community, but she was the same sick killer she'd always been and always would be.

The data was clear. Once a serial killer, always a serial killer.

Rehabilitation was not possible. The only way to stop a serial killer was to end her life. Take her off the planet where she could do no more harm.

Oak Valley was chronically short-staffed, and management felt lucky to have a well-qualified nurse like her. The CEO said anyone could make a mistake and Vance had paid for hers with five years in prison. She would find work somewhere, he said, so why not Oak Valley?

Reed figured the CEO didn't know about the ten babies Vance had killed. Reed had delivered the horrific news to the parents and stared at the tiny caskets at their funerals. All these years later, the memories were chilling.

Vance had always been a master at playing the long game, even when the dead babies were hard to explain. But at the assisted living facility, where murders can remain undiscovered, Vance had found an environment where she could operate for years and years without suspicion.

She'd still be killing if he hadn't stumbled upon her again. When a friend's uncle died unexpectedly, she'd asked Reed to help her make decisions about the funeral plans. They'd met the uncle's nurse. His friend had hugged her, teary-eyed. "My uncle said you were such an angel to him."

Out of context, years later, Reed hadn't recognized the bitch at first. But something about her seemed off. Later, he did a fast background check on the new Nurse Vance, which came back too short and too clean. He dug deeper and discovered her conviction under her real name.

Vance was no angel. She was an angel of death, that's what she was. Reed identified seven Oak Valley patients who had died of respiratory failure during her brief six-month employment, a sharp spike in mortality.

Reed kept digging, but she was cunning and sly, and she'd learned to be even more careful over time. Vance was smarter about using the powerful new drugs that had been developed while she was in prison, too.

Despite his best efforts, Reed could find no hard evidence sufficient to arrest her again. The evidence he'd gathered wouldn't support a warrant to exhume the bodies and prove his suspicions. Reed's anger had boiled over.

He put the empty hours watching the Garrison house to good use. He'd monitored her internet use and tracked her movements and listened to her conversations. His opportunity came when she scheduled a winter vacation in Jamaica.

On the day she was scheduled to leave, Reed watched from across the street while Vance waited for a taxi that would never come because he had canceled it. She shifted her weight from one foot to the other, glanced up and down the street, checked her watch, more anxious about missing her flight with every passing second.

When he judged that she felt desperately late, he pulled his car up to the curb. "Aren't you going to miss your flight? Can I offer you a ride?"

"Oh, yes! Thank you!" She'd seemed pathetically grateful.

"Hop in. I'll stow your bags in the back." He'd retrieved the syringe and the chloroformed mask from the back before he placed her bags inside.

She was buckled into the passenger seat when he'd slipped in behind her and put the mask over her mouth and nose. He'd forced her head back against the headrest until she stopped struggling. The chloroform was a kindness she hadn't deserved but made his work easier.

Off the main road, he'd found a winding two-lane and then a

fire trail. Parked behind a stand of trees, well out of sight of any potential witnesses, he'd unlocked the front passenger door with the remote.

He removed her boot and sock from her right foot and injected the massive neuromuscular blocker overdose between her third and fourth toes.

Because she was already unconscious, she didn't feel herself suffocate. A kindness she'd denied all her victims. She'd deserved the pain and horror of fighting to breathe until the very end, but he simply couldn't torture another human like that. Even her.

He tossed the empty syringe along with her boot and sock into the footwell and pushed her leg inside. Less than five minutes had elapsed since he'd pulled in behind the stand of trees. Storing the body in a cold place had also been ridiculously easy, given the weather in January.

Reed felt no guilt in killing Vance. The guilt he felt was for the innocent lives not saved because he hadn't killed her sooner.

A raccoon ran across the road, snapping him out of his reverie. His headlights flashed and eerily reflected the animal's eyes in the dark night. Reed shivered as if he'd awakened from a trance. He saw familiar landmarks along the roadway, but he took almost a full minute to comprehend where he was and how he'd arrived there. He wasn't far from his destination.

The surveillance base was only a couple of houses north and across the road from the target. Assistant Director Deerfield had set up the place. He'd called in a favor from the owners, who spent winters in Grand Cayman.

Reed glanced at the clock a couple of miles before he reached Garrison. He was too early. If he showed up now, Brice might ask questions Reed didn't feel like answering. The experience with the raccoon had spooked him. Maybe the cancer had moved to his brain or something.

He stopped at a chain restaurant and went inside. He washed up and ordered but didn't eat because of nausea, which often flared at the most inconvenient times. He sipped black coffee and waited for the time to pass.

He'd be on duty alone this shift. Which was against policy, but everything about watching the Garrison house was against policy. The Special Operations Division and the Special Surveillance Group were not running the surveillance, partly because that level of expertise wasn't necessary here, Deerfield said. There were other reasons, too.

Budget tight, necessity slim to none, resources had been reallocated after a couple of fruitless weeks. The word came down the food chain from the top. Only two shifts, twelve hours each, one man. Anything happened, call for backup. They'd worked like that for a while, too. Which suited Reed fine.

He had volunteered for the night detail. His wife had left him long ago, and he'd be sleeping all night anyway. Figured he might as well get paid for it. When Brice found Webb's body, Deerfield modified the schedule again. Not that it mattered anymore.

This was the last shift. Everything would change today, one way or the other.

# CHAPTER THIRTY-SEVEN

*Sunday, January 30*
*11:15 p.m.*
*New York, New York*

GASPAR WAS SOUND ASLEEP when the house phone rang.
He reached for the receiver. "Yes."

"This is room service. Do you still want your order, sir? He's
outside your door now."

"Yes, thank you. Sorry." He struggled off the bed and
staggered to the door. When the waiter pushed the table inside he
held out two padded manila envelopes as well. Gaspar thanked
him and added a generous tip to the bill, which smoothed out the
problems.

He poured coffee with cream and sugar and swigged two big
mouthfuls before he opened one of the envelopes, turned on the
new cell phone and pushed the redial button.

The Boss picked up immediately. "I thought maybe you took
a vacation."

"No such luck," Gaspar replied, swigging more coffee to wake up. "Something wrong with the phones we had?"

"Unclear. Easier to start over. You've heard nothing from Otto?"

"Correct."

"Finlay?"

That was a test question. If Finlay had called, the Boss would already know about it. "I was sleeping until two minutes ago. Want me to check?"

"Later. First, I have new intel to give you."

Gaspar forced himself to concentrate through his sleep fog. "Ready."

"Deerfield has had Farid Petrosian in protective custody for two weeks. Farid refused to talk until his family was set up in WITSEC and Farid's immunity order was entered by the court. That happened on Friday morning."

"Ah." The situation was coming into clearer focus. Farid wouldn't have told Deerfield everything until his conditions were met. So Deerfield learned new information on Friday morning that dropped an opportunity in his lap and started things in motion. "Farid told Deerfield about the woman in the bathtub."

"He also told Deerfield that a man brought her inside and placed her there. He said she was already dead. What he didn't know was the identity of either the victim or the man."

"How did Farid get this information?" he asked.

"He has eyes inside and outside the house." Cooper paused. "Particularly on the master suite. For obvious reasons."

"Ah." He'd been told the electricity was turned off at the house. Battery operated surveillance cameras with motion sensors weren't reliable. Among other issues, the batteries didn't last forever. As they weakened, the motion sensors became erratic. "Does Farid have recordings?"

"Deerfield claims not."

"Before he paid you a visit in Phoenix, you'd have believed him. Now you don't."

"Precisely. Deerfield is—let's call it agile around the facts."

"He worked quickly after Farid told him about the body, I'll say that." Gaspar refilled his coffee, but the first cup had done its job. All senses were on full alert.

The Boss said, "I sent you new files. Info on the victim. Here's a news flash. It's not Jodie Jacob."

"Good news for Jacob. Who put the body in the tub?"

"He says Farid doesn't know. Couldn't even give an accurate description because the guy was covered crown to sole, including a face mask because of the oil paint fumes."

Gaspar said, "You think Deerfield has seen the recording and knows who it is."

"Of course," the Boss replied.

Gaspar said nothing.

"Only three possible members of Deerfield's team could have placed the body. Brice. Poulton. Smithers. I sent those files as well."

"You have a best guess at this point?"

Cooper said, "I don't want to influence you. Look at the materials, we'll talk again."

"What about Otto?"

"Deerfield says he doesn't know where she is. Finlay says the same. We're all working on it." Cooper paused briefly as if he might say something else. And then he simply signed off. "Get up to speed and call me back."

Gaspar set up the laptop, connected to the secure server and

downloaded five files. One for each of the three agents. One for
Jodie Jacob. The last one was labeled Valerie Vance a/k/a
Valerie Webb. He refilled his coffee, snagged a sweet roll, and
began with Webb, the victim in the tub.

Valerie Webb's file consisted of three photos and a short
bullet point list of relevant facts. He looked quickly at the photos
and then put them side by side on the screen with Jodie Jacob's
photos. The two women could have been sisters, but the human
genome often produced lookalikes. Hell, Jacob's father, Leon
Garber, was no saint. He might easily have fathered both kids.
Not that it mattered why the two resembled each other.

Gaspar moved on to the bullet points. He read through them
quickly. Valerie Webb was a suspected serial killer. At least ten
infants under her care had died of respiratory failure when she'd
worked as a nurse in Albany. Resources for criminal
investigations and overcrowded judicial systems being what they
were, Webb was only tried and convicted on one count of
criminally negligent homicide.

Two of the bullet points in this section were highlighted. The
first was Webb's pro bono lawyer's name. Jodie Jacob. The
second was the investigating detective. Terrence Poulton.

Webb served almost five years and was released for good
behavior due to prison overcrowding. She changed her name and
moved to work in an assisted living facility called Oak Valley
not far from Garrison. During six months of employment, seven
unexplained respiratory failure deaths were reported. None were
the subject of a criminal investigation, even after the on-site
pharmacy discovered high doses of mivacurium chloride, a
powerful drug used to temporarily paralyze a patient's ability to
breathe, had gone missing. Webb had left for a one-week
vacation on January 17th and failed to return to work.

The only highlighted bullet point in this section explained that an overdose of mivacurium chloride, a neuromuscular blocker, caused suffocation by the inability to breathe and the victim remained conscious until death.

Gaspar shuddered. One of his daughters had asthma, and every attack terrified him. Few things in life were worse than being unable to breathe. Only a depraved killer would torture victims like that. He couldn't work up an ounce of sympathy for her. Whoever killed Valerie Webb did the world a favor.

Jodie Jacob's file was short and sweet. It contained nothing Gaspar didn't already know.

The other three files on FBI Agents Smithers, Brice, and Poulton were equally unremarkable except for one bullet point, which was also highlighted.

Terrence "Reed" Poulton's brother, Anthony "Rusty" Poulton, was one of the lead agents in the failed bathtub murders case. Tony Poulton's file notes reflected his final conclusion back then. The serial killer responsible for the murders, he said, was Jack (none) Reacher. He vowed to find the evidence to bring Reacher to justice, even if the search lasted the rest of his life.

Which, sadly, it did. Tony Poulton had died before completing his vow.

Gaspar wondered whether Poulton's brother had assumed the duty. He'd never laid eyes on Terry Poulton, but he figured in a contest between them, a betting man would put his money on Reacher.

He fortified himself with another cup of sweetened coffee and drank half of it, thinking about Farid Petrosian's motives for a bit before he called the Boss again.

# CHAPTER THIRTY-EIGHT

*Monday, January 31*
*12:25 a.m.*
*Upstate New York*

KIM RUMMAGED IN THE small desk until she found a sheet
of stationery and a pen. She handed them to Jodie. "I need to get
a sense of the hallway from here to the kitchen, the exit, and the
garage. Sketch our escape route for me. Add anything else you
think is relevant."

Jodie took the pen and paper. She used her book as a lap
desk and drew quickly. When she finished, she handed the
sketch to Kim.

"How many people are here in the house with you?" Kim
asked while studying the layout Jodie had drawn.

"Only two. The man who let you in tonight is Herman.
He lives here with his wife, Irene. I don't know the last names.
They won't say, and I've looked everywhere for ID and haven't
found any."

Kim thought that odd, but the entire situation was strange.

Captors without surnames were the least of her worries. "So who are these people?"

"I have the impression they're live-in help. From a few things they've mentioned, they might live in the carriage house in the summer. But in the winter, Irene does cooking and typical household chores and Herman takes care of everything else inside and out."

"Who owns this place?"

Jodie shrugged. "I have no idea. I've only seen Herman and Irene."

"What kind of vehicles do they have and where are they?"

Jodie pointed to her drawing. "There's a big garage behind the house that was converted from a horse barn. I've seen Herman go in there for the small tractor he uses to clear the snow. He has a battered old pickup with a back seat in the cab. Diesel, I think. I've heard the engine and smelled the exhaust a few times."

Kim nodded. "Are those the only vehicles?"

"I don't know for sure. There may be more. There are quite a few buildings on the property. This place is huge, you know."

"How huge?"

"About fifteen acres, give or take. It looks like more because there's hundreds of acres of protected state land around it." Jodie paused. "That's why I said escape on foot was impossible. There are no neighbors that I've seen. Only the one road, which is out front. We're miles from a store or anything like that. Plus, the temperatures have been sub-zero at night and damn cold in the daytime."

Kim nodded, taking it all in. "Is there an alarm system on the house or an electrified fence around the property? Anything like that?"

"I've seen a few of those stickers on the windows saying the house is monitored. I imagine it must be. Or they might have bought the signs at the hardware store. Who knows?" Jodie replied.

"It would help to have weapons. Have you seen any firearms around the place?"

"No handguns, if that's what you mean. I carry a .22 in my purse, but the driver made me leave it in the car before he'd let me out. I don't know what he did with it. Took it with him, probably." Jodie shrugged. "This is a working farm, so it's likely there are shotguns or rifles somewhere. Maybe explosives out in the barns."

Kim walked to the big windows and leaned close to the cold glass. She cupped her hands around her eyes to reduce glare from the interior lights and tried to see outside. It was too dark to identify anything.

"How about dogs? It's too cold for dogs outside, probably none out there. Any dogs in the house?"

Jodie cocked her head as if she needed to think about it, which told Kim all she needed to know. As long as Jodie had been captive here, she'd have seen or heard any inside dogs.

"Where exactly is the garage with the truck?" Kim handed the sketch to her. "Show me on your drawing."

"The driveway you came on from the road runs along the left side of the house and around to the back. The garage is at the end of the driveway." Jodie gestured around the opposite side of the house and marked her sketch as she talked. "If we go out the back door through the kitchen, Herman has probably plowed a trail through the snow. So we'd maybe have to go about a hundred feet or so."

"Is the garage locked? How can we get in?"

"I don't know. I tried to get inside before and couldn't pull or push the doors open." She handed the paper back and shook her head. "I'm not sure they were locked, though. Maybe just super tight. Layers of old paint or swollen wood or something."

"Why do you think they weren't locked?"

"Things are pretty relaxed. Probably because this place is so remote. At least in the winter, it's not likely to be bothered by vandals. And if someone besides Herman does approach, which has only happened once, by the way. Tonight, when you arrived." Jodie paused to let the significance of her statement hang in the air. "There's plenty of time before they get all the way in here from the road to do something."

Kim still had her coat and boots on, but Jodie was dressed in pajamas, robe, and slippers. "Where are your clothes? Can you get dressed quickly? Find a coat and boots without waking Herman and Irene?"

Jodie shook her head. "My room is upstairs, and every one of those old stair treads squeak. I can grab Irene's stuff by the back door. Safer to do it that way."

"Okay. No stairs. Let's assume they do have guns." Kim paused and looked around the room, remembering the hallway and the doors leading off from it near the front. "Where would they store guns on this floor?"

"I've tried scouting out every room in this house. I haven't seen a gun cabinet or gun safe or any cleaning supplies or ammo. I'm an Army brat. My dad was a general. Trust me when I say that I know what to look for." Jodie shook her head. "We can search again, but it might take a while. There's a lot of rooms. The best we're going to do quickly are knives in the kitchen or garden implements in the garage."

"Okay." Guns were always Kim's first choice. But Jodie's

searches came up empty, which meant either guns didn't exist or would take too long to locate.

"When do you want to do this?" Jodie asked.

"We should go now. It's full dark. Herman and Irene are probably sleeping. After daylight, we'd need to subdue them both first. Doable, but an unnecessary complication." She looked at the sketch one more time. She crumpled it and tossed it into the fire. "We don't know what plans they may have for us tomorrow. It's better to go now, while we can."

Jodie nodded tentatively.

The sketch burned to ashes and swirled into the smoldering logs.

"Don't worry. You've done this before, and you're still alive, right?" Kim joked, but Jodie didn't crack a smile. "Look, if we do get stopped, Herman and Irene aren't going to kill us. They're babysitters, not assassins. Okay?"

"Okay," Jodie whispered. But she didn't sound like she meant it.

"What about keys for the truck? Where are they?"

"Herman came in through the back door carrying groceries from the market a couple of days ago. I was having breakfast. Irene met him at the door and took the bags. He shrugged off his coat and hung it on a peg." Jodie closed her eyes a moment. "I think he left the keys to the truck on a small shelf there when he went back out to shovel the walks. We can get them on the way out."

Kim nodded. She looked at her watch and noted the time. She closed her eyes, mentally rehearsing the process of getting out of the house, making their way to the garage, getting inside, starting the truck, and driving away. She opened her eyes and looked at her watch again. Start to finish, less than five minutes if they were lucky.

"When we reach the road, which way do we turn? Left or right?"

Jodie said, "You turned right into the driveway from the road, didn't you? That's how we came in. If I'm correct about where we are, and I think I am, we turn right out of the driveway to go the opposite direction. And then we hope I see a recognizable landmark soon."

"Sounds about as good as we're going to be able to do with what we have at hand," Kim replied.

"My phone is upstairs. But you have one, right? Maybe we can pick up a cell signal within the first five or ten miles."

"Speaking of phones, are you sure there's no way to communicate from here?" Kim watched Jodie's expression, which didn't vary much. "What would they do in case of a fire, for example? This old house is a tinder box. It would go up fast. There must be some way to call in emergency services."

"I don't know what they would do." Jodie shook her head slowly. "Maybe they have a landline in their bedroom. Or maybe they have a satellite phone or something like that? Otherwise, I've been looking for a way to call for help. None of the rooms I've checked have phone jacks. I've never seen either of them talking to friends or anything."

The fireplace logs had all but died, and Kim noticed the draft. Old houses were always cold. This one didn't seem to have central heat, either.

Jodie was still thinking, but she shook her head. "There is a mailbox at the end of the driveway. Herman drives out there every day to pick up the mail and the newspaper, which also comes by mail a few days after it's published. We have broadcast television. They capture the signal with an antenna. As far as I know, that's all there is."

# CHAPTER THIRTY-NINE

*Monday, January 31*
*12:35 a.m.*
*New York, New York*

GASPAR FELT SIMULTANEOUSLY EXHAUSTED and wired. He reviewed the file materials on Farid Petrosian and his brothers again quickly. All three were despicable human beings, although, in his own mind, Farid was a better source than Samir or Tariq. Gaspar was a pragmatist and understood the politics of necessity. He had often dealt with scumbags because he had little choice. With the Petrosian brothers, none of the options were good. The best that could be said was that Samir and Tariq were twice as bad as Farid because there were two of them.

In the end, Gaspar followed orders, as he often did when all choices were bad. He dialed the Boss, who must've been waiting by the phone.

Cooper said, "Deerfield's flight plan is taking him into Stewart and then by helo to West Point where he'll get a limo to the house in Garrison."

"How did he get permission to land at West Point?"

"Same way I did, probably."

Gaspar raised his eyebrows, genuinely surprised. "You're going to intercept Deerfield at West Point?"

"No, but you are. There is a helipad on the roof of your hotel. The pilot will pick you up at 0200 hours. You'll intercept Deerfield at West Point and persuade him not to continue with this folly."

"What do you suggest I tell him that will make a difference?"

Cooper was silent for a few moments. "Tell him if he persists along this course, he'll be so screwed before the day is over that he'll never recover."

Gaspar was doubtful. "You think that'll be persuasive? The guy's trying to take you out. He must have a counter plan for that approach, don't you think?"

"Just tell him what I said. Suggest he return to New York City while he still can."

"What are you not telling me?"

"All the things you don't want to know."

Gaspar waited a couple of beats and then changed the subject. "Farid Petrosian seems like a weasel, doesn't he?"

"What else would he be?"

"I don't trust him."

"Join the crowd."

"Who are the two operatives Deerfield is looking for?"

"Deerfield says two Petrosian debt collectors, a man and a woman, were executed by Samir and Tariq and dumped there. They were loyal to the old man and to his kids, from all accounts. Samir and Tariq said they were skimming. Which they denied." He paused. "We confirmed that Herman and Irene

Amon disappeared around the same time the foundation was poured for the addition to Farid's house."

"You think the bodies are under the house like Farid claims?"

"Would you bury two bodies under your five-million-dollar house?"

"Unlikely I'll ever own a five-million-dollar house." Gaspar frowned.

Farid could be jerking Deerfield around here. WITSEC was in place for Farid and his family. Farid's immunity order was signed, according to the online court files.

He asked, "Deerfield has a lot riding on this. He's held up his end of the deal. Suppose Farid doesn't deliver? What will Deerfield do?"

"All I can tell you is Deerfield doesn't expect that to happen," Cooper said. "He's got no Plan B."

Gaspar accepted the answer. But most poker players would bet on Deerfield's strategic plans, not Farid Petrosian's. "Where's Otto?"

"Still working on that."

He barely held his temper. "Are you making any progress?"

"Not yet."

"You still have eyes on the Garrison house?"

"Of course. Inside and out. Your helo arrives promptly at 0200. If I find anything more you need to know, I'll send it. Don't be late." He disconnected the call.

Almost as if he'd waited politely for Cooper to hang up, Finlay rang next. Had Otto no longer been at risk, Gaspar would have ignored the call.

"Have you found her?"

"You'll be the first one I call," Finlay replied. "Farid Petrosian is a liar."

"There's a news flash," Gaspar said dryly. "Next you'll be telling me both of his brothers are thieves."

"Roger that." Finlay chuckled. "The point is we've established a visual feed off the satellites around the Garrison house. Still a lot of activity out there. More than there should be."

Gaspar thought about the possible reasons. "NYPD is still processing the crime scene. Anywhere cops go, television cameras follow. Nothing unusual in that."

"We're seeing activity in the back and sides of the house. At least two separate actors. Not cops and not reporters."

"You can read photo ID from space now?" His sarcasm might have been wearing on Finlay's nerves. He hoped so. He was tired of the cryptic hints. It was long past time for straight talk.

"We're seeing two singles. Hunkered down, away from the house. Big guys. Too big for the cops and reporters on scene and no new arrivals on the front side for several hours," Finlay explained.

"Good to know. Weapons?"

"Both armed, but limited battle rattle."

He understood. They were dressed for stealth, not the full gear they'd be wearing if they didn't care about making noise. Which didn't mean they lacked powerful weapons.

"How'd they get there?"

"Good question. The only answer I have at the moment is separately, early, and quietly," Finlay said. "No incoming motorized vehicles from the riverside or from the neighboring houses in the past couple of hours. We're checking the earlier feeds."

"Thanks for the intel," he replied. The separate arrival was odd. The rest made sense, given the conditions on the ground.

The stealthy approach, arriving early, suggested a military option had been deployed. Go in early and wait. Stand by to stand by, as they said when he was in the Army. Cooper could be responsible for it. Which might be why he was being sent to West Point. Hell, Deerfield might be pulling those strings, too.

Given Reacher's recent phone messages to Otto, Gaspar couldn't rule him out, either.

Finlay didn't say anything for a while.

Gaspar glanced at the clock. His helo would be here soon, and he still had prep to do. "Was there something else?"

"A guy like Deerfield has a lot of enemies," Finlay said.

"Roger that," he mocked Finlay's earlier response. "Well deserved from what I hear."

"Watch your back out there," Finlay said, which rubbed him the wrong way, like an insult to his tactical skills. Did Finlay think he didn't know how treacherous the situation was?

"Yeah. I'll do that," he growled. "You find Otto."

# CHAPTER FORTY

*Monday, January 31*
*12:55 a.m.*
*Garrison, New York*

POULTON WAS FIVE MINUTES out. He'd arrive on time to relieve Brice at 0100 hours as scheduled. He needed sleep. Smithers was due to take over at nine in the morning. They were covering eight-hour shifts now while NYPD was on the scene until the Petrosian matter wrapped up. Arrests should happen before the day ended.

After the body in the bathtub was discovered in the Garrison house and the scene was handed over to NYPD, the surveillance schedule continued with twelve-hour shifts on Friday, as before. Smithers took the day shift, and Reed was there at night. The schedule that provided a perfect alibi and simultaneously enabled him to do what he needed to do for the killers on his bucket list.

Brice was added to the surveillance schedule when Deerfield moved them to eight-hour shifts on Saturday after Webb's body turned up. Deerfield was the man in charge, so he ordered the duty roster along with everything else. When he reshuffled the Saturday and Sunday shifts, no one questioned him. Poulton figured Deerfield either wanted a snitch hanging around all the time, or he wanted Brice out of the way.

Poulton had always been uneasy around Brice because he was the boss's son-in-law. Since Brice's divorce, he'd been like a barnacle on everybody's ass. But when Deerfield found out about the body in the bathtub, Poulton was willing to bet that Brice told him something that raised his suspicion. Deerfield was a smart guy. But he wasn't that smart. He wasn't clairvoyant, either.

Poulton had retraced his actions several times, and how Deerfield had learned about the body remained unknown. But Brice must have been the one. Before Friday, no one had been in that house since Poulton put the body there, he could say that for sure.

Whatever the source of his information, after he found out, Deerfield made two big changes to the operation.

First, he'd sent Brice into the house to discover the body on Friday. Only if he'd already known what Brice would find did that move make any sense. Up until Friday, the whole operation was designed to keep the house uncontaminated until Deerfield got the search warrant lined up. Something significant had caused him to change his plan. Unless he believed one of the Petrosians had killed the woman, Deerfield's motive for disturbing the house early must have been a powerful incentive.

Poulton figured everything else that happened flowed from sending Brice inside Friday morning. Several birds, one stone. NYPD flooded the place with personnel, which definitely kept the twisted Petrosian brothers away from the bodies buried in the foundation. And the salacious details of a revitalized serial killer roaming Upstate New York was designed to attract media attention. Poulton counted on the media to lure Reacher out of hiding, but he wasn't sure about Deerfield's motivations where Reacher was concerned.

The second thing Deerfield did on Friday was confounding, though. Poulton didn't understand it, although he'd tried.

For some unknown reason, he'd officially pulled Agent Otto into the mix. He'd reached out to her through channels. There'd be paperwork and expenses involved, and formal reports would be filed. The budget had been cut to the bone, they were keeping the Petrosian case on the down low until the indictments could be served, and then he inexplicably turned the internal spotlight on the whole operation.

Deerfield's excuse was that he wanted fresh eyes on the crime scene. But hell, everybody on the team except Deerfield was already fresh eyes on the bathtub murders serial killer. Poulton only knew the prior case existed because his younger brother worked it originally. After the case went south, Tony was never the same. He volunteered for high-risk assignments and behaved recklessly way too often. As far as Poulton was concerned, Reacher and the unsolved bathtub murders actually killed Tony's will to live.

Poulton hadn't figured out why Deerfield wanted Otto here. Something to do with Reacher, he felt sure. Maybe Deerfield knew about his bucket list and wanted to help him with Reacher. Which was probably wishful thinking.

But it all worked out, anyway, because Poulton was lucky.

The victim in the bathtub was taking longer to identify than normal. Partly because Deerfield planned it that way. He was in no hurry to have that particular mystery solved. Which was why he'd made Brice wait to report the homicide until late on Friday.

Government offices worked light crews on weekends, and many private healthcare offices were closed. Unless requests were expedited, everything waited until the work week started up again.

Which was okay. Properly refrigerated, most dead bodies could wait a while.

Poulton had taken care of the rest. He'd made sure the factors that cops normally relied upon for quick victim ID were missing. No purse or wallet with the body. No jewelry, nothing engraved, no smartphone. The body itself was the only thing the coroner had to work with, and this one was damaged by the oil paint.

It was helpful that Detective Grassley had tunnel vision. She was doing her best to name the victim Jodie Jacob, but she slammed into one roadblock after another. The body's fingerprints were not usable. Jacob's DNA was not in any of the databases. Valerie Vance, a/k/a Valerie Webb, had DNA in the system, but a broader search than Grassley had done so far would be required to find it.

More problematic were dental records, and for the same reason. Grassley laser-focused on Jodie. Jodie grew up on Army bases around the world, and she spent several years working in Europe. Which meant her dental work was unusual and should have made it easier to identify. But finding those records required contacting each of the bases and tracking the records down. A local dentist might have solved this issue, but Jacob was young, and her teeth were good, and she'd lived out of the country for a while. She might not have a local dentist at all. If she had one, Grassley hadn't located him yet.

Grassley ran into similar roadblocks with medical records. She'd requested records from Jacob's last known health insurance company, contracted by the Spencer and Gutman firm.

Grassley had made no progress on that front yet, either.

Meanwhile, with all of that going on, Deerfield inexplicably left town. He told no one where he went or why. He was on his way back now.

By mid-morning, Brice would have the warrants for examining the bedroom foundation with high tech equipment. If the initial tests confirmed the two victims and the guns used to kill them were buried under there, as Farid told Brice, Deerfield would have the final evidence he wanted. Farid's testimony and the records he'd stolen before he turned against his family to save his own neck, would ensure that both Samir and Tariq Petrosian would be in custody by late afternoon.

Poulton was more than ready to finish up. He was exhausted. What with his bucket list and dealing with Vance, on top of his job, he'd been working non-stop since the woman in the red sedan showed up.

The morning after he put Vance inside the Garrison house, Deerfield had texted, "Pick up Jacob and park her at this address until further notice."

Earlier today, Deerfield's orders seemed a bit unhinged. He'd texted, "Pick up Otto. Otto and Jacob no longer needed. Eliminate both. Leave bodies outside."

Deerfield probably couldn't be tied to that farmhouse and would disavow all knowledge, of course, which dovetailed nicely with Poulton's own plans.

Reacher should show up at the Garrison house after daylight. He'd want to see the crime scene for himself because he thought he was a smart guy and a better investigator than everyone else. Maybe he was. Poulton didn't care. His work was almost done. He needed only to kill Reacher for Tony, and then he'd be ready to die.

Poulton pulled in, parked alongside Brice, and went inside the safe house. He checked the video feeds first. He saw fewer NYPD personnel hard at work across the road at the target house, which was to be expected. They'd been there since Friday night. Even working short-staffed, they should be finished soon.

The gaggle of reporters had dwindled, too, but those who remained did their best to capture all activity just in case the NYPD found something tonight. Television was a visual medium and live feed produced better ratings than recorded video. Viewers had wised up. They knew video could be edited. Poulton grinned.

Brice walked in from the kitchen. "I don't know how you can stand this duty, man. Boring as hell to hang out in this house for eight hours, let alone twelve."

"Well, at least you had exciting TV to watch." Poulton tilted his head toward the video display. "For days and days, what we saw was nothing at all going on over there."

"All but two TV crews gave up about an hour ago. They'll leave when Grassley does." Brice shook his head. "Nothing much happening now, frankly. Crime techs are almost done. Everybody should be cleared out before 0200."

"Grassley say how the murder investigation's going?"

"Not much progress. Jacob's red sedan was parked in her apartment's garage. Grassley had it towed to the lab for processing. The coroner hasn't completed the autopsy and still has no ID or cause of death. The consensus is that the victim suffocated, but no clue how." Brice paused to recall more news to report and shrugged when he came up empty.

Poulton nodded. "I imagine removing that paint from the body can be time-consuming. They still may find something."

"Possibly. This case is going to kill me yet. I'm gonna stop over there and talk to Grassley now before they bug out." Brice swiped a hand over his tired face. "After that, I have to go babysit Farid, so he doesn't freak out even worse than he already has."

Poulton cocked his head. "You're getting pretty tight with Farid. He telling you any secrets the rest of us don't know?"

"Hard to know what to believe when we hear it from these thugs." Brice shrugged, which wasn't an outright answer. "I'm due at the courthouse at seven, and I should have the warrant in hand before eight. See you later."

Brice left through the side door and backed his big SUV down the driveway. Poulton watched him go on the video feed, wondering what Farid Petrosian had said to Brice. Whatever it was had put an extra spring in Brice's step the past couple of days. Which could mean that Deerfield didn't know about it, either.

Yet, Deerfield's order to kill Otto and Jacob had come out of the blue. Somehow, the situation had definitely changed. Poulton frowned, trying to puzzle the intel from the facts he already knew. Could have something to do with the blonde in the red sedan who came to the house that day. Or maybe something about the bodies buried in the foundation. Hell, it could be almost anything.

Brice pulled into the driveway at the Garrison house and went inside.

All of a sudden Poulton was overwhelmed by exhaustion. His usual symptoms, itching, nausea, and vomiting came without warning. Some days, the abdominal pain and back pain were so debilitating that he could barely move. He'd lost thirty pounds he couldn't afford to lose. He'd learned why when he received his death sentence a few weeks ago: pancreatic cancer. Doc told him plainly that his time was short and said to make the most of it. Good advice.

What he needed right now was sleep while NYPD remained on scene. He could count on Grassley to sound the alarm if anything unexpected happened in the next hour. He stretched out on the sofa and dropped quickly into oblivion.

# CHAPTER FORTY-ONE

*Monday, January 31*
*2:15 a.m.*
*Upstate New York*

KIM LOOKED AT THE clock on the mantel. Already past two in the morning. She came from a long line of farmers like Herman and Irene. Even her parents maintained a large vegetable garden. To a man, every single one of her relatives was an early riser, even in the winter. Her window of opportunity was closing quickly.

"This situation isn't getting any better," Kim said. "We've got to go. Right now. You lead the way, and when we get to the garage, I'll drive us out of here. Are you up for it?"

"What choice do we have?" Jodie seemed stronger now than she had been since Kim arrived. "I've been sitting here for days expecting someone to find me. We could grow old waiting. Obviously, we're on our own. So let's do this."

Kim nodded. "I heard Herman lock the door when he left us in here. Do you know where the key is?"

Jodie's eyes widened. She walked to the door and grabbed the crystal knob. It didn't turn, and the door didn't budge. "He's never locked me in before. He must be worried about you."

"Then he's smarter than he looks." Kim examined the doorknob. It was a reproduction, definitely not as old as the house. But the door lock was intended for privacy, not security.

She rummaged through the desk drawers again, this time she found a brass letter opener. She used it to unscrew the doorknob and remove it from the door. She ushered Jodie into the hallway. She replaced the doorknob. Then she relocked the door in case Herman came down to check. Might give them an extra few seconds if they needed it.

She gave Jodie a little push to get her moving. Kim belted her coat, slipped the letter opener into her pocket, and followed Jodie down the hallway toward the kitchen. They moved quickly and quietly along the path Jodie had sketched, with only ambient light from the kitchen appliances to guide them.

Inside the kitchen, Kim closed the door and waited, listening for any warning noises.

Jodie hurried across the kitchen floor to the opposite side of the room where an exterior door exited to the back. She stopped at the pegs on the wall and grabbed a faded red barn coat. She slipped her arms into the sleeves and her feet into snow boots simultaneously.

Irene must be a big woman, Kim realized. The coat and the boots were several sizes too large, but Jodie was able to walk, and she wouldn't freeze instantly when they went outside. As long as she didn't trip, she'd be fine.

On the next peg was a flashlight. Jodie lifted the webbing loop off the peg and slipped the flashlight into the barn coat's oversized right pocket. She searched the counter frantically looking for the truck keys. From the panicked look on her face when she glanced up, Kim assumed the keys were not there.

Kim hurried across the room, leaned close to Jodie and whispered, "Don't worry. I'll get the truck started."

"How? Hot-wire it?"

Kim shrugged. She'd have to look at the truck first. "I'll figure it out."

So far, so good. She pushed Jodie aside to examine the door. The last thing they needed was a blaring alarm. She saw no cameras or keypad nearby. She checked the door for wires, motion sensors or other indications that the door was armed and found none.

New wireless systems on the market could also be operated by remote or cell phones, but there were no cell signals here. Kim crossed her fingers and hoped that there was no alarm system at all. Or at least, no system that somehow employed cutting-edge technology lacking in the rest of the house.

Kim nodded. Jodie opened the door and slipped outside. No alarm sounded. Nothing she could do about any silent alarm, so Kim followed Jodie and pulled the door closed behind her.

They hurried single file along the shoveled path toward the garage. Kim glanced back over her shoulder. No lights had turned on in the upstairs windows where the bedrooms were located. With luck, Herman and Irene were still sleeping.

Jodie reached the garage first. She grabbed the knob on the side door, and Kim yanked her arm back. The garage could have a separate alarm system. She checked quickly and again, found nothing.

She nodded. Jodie opened the door and went inside. Kim followed, stepping into a blackness so complete she might have been sealed in a coffin.

She reached into her pocket, pulled out one of the burner phones, and pushed a button to light the dim display. She touched Jodie's arm.

"Are there any windows in here? Can we use the flashlight?"

Jodie pulled the flashlight from her pocket and handed it to Kim. She slipped it into her pocket, beam pointed toward the floor, and turned it on.

The diffused beam was bright enough to locate Herman's big truck parked in the second bay.

Even better, the beam revealed the first bay, where the armored Mercedes she'd arrived in was parked.

She touched Jodie's arm and pointed toward the sedan.

"Let's try that first," she whispered.

Kim hurried over to the sedan and opened the driver's door. The push-button start was a plus. The keyless entry fob was probably somewhere inside the vehicle. She motioned Jodie into the passenger seat.

She ran to the truck and found the garage door opener. She brought the opener back with her and jumped in the driver's seat. The dashboard had an overwhelming number of gauges and lights and switches. She hoped most of them were nonessential. No way could she master them in the next two minutes.

Instead, she adjusted the mirrors and the seat so that she could reach the pedals, hold the steering wheel, and see over the long hood, all at the same time. In theory, at least. That's all she could do.

Jodie was already belted into the passenger seat. Kim handed Jodie the garage door opener. "I want to start the car first and be ready to go when the door opens. If the fob isn't inside the car somewhere, it won't start. Then we'll take the truck. Push the door opener when I tell you to, okay?"

Jodie said wryly, "I'm a New Yorker now. I don't drive often. But I can push buttons."

Kim nodded and pushed to start the ignition. The big sedan's engine sprang to life like a resting tiger, ready to lunge. "Now. Open the door now."

She put the transmission in drive with her left foot on the brake and her right foot resting on the accelerator. The transmission's indicator on the dash showed the parking brake was engaged.

She looked at the lights and buttons until she found the release and the indicator disappeared.

At the same time, Jodie opened the big double steel garage door. The door lifted out and then rolled back slowly, all in one piece. As soon as it was high enough off the ground to slip the sedan underneath without scraping the roof, Kim accelerated.

The big sedan rolled out. When they cleared the garage, Jodie pushed the button to lower the door.

At the end of the driveway, Kim turned right and headed east, the opposite direction from the route her driver had used. After they drove beyond the boundaries of protected state land, she heard a train whistle in the distance. She remembered seeing the train from the back seat on the way to the farmhouse.

The train tracks ran parallel to the road, which had to mean civilization around here somewhere. They came to a crossroads with a four-way stop. To the right was a grade crossing for the train.

"Should we turn here?" she asked Jodie.

"I don't think so. The interstate should be ahead. I think it's more farmland in that direction."

Kim crossed the road and kept going, parallel with the tracks. They traveled eleven more miles before she saw the first sign for Interstate 87.

Three miles farther and she picked up a cell signal on Gaspar's burner phone. She saw six message envelopes on the screen. Four were from Gaspar.

The first three messages were short variations on the same plea. "Call me."

He left the cryptic fourth message at 1:45 a.m. Which probably meant this burner cell phone had been discovered and he didn't trust it anymore. "Orders. Garrison. Call me."

She grinned because he mimicked the message Reacher left earlier on Finlay's burner. As the meaning sunk in, she began to worry. Gaspar was in no condition to go into the field at all. And why would the Boss order him to Garrison, anyway?

She pushed the call back button. Gaspar's burner rang several times and then kicked over to voice mail. She left him a similarly cryptic message because he'd signaled that the phone was compromised, and she had no idea who might hear it. "I'm fine. See you soon."

The fifth message was short and to the point. From the Boss. "Video attached. Watch now."

She didn't recognize the phone number on the sixth message, which was sandwiched between Gaspar's and time-stamped Sunday night at 10:45 p.m. The message lasted six seconds, including a worrisome short pause at the beginning and the end. She listened to it twice.

Kim glanced over to check Jodie's reaction as she said, "There's a message you need to hear. From Reacher."

Jodie's eyes widened, but she said nothing.

Kim played the message aloud so both could hear. "Stay away from the house. They don't own me. Never did. Never will. No matter what."

Kim said, "Do you know what he means?"

Jodie cocked her head. "He might be talking about Deerfield. Sounds like something he said a long time ago about the Petrosians, but I can't remember exactly."

Kim pulled into a gas station. The Mercedes was still half full, and she didn't have a credit card or cash on her anyway.

"Why are we stopping?" Jodie asked.

"My boss sent me a video. He said to watch now. Which usually means something essential." She downloaded the video and queued it to play. The time stamp said 2:55 a.m. today. She glanced at the clock. Half an hour ago.

She pushed the play button.

The video was recorded from a satellite above the Garrison house. The images were night vision and heat sensitive thermography. She ran through it once quickly.

The whole video consisted of a series of spliced sections. Each section showed warm bodies at various locations around the exterior of the house, amid unidentifiable objects too cold to result in strong images on the inferior phone's tiny screen.

"What is it?" Jodie asked.

"The Garrison house. Looks like people on the property," Kim replied and pushed the play button again.

On the second pass, she looked closely and counted three humans in six different scenes spliced together to create one video.

Two big men knelt near the master bedroom patio.

Another big man crouched down and ran across the back, near the river, from a location on the north side of the property line to a location on the south side. When he arrived there, he knelt.

All three seemed to be busy with their hands.

The single man ran from the river to the house and entered through the front door.

The two-man team crouched near the hedge separating the north side property line from the neighboring property. They were so deep in the hedge and so still that she might have missed them with normal night vision. Only the heat signature marked them.

"What are they doing?" Jodie asked.

"Impossible to tell. Nothing good, probably."

The video clip changed to the interior of the house, which was pitch black, too. The heat signature of the big man who had entered through the front door made its way to the kitchen first. Then he headed down the hallway toward the master suite. He didn't stay long in any one area except the master bathroom. He stood for a full minute near the bathtub's location. After passing back through the master suite, he left by the front entrance.

Something about the way he moved seemed familiar to Kim, but she couldn't identify him. It could have been Reacher, maybe. Or Smithers. Or maybe just a big guy with some covert ops training.

The video was spliced one more time. The single man hurried away from the house and the river. The two-man team stayed in place by the hedges.

She watched the video again before she passed it over to Jodie. "Take a look. Tell me if you recognize anyone. Or if you can guess what they're doing."

She didn't know what was going on at that house, but she felt a strong sense of urgency to get there now. She rolled the big Mercedes onto the road toward Garrison, increasing her speed wherever possible.

# CHAPTER FORTY-TWO

*Monday, January 31*
*3:05 a.m.*
*Garrison, New York*

POULTON AWAKENED WHEN HE heard a helicopter overhead. In the weeks he'd been sitting on the house, he'd heard the big birds arrive and depart West Point several times during the quiet hours. He looked at the video feed and scowled.

"What the hell?" The target house was dark. The driveway was unoccupied. The video images looked exactly as they had for days and days before the body was discovered.

He rubbed the sleep from his eyes and stared at the screen, not quite comprehending. Grassley and her NYPD team had departed. Media followed cops like kids followed ice cream trucks.

After three days of that solid buffer preventing Samir and Tariq Petrosian from contaminating the evidence or damaging the burial site, Poulton was the only line of defense again.

He had no idea how long Grassley had been gone. The two Petrosians could have done almost anything while he'd been sleeping. Maybe they already had.

*Shit!*

He pressed the rewind on the video recording to the start of his shift. He saw Brice arrive at the house and go inside.

Ten minutes later, all the crime techs came out and loaded their equipment into the vans. The two-man teams in each of the remaining television vans approached and recorded a short statement from the lead tech, Brennan. She must have wrapped it up for them because both teams returned to their vans and departed when Brennan left.

Only Grassley's unmarked sedan and Brice's unmarked SUV remained in the driveway. Half an hour later, Brice and Grassley came outside with arms around each other and laughing together. Poulton's eyes practically bugged out of his head when they shared a passionate kiss before they got into their cars and drove away.

*Grassley and Brice were having an affair?*

*Holy Shit!*

After Brice and Grassley left, the house and grounds became totally dark again. The time stamp was 0148. One hour and seventeen minutes before the helicopter had awakened him. Poulton had seen many bad things happen in way less than seventy-seven minutes.

Reacher could be inside right now. Or he could have come and gone already. Poulton might have missed his opportunity to get rid of him once and for all.

The weakness in this surveillance had always been its limitations. The budget was so tight that they only had views of the front entrances, Deerfield had said. When Poulton argued for more, he remembered now, it was Brice who said front surveillance was enough because no one was going to swim or take a boat to approach the house from the back in January.

The whole team figured there was the potential for satellite imagery if they had a legitimate reason to request it. Since the whole surveillance operation was off the books, Deerfield couldn't very well ask for satellite coverage though, could he?

Poulton zipped through the rest of the recording. He might as well have been watching a still photo. Nothing changed. Nothing moved. Nothing happened. He relaxed slightly. Maybe he'd dodged a bullet here. Maybe he still had a chance.

Without warning, a hard stab of pain shot through his core. He felt weak as a kitten. He plopped onto the chair and tried to control his breathing and hold back the vomiting. Sometimes, he could, but more often, vomiting won the battle. After a bit, the pain subsided and so did the nausea. A few minutes more and some of his strength returned.

He ran a shaky hand through his hair. He glanced at the clock. Almost 0351 hours. Smithers wasn't due to begin his shift until 0900.

Poulton couldn't leave the house unattended for five more hours. He had to get over there. After everything he'd done so far for the chance to get Reacher, he couldn't give up now.

He found his coat and gloves, his pistol, two rifles, and ammo. He tossed everything into the back of the SUV and drove across the road. He parked in the driveway near the garage.

Shortly after that, he heard the helicopter overhead again.

# CHAPTER FORTY-THREE

*Monday, January 31*
*3:05 a.m.*
*West Point, New York*

GASPAR ASKED THE PILOT to lower the helicopter to hover briefly over the Garrison house and grounds. He'd only seen the house on recorded video from various distances. A personal look was always preferable.

"This is a residential neighborhood, and it's three o'clock in the morning. You'll have the neighbors complaining to HQ. The last thing I need is trouble with my bosses," the pilot said.

"You're right," Gaspar nodded. "Just do a slow pass, then. I'll take a quick look."

The pilot seemed unhappy with the decision, but he'd been told Gaspar was his CO for this trip, so he grudgingly complied. "No spotlights, though. There's regulations about all this. You won't see much in the dark."

"Thanks," he said, knowing the pilot was right as soon as he saw the place in the distance. In the earlier satellite imagery, the house had been lit up by floodlights and bustling activity. Now it seemed deserted, as Otto had described it to him originally.

Even in the dark, though, he could see the footprint of the house sprawled across the lot. With the addition on the back and the other renovations, the architect must have redesigned the roof as well. If Reacher saw his old house from this angle, he probably wouldn't recognize it.

Without enhanced visibility, Gaspar couldn't see any personnel on the ground, covert or otherwise. He had heard nothing more from Finlay or Cooper while he'd been in the air. No contact from Otto, either. At this point, he figured not hearing from her was the good news.

Her abduction was no common kidnapping. First, she disappeared in front of a five-star hotel into an expensive Mercedes.

No ransom demand had been made. No body had been found. Both Otto and the Mercedes were still missing.

She would have contacted him if she could. The longer she remained missing, the less likely she'd been harmed, and the more likely something else was going on.

Which meant that the Mercedes driver was uncommon in several ways. He was bold enough and skilled enough to successfully abduct an FBI agent. He cleverly disappeared from all forms of surveillance. And he had exploited the limits of communication technology to keep Otto silenced.

Not many men had such capabilities. Not even in New York City.

Gaspar knew at least three who were more than capable. Either Finlay or Cooper could have done it. Deerfield, too. He didn't trust any of them, and he didn't believe them when they said they couldn't find her.

The only potentially good news was that none of the three would kill her. Once she resurfaced, though, they might wish they had.

Not long after they flew over the house, the pilot landed on the helipad at West Point. There was no sign of Deerfield's helo.

"I'm going to need a ride back to the city, and maybe back to that house across the river," Gaspar said to the pilot. "Can you stay here and stay ready on my request or do I need orders from higher up?"

"I can do that. There's an official-looking limo departing in our two o'clock position. Any chance your guy arrived early?"

Gaspar shrugged. "Can you check with the tower? I didn't see another bird headed out as we approached. Did you?"

"Negative. Hang on."

The pilot changed frequency and spoke to someone in traffic. Gaspar felt the rotors spooling up again and knew the answer.

"That's your guy. So you want to go across the river and land over there, right?"

"Do we have another option at this point?"

"Not if you want to catch up with him," the pilot said. "The good news is we should get there first. He has to drive around to the bridge, and we can fly over the river."

"Let's do it. Sorry to get you in trouble with the neighbors."

"Can't be helped." He lifted the helicopter off the ground and when they were high enough, turned in a wide circle to head back. A few minutes later they were approaching the Garrison house again.

This time, the scene was totally different. A black SUV had pulled into the driveway and parked near the house. Gaspar assumed it was an unmarked FBI vehicle. The back of the house all the way to the river was still dark and seemingly quiet.

As the helicopter approached, he saw snowmobiles parked in the shadows behind the hedges. Finlay had said there were two actors on site. Gaspar wondered who the hell they were and why they were there.

The pilot asked, "Where do you want me to set down?"

"What are our options?" He saw two more vehicles approaching the house from opposite directions. The first was Deerfield's limo. The second was a black Mercedes sedan, similar to the one that had abducted Otto. The snow-covered road had a single lane in the middle and more snow was piled high on the shoulders. Which was no problem because both the vehicles were headed to the Garrison driveway.

"If you don't have to be right on the lawn, there's a big open apron on that driveway across the road. Can you walk that far?" The pilot asked.

No. He couldn't walk that far. He didn't even pretend that he could. Instead, he scowled when he said, "How about you set down in the road in front of that limo before he reaches the driveway? Is that doable?"

The pilot glanced across, "Will it get me court-martialed? That's not one of the Joint Chiefs in there or something, is it?"

Gaspar laughed. "Honest truth? I'm not sure how much power that guy has. But we're about to find out."

"What about the Mercedes? You want to block him too?"

Gaspar nodded. "I can't think of anything I'd rather do at the moment."

The pilot said nothing more as he positioned the helicopter to land on the road blocking Deerfield's limo.

If Deerfield wanted to snowshoe past the helicopter, he was welcome to do so. Gaspar was out of patience with all of them.

# CHAPTER FORTY-FOUR

*Monday, January 31*
*3:50 a.m.*
*Garrison, New York*

THEY REACHED THE TURNOFF to the road for the Garrison house. This was the south entrance, and Kim had never driven in this way. But Jodie had, so she navigated from the passenger seat.

Jodie said, "This road was always the thing Dad disliked about living out here. Too narrow. A couple of SUVs trying to pass can easily lose their side mirrors if they don't move over onto the grassy shoulder."

"And you know the residents aren't thrilled with people driving on the grass, right?" Kim said.

Jodie nodded. "You've lived in a rural area, I take it?"

"My parents do." Kim had had the Mercedes headlights on high beam for miles now, but along this road, they were a necessity. She was driving in a tunnel of snow piled high on both sides. At this hour of the morning, she hoped they'd make it all the way to the house without running into oncoming traffic.

Jodie said, "Your partner is meeting you out here, you said. Do we know why?"

Kim shook her head. "Not exactly."

Finlay's burner phone rang in her pocket. Kim poked around until she found it. "Otto."

"Welcome back," Finlay said as if she'd been on a nice vacation. "Have you talked to Gaspar?"

"Not yet. We're playing phone tag."

"Cooper?"

"No. Why?"

"Are you alone?"

"Jodie Jacob is with me."

Finlay paused for such a long time, she thought she'd lost him until he said, "The situation has been developing fast since you left here last night."

Which probably meant Jodie Jacob being alive was news to him, and he didn't intend to admit as much. "Give me the highlights."

"Deerfield is on his way to Garrison. He's planning a big press conference this morning when he'll announce the arrests of Samir and Tariq Petrosian as soon as they confirm the two bodies buried under the house."

"That would be impressive," Kim replied. "*Are* there actually two bodies under the house? I suspect not."

"According to Farid who told Brice who told Deerfield. Two collectors. Herman Amon and his wife, Irene," Finlay said.

"Poor Deerfield misses again." She cocked her head, and a grin stole across her face. "This will definitely be embarrassing."

Finlay paused, and then he laughed out loud. She'd surprised him twice in one conversation, which didn't happen often.

He asked, "How'd you figure that out?"

"Pretty easy. Those two collectors are still alive."

"What makes you say that?"

"I met one tonight. Herman Amon. And Jodie has spent quite a bit of time with the other one, his wife, Irene." Kim paused.

"Which could mean there are no bodies buried there. Or two different members of the Petrosian gang." He paused. "Either way, Farid has been feeding Brice false information."

"Has he?"

"Maybe not intentionally," Finlay said. "I'm told Brice is a few cards short of a full deck."

Kim replied, "Turns out, he's not as dumb as he looks."

"How so?"

"Let's just say Brice is not guileless. I'm not completely clear on the details. When I am, you'll be among the first to know."

"Anything I can do for you at the moment?" Finlay asked.

"You already know something is going on at the Garrison house tonight, I assume. Cooper sent me the video. Three actors. All did things at the house."

"Three?" Finlay's voice became clipped and stern.

"Yep," she replied. Curiously, he seemed more surprised by the number of actors than their presence. Had he sent them?

"When did this happen?"

"Less than an hour ago."

"I'll call you back," he said and hung up.

Jodie smiled. "He's a chatty one, isn't he?"

"Sometimes. But not tonight."

# CHAPTER FORTY-FIVE

*Monday, January 31*
*4:02 a.m.*
*Garrison, New York*

AS THE PILOT SET the helicopter down, Gaspar noticed a guy jump into the SUV in the driveway and speed south. Where was he going in such a hurry?

The rotor blades slowed and quieted. A minute or so later, Deerfield's limo came around the curve, and the driver mashed the grabbers. The back end of the limo fishtailed, but it stayed between the snow bunkers and stopped before hitting the helo.

The driver got out first. Houston Brice. He trudged across the snowy pavement, sliding here and there until he reached the helo's door and stepped inside.

"What's going on here? We need to get into that house," Brice was antsy, nervous. Perspiration popped out on his forehead and upper lip, even in the cold.

Gaspar tried to neutralize his feelings toward the dweeb, but the guy was so easy to dislike on sight.

"You have Deerfield with you?" When Brice nodded, Gaspar said, "My orders are to discuss the situation with him personally."

Brice replied, "Come into the house. We can talk there. It's warmer. There's coffee."

Like a guest invited to dinner, Gaspar said drolly, "Thanks, but I can't stay. I have a message for Deerfield, and after I deliver it, I'll be on my way."

Brice seemed nonplussed. "Uh, look. Deerfield is my father-in-law. And my boss. I really can't just go over there and tell him I tried to reason with you and you said no."

"Why not? That's the truth." Gaspar cocked his head. "Look, Brice, this isn't your problem. It's his. He can solve it. I'd have done this over at West Point, but he knew I was coming and ducked out ahead of me. So now I'm waiting here."

Brice took a deep breath. "Okay. I'll tell him."

He stepped out of the helo and walked back to the limo. He opened the rear passenger door, talked for a few moments. Then he stood aside, and Alan Deerfield stepped out.

Brice stayed with the car and Deerfield walked toward the helo. He'd taken about three steps in the snow when Gaspar heard the crack of gunfire and saw Deerfield's head bounce sideways before he went down. Brice ducked behind the limo's engine block half-a-moment before another shot came from the area behind the house.

The helo pilot started the rotors while two more rounds kept Brice hiding behind the vehicle. He looked desperately at Gaspar as if he might try to bolt for the helo. Gaspar waved him over. Brice didn't move.

The shooter was standing near the hedges on the north property line of the house. Gaspar saw a couple of sparks in the darkness.

The pilot said, "We've gotta go. Is he coming?"

Gaspar waved Brice aboard again, but Brice shook his head. Gaspar couldn't get over there and drag him back. If he didn't come on his own now, maybe he could drive out after the helo moved.

The pilot said, "Well?"

Gaspar pointed his thumb and jerked it up a couple of times. He fastened his harness and stared into the dark hedge looking for the shooter as the pilot lifted the helo up and away, toward Manhattan.

Over the roar of the blades, he heard more gunfire. When he looked down again, he saw Brice dead on the ground near Deerfield, blood soaked across the snow like a thirsty sponge.

Two men ran away from the hedge that served as the sniper's nest, full out toward the snowmobiles near the river.

In his peripheral vision, he saw a huge man standing near the opposite corner of the property, nowhere near where the shooter must have stood.

As he watched them, in the foreground a monstrous explosion roared to the sky when the Garrison house exploded, shoving the helo higher and harder through the air.

From his position above the billowing orange cloud, Gaspar saw the two men reach the snowmobiles and jump aboard.

When they started their engines, both snowmobiles exploded, one a half moment sooner than the other. Body parts were thrust off the seats into the icy cold river.

He swiveled his head and peered directly toward the huge man standing in the shadows. He saw only darkness now. He blinked a couple of times to clear his vision, but nothing changed. Maybe no one had been there at all, and only a trick of the firelight made it seem so, but Gaspar didn't believe that and neither would Otto.

# CHAPTER FORTY-SIX

*Monday, January 31*
*4:02 a.m.*
*Garrison, New York*

POULTON HAD WATCHED THE helicopter land, blocking the road north of the driveway. The only way out of there was to the south. If anyone else had pulled into the driveway behind his SUV, he'd have had no escape route at all.

Before the helicopter settled completely, he'd tossed his weapons into the passenger seat of the SUV and jumped into the driver's seat. He'd thrown the transmission into reverse and accelerated fast out of the driveway. At the road, he'd turned south, high beam headlights breaking a wide trail in the dark.

He'd traveled about a mile when Farid Petrosian's house exploded into the night sky like an atom bomb in a snowy desert. The blast rocked the big SUV on its springs, but Poulton kept going. The first explosion was followed by two more—smaller ones close together.

He looked into his mirrors to see behind him. The Mercedes was still stuck in the snow bank. He couldn't see the helicopter or anything else around the big bend in the road.

"Whoop! You are one lucky bastard, you know that, Reed?" He shouted inside the cabin, like a reflex. Shocked to be unharmed. His whole body shook with equal parts terror and relief.

If he was back there, Reacher had to be dead. Which was just fine with him.

# CHAPTER FORTY-SEVEN

*Monday, January 31*
*4:10 a.m.*
*Garrison, New York*

KIM ROLLED HER SHOULDERS. She'd been sitting in the uncomfortable position behind the wheel for too long. She'd be glad to get out and move around.

"Not much farther. Maybe another couple of miles after we go around that next bend," Jodie said.

"Good to know," Kim said.

Before they reached the curve, an explosion ripped through the quiet night. Bright orange light projected high in the sky up ahead. Two smaller explosions followed almost immediately.

Jodie gasped, and her hands flew to cover her mouth. Kim didn't say what they were both thinking. The men they'd seen on the video must have rigged the Petrosian house to explode. But why three explosions?

Kim accelerated faster along the snow-covered pavement. She approached the big curve and slowed to go around safely.

As the sedan rolled around the bend and straightened out, a pair of blinding headlights came at her from the opposite direction.

"Lower your high beams, and maybe he'll lower his," Jodie said.

"I'd love to if I knew where the hell the switch was." Kim kept both hands in a white-knuckled grip at nine and three on the wheel while she let up on the accelerator.

The big vehicle's headlights came straight at her.

She reduced her speed a little more and whipped her head from right to left and back. There was nowhere to go. The wall of snow on both sides of the tunnel was impenetrable.

"There's a driveway on the left up ahead. Maybe another twenty feet. Turn in there and let him pass," Jodie suggested urgently as she pointed.

# CHAPTER FORTY-EIGHT

*Monday, January 31*
*4:13 a.m.*
*Garrison, New York*

POULTON ROUNDED THE FIRST big curve in the road. From his higher vantage point, he saw the black Mercedes he'd left in the farmhouse garage, headed toward him. The big sedan was traveling in the dead center of the road, bright headlights pointed directly forward along the snowy road ahead.

With both vehicles' headlights set on high beam, he couldn't see the other driver. Which meant the driver couldn't see him either.

When the road was clear, it boasted two lanes with sufficient room for cars to pass, one traveling in each direction. But in the winter, drivers treated the road as one lane right down the middle. With all the heavy vehicles coming in and out since Friday when they found the body, the center lane had been plowed clear enough. But massive snowfall had piled three feet up on each side.

Poulton had three advantages. He was more familiar with the road. And his SUV was both four-wheel drive and higher off the ground than the Mercedes, which meant it was less likely to get stuck in the snow. If the Mercedes wanted to survive and not get stuck, the sedan's only choice was to stand down.

Poulton hung in the center lane and pressed the accelerator, barreling straight toward the Mercedes, prepared to slam into it head on unless it moved aside.

He flashed his lights, to be sure the driver saw him coming.

He kept his foot on the accelerator.

The Mercedes began to slow. There was a driveway coming up soon. The Mercedes could turn in and wait for the big SUV to pass. If the driver recognized the safe harbor in time.

Poulton kept his foot on the accelerator. The gap between the SUV and the Mercedes closed at an alarmingly fast rate.

Before the Mercedes reached the upcoming driveway, Poulton tapped his horn and flashed his lights, and flipped his turn indicator.

# CHAPTER FORTY-NINE

*Monday, January 31*
*4:18 a.m.*
*Garrison, New York*

HEART POUNDING, KIM SQUINTED into the spotlights and saw the other driver flash his turn indicator. "Is he saying he's going to turn in or he wants me to?"

"I don't know."

"Hang on. We'll get there first. Then he can go around."

She pushed the accelerator to speed up while he raced relentlessly toward them. She turned the wheel too late to avoid the snow piled at the driveway's entrance and plowed the right front wheel into the opposite snow bank.

She slammed the transmission into reverse to reposition, but the tires spun in the snow. She slammed into drive and tried again. Same result. She couldn't move the big Mercedes all the way off the road.

The other vehicle kept coming.

Now that the opposing headlights weren't quite so blinding, she saw he was driving a big black SUV. An unmarked FBI vehicle like the ones she'd seen at the house on Friday night when she first arrived.

He rammed the SUV straight ahead, slamming into the right rear bumper of the Mercedes on his way past. If the Mercedes had been lighter weight, he'd have shoved the big vehicle a dozen feet or more.

As it was, the impact knocked Kim to the side. She winced in pain when she hit the door with her arm and shoulder. And when her head struck the reinforced window with a loud whacking noise, she knew she'd have a goose egg there for a while.

Jodie cried out as she whiplashed sideways, too.

When Kim regained her breath, she said, "That's Poulton, one of Brice's men."

"Did he trigger those explosions? Is he fleeing the scene of a crime?" Jodie exclaimed.

"Dunno. He's in too big a hurry, for sure," she said quickly. Which was when she remembered something else about Poulton. He had red hair and sandy eyebrows and freckles. And blue eyes. She'd seen him only a few hours ago. "He's also the driver who abducted me."

"Are you sure?" Jodie asked.

"Positive." Kim nodded. "There's no one else out here. I'm going after him. Make sure he doesn't get away."

"You don't even have a gun. How will you stop him?" Jodie asked.

"I'll call 911. Get some help. Then I'll come back for you."

"Wait. You said Poulton? There was a Poulton on the old bathtub killer case." Jodie seemed shredded by indecision until she made up her mind. "I'll go up ahead and try to get you some backup."

"Okay. Go. Go."

# CHAPTER FIFTY

*Monday, January 31*
*4:18 a.m.*
*Garrison, New York*

POULTON SWERVED LEFT JUST in time. Even so, the big
SUV clipped the Mercedes right rear bumper and pulled it away
from the sedan's body as he kept going.

Once the Mercedes was out of the way, he accelerated again.
The road was two-lane for several more miles. He needed to get
off this damn road.

He held onto the steering wheel with both hands and drove
on. He knew precisely where he was going.

He had found the perfect spot on the day he'd abducted Jodie
Jacob. He knew he could use it effectively if the opportunity
presented itself. Which it would at some point, he'd felt sure.

This far north of Manhattan, the narrow road ran east and
west for miles between farms without interruption. The railroad
ran the same route. Smaller state roads crossed the railroad at
irregular intervals, and at every intersection, a guard system was

in place at the grade crossing to warn drivers when the train was coming.

A shockingly high number of drivers failed to stop, he'd learned. Sometimes the warnings didn't work. Some didn't see or hear them. Some drivers ignored the warnings and proceeded through the grade crossing knowing the train could be coming at a high rate of speed.

Some vehicles managed to cross and clear the tracks before the train pushed through. The lucky ones.

Too many never made it all the way across. Poulton had covered the aftermath of enough train wrecks in his life. Proceeding against the warnings was a mistake most drivers rarely lived to regret.

When a train and vehicle collided, regardless of the vehicle involved, the outcome was gruesomely predictable. The train always won, even if the train suffered consequences. He'd researched train wreck videos online. He'd watched hundreds of them. One after another, the train slammed into cars, trucks, SUVs, vans, buses. Didn't matter. The trains always crushed it.

He'd checked the schedules for the track running parallel to State Road 793. Freight trains came along this particular track with predictable frequency. All he needed to do was reach a grade crossing at the right time. Which was surprisingly easy. He'd practiced a few times. He knew what to do.

The speed limit was fifty, but Poulton sped along the deserted road at seventy-five miles per hour. The train's engine was ahead, moving at fifty-eight miles per hour, pulling ten loaded freight cars behind. He nodded, pleased. This train was perfect.

He felt the pain and nausea starting again. It wouldn't last long.

# CHAPTER FIFTY-ONE

*Monday, January 31*
*4:18 a.m.*
*Garrison, New York*

JODIE JUMPED OUT, AND Kim reversed the Mercedes clear of the snow bank after a couple of tries. She turned the big car south and pushed the accelerator. When she looked into the rearview mirror, she saw Jodie trotting along the road wearing Irene's big coat and sloppy boots.

After that one glance, Kim concentrated on her driving. Poulton had a solid head start, and the snowy road's curves slowed her down, but she'd catch him after they got off the two-lane.

When she reached the intersection at the state road, she increased her speed, searching for Poulton's SUV. She saw taillights up ahead. He was driving like a bat out of hell on the clear pavement.

She glanced at her speedometer. The big Mercedes cruised along easily at seventy-five like it was standing still, but she wasn't gaining on Poulton at all. She pushed the accelerator harder.

So focused was she on the chase that she heard the train before she saw it. Poulton was racing the SUV alongside the train, gaining ground.

He pulled even with the engine.

Was he crazy? What the hell was he doing?

The Mercedes' navigation system showed a grade crossing two miles ahead, which answered her question. He planned to cross the tracks. He'd scoot across in front of the engine with mere moments to spare, leaving her behind.

She'd be stuck on this side until the train passed while he sped away on the other side.

Poulton slowed, confirming her suspicions.

Kim accelerated to overtake him, but he swerved in front of her every time she moved, staying ahead of the train's engine and effectively keeping her behind.

The crossing loomed.

The warning lights flashed, and the gate descended slowly, landing at the bottom with a little bounce.

Warning bells began next, ringing loud enough to wake the dead.

Kim tried to pass him one last time. He blocked her again. She floored the accelerator to ram his SUV with the Mercedes. She'd lost her chance.

Poulton had timed his approach to the crossing when the train was too close to stop and turned his wheels before the Mercedes made impact.

He revved his engine, and the SUV jumped forward fast and hard, like a big racing stallion.

The SUV rammed the thick wooden gate, which broke and splintered, sending chips into the air.

Kim repositioned and pressed the accelerator again, but she couldn't catch up.

Out of options, she slammed on her brakes, well back from the crossing to let the train pass.

Everything after that seemed to happen in an instant.

Inexplicably, instead of crossing the tracks and zooming away, Poulton mashed his brakes.

His vehicle screeched to a stop, resting across the tracks, mere seconds ahead of the oncoming train.

Poulton stared through the side window as if mesmerized by the relentless machine bearing down on him.

"What the hell are you doing?" Kim screamed although he couldn't possibly hear her.

The engineer blasted his horn and heroically attempted to reduce the train's rate of speed in the brief interim. The heavily loaded freight cars behind him never slowed.

The train's momentum carried it barreling ahead, even as the emergency brakes squealed. Smoke and sparks flashed from the wheels fighting the rails for traction.

The crash was inevitable. Kim could do nothing to stop it. She reversed to move farther back from the crossing to avoid the shrapnel that could turn Poulton's insane suicide into a homicide, too.

The train slammed Poulton's vehicle on the driver's side and barely slowed.

A horrible crunching sound filled the air.

Instantly, the black SUV was gone. Whooshed ahead by the engine faster than Kim's brain could process.

Poulton couldn't possibly have survived.

The train pushed the SUV a thousand feet up the tracks before it came to rest.

Along the way, the force of the impact created a fuel leak. Gas poured onto the tracks.

The fuel sparked, and Poulton's SUV erupted.

The first explosion was followed by a second, and a third, and a fourth following the fuel leak's path along the tracks.

Weaponized pieces of steel, glass, plastic, gravel, and dozens of other materials shot out in all directions.

The bullet resistant Mercedes withstood each assault.

The train's brakes continued to squeal much longer than she expected.

After what seemed like an eternity, the train finally came to a stop.

The conductor jumped down into the snow and helped the wounded engineer down after him.

Kim could do nothing except stare in horrified fascination.

# CHAPTER FIFTY-TWO

*Wednesday, February 2*
*3:57 p.m.*
*John F. Kennedy Airport*

KIM LEANED BACK IN her chair, still thinking about the case, as she watched Smithers rushing toward them. He was running late. They wouldn't have much time to talk.

She and Gaspar were booked on separate planes to separate cities once again. She was headed home to Detroit, and he was returning to Miami.

They'd been debriefed for several hours by the Acting Agent in Charge of the New York Field Office yesterday. They'd promised to return for testimony if needed.

Since then, she'd worked out a few things on her own or with help from the Boss. She knew the woman in the tub was Valerie Webb. Since Poulton set up the false green paint bathtub scene, it was fair to assume he killed her.

But too many questions remained, and Smithers had some of the answers. After he settled in, she got directly to the point.

"It was Brice all along, wasn't it? Then he freaked out when Deerfield brought me into the mix, and he lost it. Totally panicked," she said.

"Why do you think so?" Smithers asked.

She'd begun to suspect Brice when Jodie Jacob said he'd questioned her after he'd told Kim that he didn't even know her whereabouts. Turned out, he knew where Jodie was all along.

Kim had asked the Boss to do some digging to confirm her conclusions. First up was to track down that farmhouse where she and Jodie were kept. The real owners were the snowbird parents of one of Brice's old college chums.

She said, "You told me this was Brice's operation Saturday night at Cipriani's. But he was much more than the lead agent on the black ops assignment."

Smithers raised his eyebrows as if he didn't understand. Kim believed he did.

"Initially, Deerfield must have classified Farid Petrosian as status unknown, maybe hostile, maybe friendly." Casually, she crossed her hands in her lap, as if his answers didn't matter. "Brice was Farid's handler. Deerfield was willing to do whatever it took to make sure the Petrosians didn't escape again. He thought Brice would be more vigilant and controllable than any other agent he had."

Smithers nodded this time but kept silent. Kim didn't expect him to verbally confirm. She didn't need him to. She'd asked the Boss to reaffirm. He did. Brice had sent those text messages to Poulton, claiming to be Deerfield, with orders to pick them up and kill them both. Lucky for Kim and Jodie that Poulton wasn't that kind of guy.

Gaspar said, "Deerfield trusted his ability to control Brice. His trust was misplaced. It cost him his life."

Smithers cocked his head and frowned. "Brice didn't kill Deerfield. Tariq Petrosian did. And Samir Petrosian killed Brice."

"How do you know?" Gaspar asked.

"We have forensics from the guns and the bullets. They set the explosives for the house, too."

That news made Kim breathe a little easier. She'd thought Reacher might have killed them. He was a solid marksman. And Gaspar saw him at the scene. Maybe she was being paranoid about Reacher now. Which was why she hadn't told Gaspar about chasing that guy down at Grand Central just because he was big enough and wearing work boots.

As if he'd read her mind, Gaspar gave her a knowing look.

She ignored him. "Brice put Deerfield in Tariq and Samir's sights. After that, both of them were like dogs in the road. It was only a matter of time."

"Why'd he do it? Set Deerfield up like that?" Smithers asked.

Gaspar said, "My guess? Motives were totally personal. For all of them."

"Motives usually are." Smithers nodded. "Farid wanted the family business. To get it, he had to remove Samir and Tariq and stay out of prison. His motives were very personal. What about Deerfield and Brice, though?"

Gaspar shrugged. "Brice was sick and tired of being mocked, ridiculed, and controlled by his father-in-law. Wouldn't you be?"

Smithers said, "Yeah. But I wouldn't kill him over it."

"Brice was no criminal mastermind. He got in over his head. He only wanted Deerfield to retire and get the hell out of the way." Kim shrugged. "When you wrestle with gangsters like the Petrosians, chances are you're gonna get mauled, at the very least."

Smithers nodded. "Makes sense. How about Deerfield? What was his personal motive?"

"Same thing. Different level. He wanted his boss to get out of the way, too," Kim replied, without supplying more of the facts she and Gaspar knew. Deerfield tried to blackmail the Boss with the black ops Reacher investigation and force Cooper to get out of his way. Deerfield pushed, and Cooper shoved back twice as hard.

Gaspar said, "They'd both be alive if they'd come with me in the helicopter like I asked them to."

Smithers shook his head. "Deerfield would never have done that. He was headed into the house. They planned to blow him up. He lived a few minutes less, that's all."

Kim nodded, "It was his day to die. Brice, too."

Gaspar said, "Who knew you were such a fatalist?"

"My mother's fault. I told you she's like that," Kim grinned. "She says when it's your time, it's your time. Not one moment more or less."

The departures board was flashing. Her plane had arrived and was at the gate. Once it emptied and the crew cleaned up, she'd be leaving. Her stomach was already doing backflips. She really hated flying.

Smithers said, "Two issues are still open. We don't know why Samir and Tariq believed there were bodies under the house. Or why those snowmobiles exploded."

"Farid is the most likely answer for both, isn't he?" Gaspar asked.

"One snowmobile malfunction killing one of them might have been a coincidence. But two? That's deliberate," Smithers replied. "And Farid wasn't out there. I was with him in the safe house."

Gaspar shrugged. Kim shook her head. But they'd discussed this before Smithers arrived. Reacher must have done it. They'd been worried that Reacher had rigged the house, too. He was the big man on the video who went down to the snowmobiles while Samir and Tariq were setting up the explosion. Then he went into the house, walked around, and came out. He had means and opportunity. Besides, unlike drowning naked women in green paint, blowing up the Petrosian brothers was precisely the kind of thing he would do.

Reacher's motive was probably personal, like the others. Maybe he still thought they'd killed the love of his life. Or maybe he just wanted to be sure they never killed anyone again.

Kim shrugged. "My money's on Farid, anyway."

"Why?" Smithers asked.

"Farid orchestrated the whole thing. He sent the blonde woman from the real estate agency into the house to replace the batteries in his surveillance cameras. That's how he got the video recording of Poulton putting the body in the tub. We know he told Brice who told Deerfield about it, too." Kim paused to think about it. "Samir and Tariq must have killed a couple of their crew and told Farid to bury them under the house, though. Farid lied about the names when he told Brice. He also lied to his brothers about putting the bodies in the foundation. Otherwise, Samir and Tariq would never have tried so hard to stop Deerfield from exposing them."

"Makes sense." Smithers glanced at his watch and seemed alarmed. "Sorry. I'm out of time. I'm meeting my wife in the city."

They said their goodbyes, and she watched him walk away. He was one of the good guys. She was as sure of it now as she'd been that first day. Maybe they'd have a chance to work together again sometime.

The boarding announcement for her flight broadcast over the public-address system. Gaspar's flight would be called soon, too. She tossed a couple of twenties on the table to cover the bill and the tip.

"Hang on there, Sunshine. Let's talk about true love," Gaspar said. "Reacher's in the wind again. Jodie Jacob's gone, too. Think they're together?"

"You Latinos are so romantic." Kim smiled and shook her head. "But you know what? I actually don't think they're together. Jodie said she hadn't heard from him in years. She said he would never settle down, and I had the feeling she's looking for that now."

Gaspar had seemed preoccupied all day. His flight was leaving ten minutes after hers. But he had something to say, and she wished he'd spit it out already.

"You're killing me, here, Cheech. What's on your mind?" she teased as she drank the last of her water.

"Yeah. I tried to bring this up a couple of times before. Straight up is probably the best way to say it." He looked across the table and cleared his throat. "I'm thinking about changing jobs."

"What?" She stared back.

"I've been recruited a few times over the years. Always rejected everything. But now... I've got five kids, you know? This job doesn't pay enough. Never has. And it's getting harder to stay out of the line of fire."

"That again? Come on. If you'd jumped out and tried to save Brice, you'd be dead now, too. He could have come with you. He didn't. That's not your fault, Zorro."

"I know. But the offer's good this time. A firm based in Houston. Private investigations. Pretty high end. Follow the money, take a cut. Fewer bullets flying, less travel." He shrugged.

She didn't know what to say. Of course, she wanted him to do what was best for him and his family. Selfishly, she didn't want him to quit.

But she understood the urge to go. She'd been wondering some of the same things herself lately. She couldn't make great arguments for sticking with the bureau anymore.

"I'm just thinking about it. Haven't made a decision yet. I'm in no shape to return to work yet, anyway. I'll be parked behind a desk for a while." He smiled weakly, and she smiled back. Because what else could she do?

She glanced at the departures board. The final boarding light was flashing.

"I've got to go. Give Marie and the kids a hug for me, Chico," she said as she collected her bags.

"You bet, Suzy Wong. Don't be a stranger," he replied with a grin before she could get too far away. "And what about that Treasury Agent. What's his name again?"

She walked backward for a few steps so she could keep eye contact. "John Lawton. What about him?"

"Nothing going on there?" Gaspar asked.

"You never give up, do you?" She smiled and turned and walked quickly to her gate, wondering when she'd see him again.

Her cell phone vibrated in her pocket with a text. She fished it out on the run and read the text from an unfamiliar number. "Jodie says thanks for everything. Fear of flying is completely irrational. See you when I see you. R."

FROM LEE CHILD
THE REACHER REPORT:
March 2nd, 2012

The other big news is Diane Capri—a friend of mine—wrote a
book revisiting the events of KILLING FLOOR in Margrave,
Georgia. She imagines an FBI team tasked to trace Reacher's
current-day whereabouts. They begin by interviewing people
who knew him—starting out with Roscoe and Finlay. Check out
this review: "Oh heck yes! I am in love with this book. I'm a
huge Jack Reacher fan. If you don't know Jack (pun intended!)
then get thee to the bookstore/wherever you buy your fix and
pick up one of the many Jack Reacher books by Lee Child.
Heck, pick up all of them. In particular, read Killing Floor. Then
come back and read Don't Know Jack. This story picks up the
other from the point of view of Kim and Gaspar, FBI agents
assigned to build a file on Jack Reacher. The problem is, as
anyone who knows Reacher can attest, he lives completely off
the grid. No cell phone, no house, no car…he's not tied down. A
pretty daunting task, then, wouldn't you say?

First lines: "Just the facts. And not many of them, either.
Jack Reacher's file was too stale and too thin to be credible. No
human could be as invisible as Reacher appeared to be, whether
he was currently above the ground or under it. Either the file had
been sanitized, or Reacher was the most off-the-grid paranoid
Kim Otto had ever heard of." Right away, I'm sensing who Kim
Otto is and I'm delighted that I know something she doesn't.
You see, I DO know Jack. And I know he's not paranoid. Not
really. I know why he lives as he does, and I know what kind of
man he is. I loved having that over Kim and Gaspar. If you

haven't read any Reacher novels, then this will feel like a good, solid story in its own right. If you have…oh if you have, then you, too, will feel like you have a one-up on the FBI. It's a fun feeling!

"Kim and Gaspar are sent to Margrave by a mysterious boss who reminds me of Charlie, in Charlie's Angels. You never see him…you hear him. He never gives them all the facts. So they are left with a big pile of nothing. They end up embroiled in a murder case that seems connected to Reacher somehow, but they can't see how. Suffice to say the efforts to find the murderer and Reacher, and not lose their own heads in the process, makes for an entertaining read.

"I love the way the author handled the entire story. The pacing is dead on (ok another pun intended), the story is full of twists and turns like a Reacher novel would be, but it's another viewpoint of a Reacher story. It's an outside-in approach to Reacher.

"You might be asking, do they find him? Do they finally meet the infamous Jack Reacher?

"Go…read…now…find out!"

Sounds great, right? Check out "Don't Know Jack," and let me know what you think.

So that's it for now…again, thanks for reading THE AFFAIR, and I hope you'll like A WANTED MAN just as much in September.

Lee Child

# ABOUT THE AUTHOR

Diane Capri is an award-winning *New York Times*, *USA Today*, and worldwide bestselling author. She's a recovering lawyer and snowbird who divides her time between Florida and Michigan. An active member of Mystery Writers of America, Author's Guild, International Thriller Writers, Alliance of Independent Authors, and Sisters in Crime, she loves to hear from readers and is hard at work on her next novel.

Please connect with her online:

http://www.DianeCapri.com

Twitter: http://twitter.com/@DianeCapri

Facebook: http://www.facebook.com/Diane.Capri1

http://www.facebook.com/DianeCapriBooks

Made in the USA
Coppell, TX
25 May 2021

56290460R00198